Extraordinary Secrets

Extraordinary Secrets

Robert T.R. Bradford

For my wife, Maddy, who has made my life extraordinary.

Also for my father, John Bradford, who inspired this story.

Who?

Chapter One

The Client

I am warped at best, held up in St. Louis, Missouri—downtown. *The Rome of the West,* they call it, with cheese. Blues games in the winter, Cardinals in the spring. I'm in between, making a living off of infidelity and shady individuals doing things their mothers taught them not to do.

I watched a man named Jake Nash, through his hotel window —fifth floor of the Hilton. I was across the street on the top floor of a parking garage. He was in dress slacks and a wife beater, kissing a woman who was down to her bra and panties. This woman was not Mrs. Nash. Mrs. Nash was in a board meeting across town, anxiously awaiting my text or phone call. Before I considered the call, though, I took thirty some odd pictures. It's that easy because his blinds were completely drawn back, a favor I was able to talk a cleaning lady into for a heavy tip. The laborers are truly underpaid. Then, I texted Mr. Nash and told him exactly what I was doing, exactly where I was doing it, and exactly why I did it. Oh, he was pissed. I could see him pacing back and forth from across the street as he yelled indecent words in my ear. His mistress panicked, pulled the bed sheet around her like

1

it covered her shame. Just like they do in the films that don't allow nudity. She glared at the window, those crying eyes. Then it was her time to yell. She feared the light of truth as much as Mr. Nash did, which told me she probably had someone waiting for her too, in some board meeting, in some building, secretly wondering if she will be there when he gets home. That's when I knew I had them.

That's when I asked Mr. Nash to make a counter offer.

To better illustrate what I do, I'm a private detective whose entire career consists of spying on cheaters or finding people who don't want to be found, for people they don't want to be found by. And occasionally someone, like Mr. Nash, will be desperate enough that I can leverage more money out of him to not give the pictures I took for his wife, Rita Nash. Rita Nash, the suspicious wife was the breadwinner, the one with shark lawyers, the one with enough money to pay for Nash's Hilton visits.

It wasn't ethical, what I did half the time and it was rarely clever detective work. In my mind, though, if you are low enough that someone would need to hire someone like me or you're low enough to do the hiring, you kind of deserve it. It wasn't a pretty side of me, but most of them weren't, anyway. Besides, I figured I had a free-pass. All of those dirty men doing dirty things, their mothers taught them better. I didn't have one of those.

A relieved Mr. Nash, a relieved Mrs. Nash, and two cups of black coffee later, I was back at my agency, F.K. Private Investigators. It said so right on the window. My office wasn't like I pictured it would be, in my younger days. It wasn't like the ones in the black and white movies—some forty's noir. A guy, a private eye, would sit behind his big oak desk, on a squeaky twirl chair, all askew. And someone, a pitiful someone, would stand outside my office, a silhouette would be caught in the glass of my door that would read the name, in my case, Grayson Grant, private eye.

Instead, my office was easy, eggshell white with a flimsy desk I had to put together myself. Gray carpet that was long out of style and an AC window unit that hummed a little too loudly. My partner Flynn Kiddy, who had the adjacent desk that was much nicer than mine, sat back in his chair, reading whatever trash newspaper he picked up on his way in to the office. He had a moral compass greater than my own. In our two-man investigation firm, he was the boss, the one with the actual police background and a solid fifteen years my senior.

"You keep reading that trash, Kiddy, one day you're gonna end up trash yourself."

"If I'm trash, Grayson, what does that make you?" He laughed as he said it. Kiddy was middle-aged —forty-five years old African American with a mustache as old as me.

"What's this?" I asked. On my desk sat a thick envelope with permanent marker scratched on the front. I instantly regretted my question. "You've got to be kidding me."

"In with this morning's mail. It is thicker than usual," Kiddy said, without looking up from his paper.

"My dad's growing more senile," I retorted.

"Your dad isn't crazy, he's just obsessive. All the good investigators are," Kiddy replied.

"He's not an investigator. He's just nuts. And I'm not obsessive."

"You're not a good investigator."

"Screw you."

"Not without dinner first," Kiddy said.

"Fire me if I'm not a good detective," I teased.

"You are good at what you do, but what you do, Grant, is not detective work. You know that. I know that. You don't want to be a real detective. If you did, you'd work better with the department—with the lawyers. Not the pissed off paranoid."

4

"My father isn't any of these things. He's more than obsessive, Kiddy. Obsessive would've been three or five years of this crap. It has been twenty years, Kiddy. How do you go this long without letting go? At least a little?"

"You've let go?" He questioned.

I traced my dad's stickily handwriting with my thumb. It looked so similar to my own. Nothing like my mother's handwriting: beautiful, loopy cursives. A faded memory that was still fading.

"I've come to terms." I opened up a bottom drawer in my desk, where other unopened envelopes, with the same marketed handwriting, stacked onto of each other, and tossed the new edition at the top.

"It is hard for others, Grayson. It is even harder without closure. Your pop, maybe he just doesn't have closure."

"I just wish he wouldn't bother me about it," I said, annoyed.

"Well, just offering some perspective. We're all haunted. The difference is how we choose to handle the ghost."

I'm not so sure why Kiddy ever bothered to hire me in the first place. He knew what I was the day I walked into his office. Eagerly running away with a map of St. Louis sticking out of my jacket pocket. He saw right through me.

Kiddy was the good cop I could never be. He knew that. I think that's why I got the job.

My fifth cup of coffee of the day was enjoyed in my apartment, pressing midnight. I lulled in a desk chair that was sitting on my balcony. My feet propped up on the iron railing and my eyes on the warm moonbeams that got lost in the city lights, below. I sipped slowly, wishing that caffeine still did the trick for me. Instead, I drifted, uneasily, and accidentally thought about my father.

Alan Grant was a tough guy. A car hood popped, greasy hands, sleeves rolled up, guy who had wrinkles before he should have had them. He was a good father, for a while, or maybe I was just only a good son for a season. Ultimately we were just different people. He was tall, bulky, like he's spent some time in the military even though he hadn't. I was slim, not skinny, but I wasn't muscular. Alan's skull was dressed in a brown layer of hair that slowly thinned over time. I wondered how much it had thinned since the last time I saw him. I was dealing with thick black hair. Not the kind of thick that makes me a handsome catch, the kind of thick that makes it hard to look like I'm not a deranged psychopath.

My father was a construction worker. A ditch-digger, he called himself, outside our hometown, Abingdon,

Virginia. I'm a private investigator, so perhaps the closest things he and I have in common is we know how to dig. My mother is a different story. She was a psychologist before we lost her. I suppose *that's* the only thing we have in common, actually—we both lost Elizabeth Grant.

She use to tell me about cases when I was a kid, and tried to understand the work she did. She told me about the famous Pavlov and his dog. Pavlov was a Russian psychologist who conducted an experiment where he tested conditioning. Pavlov would test this theory by ringing a bell when he gave food to his dogs. When he conditioned the animals to associate the bell with food, he took the food out of the equation. Next time he rang the bell, the dogs salivated without the presence of food.

It was hard for me to grasp as a kid. It didn't make sense to me until I got a little older. Ever since, I would occasionally find myself overwhelmed by the idea that this was happening constantly around me. Sitting on my balcony, falling asleep in my chair, trying to remember my mother's smile, I thought about how often people rang a bell and how desperate I was drooling for it.

When morning breaks, I begin my routine. One cup of coffee, three sugars—black. I try to pretend, sometimes, that I'm this hardened man who will shoot back a dirty glass of whiskey and grits his teeth as the burn washes down his throat. I'm not that man, though. I drink coffee because I need the energy. I drink coffee because somehow it is how I function. I can't rely on straight black anymore. My taste buds have rejected it. The fact is I'm quite hardened, my taste buds just don't know it.

My phone rang. Kiddy's ringtone—an annoying, repetitive tune. Something like Kiddy. I heard from him two hours before usual. When I hear from him, though, it is usually because I'm an hour late for work.

"I'm not late yet, Kiddy," I say in lieu of a hello.

"You have a client, Grayson," he said, in an annoyed, but surprised tone.

"I don't have anything scheduled today, Kiddy."

"She's a walk-in."

"I don't take walk-Ins."

"Yes, you do."

"Only because you make me."

"I do make you. But you're going to want to hear this one out," Kiddy said eagerly.

"Why?"

"Oh, trust me Grayson."

It was storming by the time I reached the office. I felt the water seep into my shoes from the parking lot to the office door. Once I was inside, I saw a young woman in a chair adjacent from my desk. She waited for me, drenched with rain water, mascara running down her cheeks. Smooth ivory skin covered in chill bumps from the splashes of rain bubbling on her body. Kiddy had already given her a hand towel from our bathroom. A hand towel in a downpour, like a matchstick in a black out. Kiddy's mind was linear. Solving the latest case without having to leave the office, I'm sure. She sat across my desk, strawberry blonde and heavy eyed. The mascara looked like shadow puppets against her white skin now. She jittered a leg up and down as she sat. Kiddy sat at his desk, pretending to read the newspaper. It was a sure sign he was nervous—and when Kiddy is nervous, I am too.

"Hello," I said, half-hoping she gave me a reason to say no to whatever reason she had for being in my office.

"Mr. Grant?" She said. There was a twang in her voice that let me know she was a Tennessee native, or at least close.

"Can I help you?" I plopped down in my squeaky seat with slouched shoulders and wandering eyes. I don't know why I was so eager to say no to this woman.

"It's my little sister," she said. There was stress in her voice. A crack of weakness and desperation and I was suddenly uncomfortable. "She—well she died."

My eyes shot to Kiddy, who I could tell by his distance and awkwardness, already knew what I was about to hear.

"Excuse me?" I said, realizing too late the insensitivity of it all.

"She was murdered two and a half weeks ago."

I sighed and forced myself to look at the woman. "I'm sorry—what did you say your name was?"

"Lexi Keats," she said quickly. "My sister's name was Miranda Keats."

"Miss Keats," I replied, trying to ignore the end of her sentence. "I'm sorry but I'm not really a homicide investigator." I heard some sort of snort come out of her nose, which was coupled with a sigh—a cocktail of scoff and sarcastic laughter.

"What do you mean you're not a homicide investigator?" she questioned. "You're a Private Investigator aren't you? What do you do? Sit around here with that guy and play Clue?"

"No, he cheats at Clue," Kiddy said, reading the newspaper at his desk.

"Miss Keats, I'm not the experienced detective you need for a murder investigation. I'm more of," I hesitated, as she looked at me. Green eyes piercing all the way through me. "I'm more like—a love investigator, you know? I find out if your husband or boyfriend is cheating on you, or if you have a stalker, or something like that. Murder investigations..." my voice trailed.

"I'm sorry, did you say *love* investigator?" Lexi asked. Kiddy chuckled.

"I'm sorry, I wish I could help. You need to talk to the actual police though, I think," I said.

Lexi shook her head violently. "No, no the police can't help me. They tried. They said they tried, but they haven't been able to come up with anything yet."

"Even if I were a skilled homicide detective," I blurted out, getting a little annoyed, "starting a case this late in the game would be extremely difficult. Even if you were talking to Kiddy over there, who by the way, is an ex-cop and probably way better at this than I am."

Lexi turned her head to Kiddy for a moment, but she wasn't looking at him.

"I'm not what you need," I finished, my voice demanded that she pick up what hope she lay before me and get out of my office. The truth was, I didn't want to help her. I didn't like admitting I wasn't good enough for her case.

"But he said you were the only one who could help me," Lexi said with exhaust in her voice.

"Who? Kiddy? He's full of jokes."

"Bad ones, but she's not talking about me," Kiddy added, thumbing through the cartoons.

"Who?" I said, cutting my eyes back and forth between the two of them.

"Your dad," Lexi said.

It felt like a joke at first. The way that the words slipped out of her mouth—like a slick, tacky comeback. "Excuse me?" I replied, knowing fully well that I was showing every single card in my hand.

"Your dad is Alan Grant, right?" Lexi asked, rhetorically.

"He used to be," I muttered.

"He said you were the perfect person to investigate my sister's murder."

"I'm sorry—you know Alan?"

She whipped her head back from Kiddy to me, her strawberry blonde hair acting like a mane. "Yes," she said, impatiently now. "He contacted me a couple of days after, well, after Miranda's body was found. He asked me how the police were handling the investigation. I told him to piss off but then he convinced me that his son was this fantastic private investigator in St. Louis and that I should check him out. I asked him what a private eye in St. Louis would do me any good, and then he told me all about you."

I chuckled for a moment, when she said my father told her I was a good investigator. I shook my head slowly and waited for her to catch on to the irony I was laying down.

"My dad told you I was a good investigator?" I started. "Like I said, I catch cheaters and liars. I'm not exactly Sherlock Holmes. I'm not even Watson."

"He said you were perfect for this case," she repeated, annoyed, as she placed a file on my desk and pushed it towards me. "He said you had experience with the killer before."

The feeling one has when everything drops to your stomach, as if one's rib cage broke into pieces and everything kept hostage inside it fell to the slimy floor of the gut, erupted inside of me.

"I'm familiar with the killer?" I asked, moving my hand to the file and flipped it open. I paused. I saw a list of names, printer copies of police notes, mugshots, and crime scene photos. They weren't of Miranda Keats, though, but of several women. The woman in the first photograph my eyes found—a beautiful woman, rope burns around her throat. The coldness of her corpse leapt out of the picture.

I picked this picture up, out of the folder, away from the rest—just to hold it.

"Mr. Grant," Lex started, "the person who murdered my sister is The Shoestring Killer, who murdered your mother twenty-years ago."

I sat at my desk, alone, hours after I told Lexi it was impossible that a killer from twenty years ago had resurfaced, hours after I made her leave my office and hours after I argued with Kiddy about the idea of taking on such a client. I sipped another cup of coffee, which must've been my fourth that evening. I flipped through the file Lexi brought with her. Despite my refusal to take her case on, she left the file anyway. She said it was a copy my father had sent her. I assumed what I held in my hand was the same as the package in the bottom drawer of my desk: All of Alan Grant's findings on The Shoestring Killer.

In 1995, when I was only a kid, a serial killer made their way through Abingdon, Virginia, killing several women, by choking them to death with shoestrings. My mother was the first of his victims, followed by our neighbor, Carol

Hanna, my best friend Jack's mother, and many women after her. The police had a handful of strong leads, but they all lead to dead ends. After a month, the killings seemed to stop but there was no criminal justice served. Everyone assumed the killer moved on to another place to haunt another town. Some thought the killer took his own life. I didn't. I always thought it was someone who never left, but waited—just waited. Another month went by without a single hint that the Shoestring Killer was still among us, but then another body surfaced. This time a man's body. The police talked to us and the rest of the families about it, but there was always suspicion that the kill was the work of a copycat. A week later, another body was found, this time matching The Shoestring Killer's M.O perfectly. It was his last mark on our town and he was never heard of again—until now.

Ever since that last kill in '95, Alan had become obsessed with finding the person responsible. He followed every news story on any homicide investigation that he could find, hoping to link it to his beloved wife, in some way or another. He was a man dreaming of ending a nightmare. I, on the other hand, refused to be haunted by my deceased mother, or the person who took her from us. I hadn't made peace with it. You don't really make complete peace with something like that—at least if you did I didn't know how—but I didn't torture myself with it.

I stayed in the office until morning, catching just a couple of hours sleep on the couch in our waiting room.

"Did you sleep here?" Kiddy asked when he came in the next morning, bright and early at six o' clock.

"I don't think you can call what I did sleeping," I said as I rubbed my eyes and lifted my head off of my own desk. Kiddy sat a cup of coffee on my desk, I sipped it quickly—my drug of choice. "I need sugar" I said.

"You don't drink yours with sugar," Kiddy replied.

"Who are you to tell me whether or not I need the sugar?"

"You don't want diabetes."

"Shut up."

Kiddy ignored my insult, stroked his thick, orange mustache and propped himself against his desk. "Well?"

"Well, what?" I asked, eyeing the room as if I missed something.

"Are you going to take the case?" Kiddy inquired.

"I thought I made myself clear when I yelled at the client yesterday," I retorted sharply.

Kiddy scratched the back of his head and motioned toward the file that I had just used as a pillow. "You were at the office all night for a reason. You've already put more time into a case you haven't even taken than you do most of the cases that you do take."

I let out something of a snort-laugh and picked up the envelope in front of me—thumbing through pages of scribbled notes and pictures. "It is a legacy of insanity, Kiddy. My old man never knew how to let go."

"Like I said, he's looking for closure," Kiddy suggested.

"He's looking for a killer."

"You gonna help him find it?"

I stared at a picture of my mother. She was beautiful—flowing locks of brown, curly hair, pearly white teeth, hazel eyes. Her smile was infectious—some people back home said I had it. Some people.

"I'm too close to this case, Kiddy," I started. "She was my mother." I put the picture on my desk, separate from the rest of the file.

"For a normal situation, I'd say so, Grant. But this isn't a normal situation and you're not too close to anything," Kiddy walked up to my desk, turned the file around to examine it himself. "I don't know, man. Maybe you should take this case. Maybe you should find out if this killer really has resurfaced after twenty long years. It's a long shot, but it would be a heck of a thing if it were true. Maybe you find your dad some closure. Maybe you'll find yourself some, too."

I sighed and stood up from my desk, waved to him while holding the file in my hand and walked out the door. I hadn't decided, when I left the building, if I would accept Lexi's case or keep walking until I got to the closest cup of coffee. That's when I started thinking about that scientist again, Pavlov and his dog. How he was able to condition his dog by the ringing of a bell. I stopped at a street corner and imagined Alan's obsession, coupled with the terrible fear that erupted in me that my father could be right. And as it happened, I was also curious. Curious like my mother raised me to be. Okay, mom, for you.

Ring. Ring.

Elizabeth's Work Journal
June 28, 1993.

My dream job has arrived. Oh, how I never thought I would see this day! All those years of hard work. Tears on satin sheets, midnight phone calls from my dorm room to my mother's house, waking her up from her chronic pain long enough to tell me: It's okay, you're going to make it! Oh how I wish she could see me now. I wish she could see that I've made it, and a charming place called Old Dominion Asylum is exactly who to thank. Dr. Liam Walker and the wonderful medical board of Old Dominion Asylum has welcomed me to be a part of their psychiatric team.

Alan is so proud of me. I'm so proud of me. This is work that means something. Truly means something. It isn't sitting in a school, listening to some teenager who doesn't care you're talking—just lingering in your office long enough for the bell to ring. No, here is where real psychiatric work needs to be done. These poor souls are in constant need of care, and if I am able to bring any one of them to some understanding within their self, the price for my tuition would be worth it.

"There is a vision for the future," Dr. Walker told me, as he took me on a personal tour of the grounds. It's a

19

beautiful building—old, years and years of history. The stone in its walls is unlike anything I have ever seen before. It is progress, the work he and his team are doing here. The team in which I now belong.

There is a myriad of patients here. These patients haven't seen true care until they arrived here, at the newly reopened mental institution. Dr. Walker's vision has saved a dying facility, and the patients brave enough to undergo his care have signed up for turn-of-the-century treatment. I'm excited to be here. I'm excited to be a part of something that I am sure will go down in history.

Alan, my adoring husband hates the name. "But Elizabeth," he belters on in his husky voice. "They're not supposed to be called asylums anymore. They're mental institutions now, right?"

But Dr. Walker wanted to keep the name. History is important and asylums being evil is a vicious stereotype. One that Dr. Walker, and myself, want to rectify.

Because nothing truly terrible happens in asylums anymore.

Chapter Two

Monsters

I never looked for monsters in my closet. They didn't hide behind my bed skirt, underneath the creaky box springs. I never saw them. There is something very real about the fear of the unknown. There's a strength in it. That's why we fear the shadows. That's why we cringe the moment before the ghost appears, but exhale the moment after we see it. At that age—that monster-seeking-behind-coat-hanger age, I knew that somehow. I knew that I wasn't going to see a monster when I looked under my bed, because the best monsters, the viciously scary—don't want to be seen.

I sipped my coffee, loaded with sugar, and looked at the laundry list of information we knew about the Shoestring murders, on a cork board in our office. I saw the faces of five women who saw a monster just before they died. The first picture was my mother, Elizabeth Grant—I forced Kiddy to hang up this one. It was for the case. Next was Jack's mother, our neighbor, Carol Hanna. A woman who was equal to my mother in loveliness and friendliness. The next photograph was Rebecca Lassiter, a beautiful housewife born and raised in Abingdon. And last was Lauren Kelley, a college student.

21

"Okay, four ladies and a dude," Kiddy said as he held up a fifth photo. "Farmer," he said, stating the man's last name, not profession. He was a handsome man—mid thirties with thick long blonde hair.

"I don't think he's a part of this," I stated as Kiddy tacked his picture up between Rebecca and Lauren's pictures.

"He falls in line between these two. Same M.O," Kiddy stated.

"But he's a guy," I said.

Kiddy turned to the picture, then back at me. "Really? I had no idea," he said sarcastically.

"I'm just saying, there's room to speculate whether or not this was a copycat."

"Either way, it is connected. It goes up on the wall," Kiddy said with a final word, as he tacked a blurry picture of a young, skinny man on the cork board. "So what do we know about these victims? "

"Nothing."

"We have to know something, Grayson."

"I'm telling you, Kiddy, most of what my dad had on file was rumors, speculations, nonsense."

"Maybe some of that nonsense needs to go up on the wall," Kiddy muttered.

I picked up Alan's envelope, and waved it in the air, staring at Kiddy. "Kiddy—my dad was grasping at straws. He has a profile on everyone my mother ever spoke to here!" I waved the envelope around as I spoke. It was like I was trying to convince Kiddy that Elvis had left the building.

"Okay so forget what leads your dad had for now," Kiddy barked back. "Let's focus on what we do know, for sure. Four of these ladies, the four we have on this board, lived in Abingdon."

"Right," I nodded in agreement.

"What about Farmer?" Kiddy asked.

I thumbed through what little information we had on the only male victim. "Joseph Farmer, he wasn't from Abingdon looks like. But his body was found there."

"Wrong place, wrong time, I guess," Kiddy stated.

"Or someone else murdered him and placed him in Abingdon, trying to pass it off," I said.

Kiddy puffed a sigh. "Seems like a stretch."

"It just seems strange to me, Kiddy," I admitted once more.

"We'll come back to that," he said as he tacked another photo on the board. This one was of a young girl, in a high school graduation cap and gown. She smiled beautifully for the camera, on a day filled of promise and future.

"Miranda Keats," Kiddy said, "Our client's sister and our sixth victim."

"She came all the way to St. Louis to hire me," I stated, still confounded by her great leaps.

"Well, you're a private investigator that is already close to the case. It's worth a little state hopping. Plus, you are dirt cheap, Grayson." Kiddy's laugh boomed too loudly, but it was infectious nonetheless. "Okay," he said, clearing his throat from the phlegm that rested inside—a mixed reaction due to tobacco and allergies. "Five women, twenty years apart."

"There's not one thing they all have in common," I started. "My mother, Elizabeth," I said, placing my index finger on her photograph, my eyes were careful not to linger at my mother's gaze, "she knew Carol Hanna. Hanna was our next-door neighbor. As far as I know, however, she didn't know Rebecca Lassiter or Lauren Kelley."

"So we can't verify if they knew each other, but it is a safe bet that's not the killer's M.O anyway, considering we have a new victim twenty years later. There has to be something else about these women. Their looks, personality, job, something," Kiddy said.

"It's not looks. My mother was tall and blonde, Hanna is a brunette, both of them Caucasian but Lassiter was African American and Lauren Kelley was a Latina American."

Kiddy flipped through a stack of notes he'd made on the victims earlier. "Therapist, baker, housewife, college student, recently graduated high school student," Kiddy sighed. "And whatever Farmer was—we couldn't get an occupation on him. None of these people have any connection."

"So the murderer doesn't work off a consistent M.O," I said.

"Most serial killers have some kind of pattern, Grayson."

"Maybe this one doesn't. Maybe this is how Shoestring has stayed hidden for twenty years, if it really is Shoestring. I don't get it, Kiddy. Why stay inactive for so long?"

"Maybe he hasn't. Maybe he's just starting to leave traces again," Kiddy said. "You gotta remember to not be so narrow minded if you're going to work cases like this one."

"No no, I get that. I just thought he finally got what he deserved," I admitted.

"What's that?"

I winced, for a moment, when I let the words slip out of my mouth: *Laces around his own throat.*

"She was touring colleges," Lexi said, sitting down at a table in a local coffee shop called *Latte Diem,* my favorite coffee house, a small mom-and-pop shop on the outskirts of the city, a place where you could see the Missouri River. "She was in Abingdon with a couple of friends touring Emory and Henry. Miranda wanted to go for a hike on the Creeper Trail without the group she was traveling with and that's when..." her voice trailed off for a moment. "I think you should come to Abington with me," she added.

"I don't think so," I said, sipping my fifth cup of coffee in under six hours.

"Why not?" There was disdain in her voice. I could hear that southern twang, again—like a folk song that went violent.

"Because I'm at a dead end, Lexi. I'm just at a dead end," I spat back, frustrated with the both of us. "I have no lead for this case. I can't find a connection between the victims, I've been on the phone with all the contacts you gave me, none of them saw anything, and no one could give me a hint of a reason why someone would target your sister. I can't even be sure this is the same killer. That was twenty years ago. Do you understand the likelihood of all this being connected?" My words ushered a wind of relief for me, but crippled the hope in Lexi. I could see it in her eyes. There was a faith that was wavering. Faith that her sister's murder would be avenged.

Faith that someone like her, who lost someone to this monster, could help her. I would've felt bad—if I wasn't so relieved.

"So what, you're just going to give up? Like that?" Lexi snapped. She was moving past confusion and on to rage. Her grip around her iced latte tightened, her eyes nearly shook.

"I'm not saying I've thrown in the towel on your case. I want to find your sister's killer but I know you want it more. I'm just being honest with you. You came to me because my dad contacted you. My dad contacted you because he's obsessed with The Shoestring Killer. That case was famous. The entire country knew about it before it was over. If no one else could figure it out what makes you think I can? I'm not going to be this savvy detective that saves your whole world. You have to understand that."

Lexi paused. The fire inside her hadn't died, but she remained silent. She stared at her coffee, twisting the cup around and around, making a liquid ring on the dark hardwood of the table. "I'm sorry Lex—" I started, but before I could finish my sentence, Lexi's arm curled back and forth like a whip, as she aimed her iced latte to my direction and splashed the icy contents onto my face, plashing over my eyes

27

and lips and the front of my shirt. I could already hear the gasps and whispers from neighboring customers.

"I came to your office looking for help. Looking for someone to believe me. I wasn't looking for Sherlock Holmes, just someone who wanted...I don't know, peace, revenge, justice—something. I drove from Nashville just to talk to you. Just to talk to someone who felt the same way I felt. You could be that person but you won't get off your hide long enough to be him."

All eyes were on Lexi and I now. I didn't budge. I didn't say a word. I just listened to the broken heart of a sister-less sister.

"I thought you and I would be kindred spirits. People that could find solace in one another. People that could help each other." She rose from the table, and flung the thin, leather strap of her purse across her shoulder. "Wallow in your dirt for all I care, but let me give you some southern wisdom—dirt don't stop the hurt." Lexi turned on her heel and exited the shop. In the afterglow of the scene, I contemplated starting after her. I also contemplated telling the staring customers to screw off. I didn't have time to do either one, though, because just as Lexi was making her grand exit, she double backed for a superior encore.

"And another thing," but *thing* came out more like *thang,* "believe me, you're not the only one to feel this pain. I saw that shoestring tied around her wrist the same as you."

"What?" the air suddenly escaped my lungs, but it didn't matter to Lexi. She'd already turned on her heel once more and disappeared in the crowded street. She left me there, alone with my thoughts—and the truth.

That night I barely slept. It had nothing to do with the coffee, I was positive I could grind beans with my teeth and it would be all the same to me. I kept thinking of a singular image, that patiently waited in my brain like an old photograph in an album that hadn't been dusted off in a decade—like the Grant family albums. I saw her wrist, my mother's wrist, with a shoestring tied in a neat bow around it.

I shook the thoughts from me the best I could, and wondered if I could possibly handle the folder that lay askew on an old pizza box in my living room. Dice were rolled and a chance was played, I picked up the envelope from before and opened it. I scattered the contents onto the table quickly— a Band-Aid to a wound. There were lots of notes, my old man's handwriting in some of them. Those, I pushed aside. I only looked for one thing—a photograph that I unfortunately found. There, in perfect color, was a shot of Lexi's sister.

There were bruises around the neck, choked to death. She was a shade of blue I hadn't seen in a long time. Her hair was stringy and kinked. The one thing I needed to see though, the only piece of the puzzle that I was looking for that I never wanted to find was ever-present: a shoestring tied around her wrist.

I sighed as I reached for my phone. My fingers trembled as I called my most recent contact.

"Kiddy," I said, after a few seconds of waiting and a few more of hearing Kiddy trying to wake up.

"What do you want?" he asked.

"It's him," I said.

"What?"

"The Shoestring Killer," I replied. I dropped the photograph back onto the table. And that is when I noticed, there in the stack, a picture of my own mother's crime scene. There she was, she looked so much like Lexi's sister. My mother was blue, her dress was torn, her neck was bruised in the same fashion, and on her wrist was also a perfectly tied shoestring.

"I don't know why I didn't think of it, before—the shoe strings tied around the wrist," I said.

"Yeah, we knew that," Kiddy sighed into the telephone.

"But the public didn't," I said. "Just the police and the relatives of the victims knew about the shoestring tied around the wrist," I exclaimed. "And unlike Farmer, whose knot looked completely different, this shoestring has the exact same knot—just like the one on my mother's wrist."

"Which means that," Kiddy's voice trailed off.

"Kiddy, he's home."

There was still speculation about Joseph Farmer's murder, it's likely that someone, at the time, could've found out about the shoestring tied around the wrist, and tried to tie a similar knot. This, though, seemed authentic. The knot seemed to be an identical match, which, suddenly made me eager to justify Lexi's feelings about the case.

I waited outside the Ramada Plaza Hotel, after persuading Lexi to stay long enough to speak to me before she left town. I parked down the block from the hotel and met her on the sidewalk outside. Her look was cold, hard, stern, but most importantly—hopeful.

"This better be good," she said. "I was just in the middle of stealing the shampoos."

"I don't want this case," I said. I could tell I'd taken her aback. "I don't want it."

"Yes, you've made that perfectly clear," she said. The southern fire of her voice became torrid. "But I have to have this case."

"I'm trying to be honest with you here. I need you to know that I don't want to do this and that it is not going to be easy for me but it will be a lot harder for me if I don't."

Lexi didn't say anything. She dug her hands in the back pocket of her jeans. The wind blew past us and a few stray strawberry blonde hairs attacked her eyelashes. "You were right, and apparently so was Alan Grant. This is the real guy."

There was a look on her face that I couldn't quite characterize. She was surprised, but not, relieved. All in all, it was probably the same feeling I had bouncing off the walls of my cerebellum.

"Well, what finally convinced you?" She asked. I held up the envelope. "Their tied shoestring was never something the police let the public know about—at least not the knot. It was their little way of detecting if any copycats came along. Even the guy they found during the murders, the shoestring was on his wrist but it wasn't an exact match. This one though, it looked identical to the one I saw on..." My voice trailed. "The same monster that killed your sister is the same monster that killed my mother."

The fear of the unknown, that lurking shadow, has a face. A real face. Something that can glare at you and wait for you to blink first. It stays in the shadows so we can't know it. We won't know it. Because how do you face a monster that is faceless? That's what happened to the people of Abingdon twenty years ago. They lost their minds over a faceless criminal who preyed on the women. I was an eleven year old kid—unknowingly living out my final days of childhood. I had a particularly intense fear of the old barn that set on our property. It was never used, and thus became the closest thing to a haunted house I had ever seen. Alan would tell me time and time again that the only things in that old shed were his fishing poles and the furniture that my mother made him get rid of when they married.

Despite my fear of the barn, which wasn't subsided by my father's efforts at all, I constantly found myself staring at it from the windows of my house—late at night, when it was the absolute scariest. My mother would repeatedly beg me not to torture myself, but I had to watch. I think I wanted to expose the shadows. I think I told myself that if I faced it, whatever waited on the other end of that darkness, it wouldn't be scary. One night, in the August of 1995, I remember waking to loud booms outside. There was a thunder roar that jolted the house, and cackles of lightning stripped the sky of its infinite blackness. I, on tipped toes, made my way downstairs and into the kitchen. I needed to know the barn was still in its place. I still needed to know that whatever evil I was determined lurked inside, wasn't taking advantage of the gruesome weather.

The night was black and the rain made it even harder to see out the windows and made it seem that our house was under the sea. I looked hard, my eyes willing themselves to see past the water, past the nothing, and find the faded red barn and all of its problems. Then, another sharp bolt of lightning lit the backyard, and the vision before me made my heart stop and my body paralyzed from shock.

Someone was on the other side of the glass—a stranger staring back. All I could see were a pair of wide unforgiving eyes looking back at me. The rest of their face was hidden, as if there weren't a face at all. The figure's mouth dropped open—as if to scream. The eyes, though, their eyes screamed louder. It was years before I went back to the barn. Because if one goes looking for monsters hard enough—one just might find one.

Elizabeth's Work Journal
July 27th, 1993.

    Old Dominion has continued to be a dream. A simple dream. Dr. Walker is a marvelous caretaker and overseer. He not only treats the patients with care and expertise but he is a fine man, an astute businessman, and a freethinker ahead of his own time. He understands the psychology of the mind better than any professor I have ever studied under.

    I have spent a month working in this asylum, and although I haven't had my chance yet to work closely with Dr. Walker and his specialists on what he calls Tomorrow's Minds, I have received several personal letters from him telling me to keep up the good work I am doing, for he has seen a real psychological change in the patients he's assigned to me; patients whose mental health diagnosis are much less severe than any of the patients he works with himself.

    Some minds might find my work naive, and it is true that there is a simplistic rubric to my style. I believe first and foremost that these patients are far more than that—they are people. People that deserve to have happiness in their lives, which is why one of my first duties as a full-time psychologist was to hire Jody.

Jody, which was just a nickname we gave him, is a wonderful man who is extremely talented, not in science, but in art. His demeanor is intoxicating—to the patients. He's a bit of a hippie. Long hair and earrings, a tattoo on his forearm and one on his collarbone. It doesn't matter his appearance. He brings an acoustic guitar and strums along for the patients. They love it, well, most of them do.

Last week Jody had the idea to bring the patients that I felt comfortable with, into the recreational room at the same time, while he played and sang for all of them. Patients like Franklin, Marcy, and Marvin listened closely, clapping along and smiling. Tony, who is more severe than my regular charges, reacted violently—but Jody never gives up. He is a gentle man and I have found that being around him...not only brightens the day for the sick, but brightens mine as well.

Alan is uncomfortable with the amount of hours I have had to put into my job. I've tried to explain to him that it is new territory for me and that once I spend some hard hours setting up my new work, I will be able to cut back on my time there. I need him to be strong now. These people, this asylum needs me more than he does. He's a strong man. Grayson is a strong boy. It's only temporary, my long hours here. I love them both so much. I don't want to disappear on my family.

I won't become a ghost.

Chapter Three

Ghost Town

"I'm having second thoughts," I said. The morning was early, there was still a thick midnight purple that drifted in the sky. I held a coffee in my hand, trying to understand what early hours felt like for a normal person.

"You'll probably have second, third, and fourth thoughts too, Grant," Kiddy said as he sipped a coffee beside me. We stood in front of the office, looking at my car as if it was going to turn on and drive to Abingdon all by itself. "And I know you're not use to taking on actual cases, but that twisting stomach feeling is normal."

"I don't think this is a good idea anymore," I said. "I'm a fry cook wearing a chef's hat, Kiddy."

"Well, at least you're humble," he remarked.

"This is a mistake. There is literally nothing good that can come from this. You know that, right?"

Kiddy sipped his drink. "Maybe," he shrugged. "Honestly, I don't know. You agreed to it, though. And I'll be honest, that's out of character for you. So, for you to get out of your comfort zone...there's a reason."

"There's no reason to believe that I can do anything that a whole department couldn't solve twenty years ago,

Kiddy!" I was flustered, now, but so was Kiddy. Kiddy flung his hand up. "Shut up, Grant," he said with a booming voice that, for once, actually made me shut up.

Kiddy was a soft spoken man, so when he walked with a heavy foot it was noticeable. He reached through the rolled down window of his car and snatched my coffee from the passenger cup holder, swigged it, and glared at me. "Don't act like you want the pity, Grayson, and don't act like you don't want this case. Congratulations, kid. You're going home."

The drive from St. Louis, Missouri to Abingdon, Virginia was pure country. Green and mountains, with the occasional sign of civilization in between and a mess of bad memories peppered in the mix. I loathed the drive because I'd only driven it once before in the opposite direction, when I left old Mother Country and never looked back—until now, I suppose. It wasn't the town—Abingdon was too tasteful, perfect, boring, to be anything near offensive or disgusting. It was everything that happened there...everything that happened to Alan, and everything that happened to me.

I drove through the night with the intentions of slipping into Abingdon unnoticed. It is silly, to think that the presence of one person could disrupt an entire town, like it was the old West and I was one of the two people that couldn't live in a town that size because it simply wasn't big enough. That's how it felt, though, for those connected to the Shoestring Killer's crime spree. All of the survivors, the families attached to the victims, the poor saps that the Shoestring Killer left alive—we were all just trying to dry our eyes while the spotlight shined on us.

I felt nauseated in the pit of my stomach when my ten-year-old SUV hit Bristol. I suddenly started reliving more memories than I wanted and regretted not fighting Kiddy harder on this trip. If anything, I would've preferred Kiddy's assistance on this case. I emailed Lexi the moment I left St. Louis, and told her that she should settle in back home in Nashville. I told her that if my lead was a solid one, I'd be contacting her in a couple of days with results.

The sky was beginning to brighten up. The harsh black of the night sky was softening to a purple-blue while the stars faded. It would be almost sunrise by the time I reached Abingdon. I would only pass the early starters, find myself some time alone, and collect my thoughts on the next move. I nearly vomited my gas station dinner at the thought of going home. Knocking on that big oak door, expecting my father to answer, open arms, smiling. I would half expect to find him in his basement with a lunatic board hung on the wall and a million strings all connecting to a faceless man in the center.

I knew if not literally, Alan's mind was mentally in that place, and it had been since 1995.

At four in the morning I hit the city limits. The child inside me expected a time warp—or a stampede of police officers, reporters, anyone with a microphone who wanted to get another quote from the grieving son of a dead mother. I expected to see faces swelled with so much pity in their eyes, would scarcely be able to withstand the pressure. I even imagined my father there, waiting at the border with a clue in one hand and a bottle of Jack Daniels in the other. Daddy isn't much of a detective either.

There weren't any of those things, though. There was only silence. A bird tweet and tires crunching on old pavement as I rolled into town for the first time since I was twenty-one. I subconsciously slouched in the driver's seat, as if I were avoiding the onslaught of attention I was about to receive. No one noticed, though. There wasn't a mosh pit of yesteryear waiting to rip me to shreds. No, in that moment it was abundantly clear that whatever punishment was waiting for me in Abingdon, Virginia, was not going to be as straightforward as a mosh pit. It would be subtle, swift, in the shadows, and hit me when I least expected it. I knew *that* for sure.

Abingdon, Virginia is a ghost town. Not in the sense that it doesn't have many people, or any kind of vibrant life. No, Abingdon has people, it has life. The town also has ghosts. Every city worth visiting has a ghost fit for a haunting, with its very own legend and story attached to it, but Abingdon is one of the few gems that has several, for the small town that it happens to be. The ghost stories have become imbedded into the culture. Heroes and villains from centuries past are told to haunt the grounds of Abingdon. Most of these ghosts are supposed to have been Civil War soldiers.

I never really believed in ghosts, not even as a kid, but it was something we all took part in, anyway. Growing up in my hometown, we all hunted for ghosts. I guess not much has changed. That's how I felt, as I drove through the small, old bricked, town. Not much had had changed. I still expected the spotlight to hit me at any moment. That some Abingdon original, somewhere, would cast sad eyes on me and ask me a question about something that happened twenty years ago, that I either don't remember or don't want to talk about.

See, the ghost town added some ghosts to the roster twenty years ago, thanks to the Shoestring Killer. The victims he took with them—they're a part of the haunt, now. And the people like me, the victims he left alive—they're the ones being haunted.

42

I settled in at the Martha Washington Inn, which was practically in the center of my Virginian hometown. A little too showy for me, but I was writing the expense off my taxes as a business trip. I caught a couple of hours sleep, which was hazy and unsettling. It was a joke to think I could get a good rest the moment I returned to home. No luxury hotel and spa would even do that for me. After I surrendered any notion of sleep, I showered, changed clothes—a pair of relaxed jeans, long sleeve t-shirt, and a Cardinals cap, all in the hopes of keeping a low profile—I headed down to the police station.

The last time I was in the police station, I was answering questions about my parents. A scared, hurt, tortured eleven-year-old kid, contemplating the reality of losing a mother to a psychopath in his own home. I sat with officers for hours as they drilled me about any suspicious characters I might have seen, how were my father and mother acting towards one another, and if I had anything I needed to tell them. It was pathetic, in hindsight, how they glared at me with open eyes, expecting a goldmine worth of knowledge to come pouring out of my mouth. As if I were some untapped secret—the one with the lead. As I entered the police station for the first time in twenty years, I realized that now was the time I had that untapped secret—a wealth of information ready to pour out of me, and I only hoped they had a cup big enough to hold it.

"I need to speak with the Chief of Police," I said hastily to a woman who sat behind the front desk. She had thick buggy-eyeglasses with equally thick eyebrows hovering over them. She was in her late sixties, at least, and squinted at me like the out-of-towner I'd wished I could have been.

"I need a new hip," she scoffed. "It sure is lovely to think about all the things we need, isn't it?"

Taken aback, I frowned and repeated myself. "Excuse me, but I need to speak to the Chief of Police."

"Is this an emergency?" she sighed.

"Well," I stuttered.

"It is or it isn't, pretty boy. Which one is it?"

"It isn't—yet. But it will be."

"That's about as ambiguous as it gets, huh?"

"Listen blue hair," I blurted out. "I get at your age you like to ride the slow lane but this is important." My usual demeanor aimed at a police officer was not a good idea, but I was already in too deep. She glared at me for a moment, clearly gritting her dentures.

"What's your name?" she asked as she picked up a clipboard near her.

"Grayson Grant, P.I." I felt fake. She eyed me over her buggy glasses, I suppose because she had her reservations that I was a private investigator as well.

"Grayson Grant?" she asked. Her tone was softer now. "Alan Grant's boy?" My heart sank. My instinct was to lie, and lie hard, but it was too late. I could already see a twisted wrinkled smile curve upward on her face. "I should've recognized you from the moment you walked in here. You look like him. Look a little bit like your mom, too."

I eyed the station for a moment, hoping that no one heard our conversation. If anyone did, they didn't let on. "Wait here," she said, but my ears had already tuned her out. I sat by the desk, resenting Kiddy for talking me into this in the first place. In my dull moment, I sent him a text message:

I want a raise when I get back.

"Grayson Grant," I heard a voice call out that struck me—soft, but authoritative, and familiar. My eyes shot from my cell phone to the voice. Standing in her bright blue uniform was Jolene Wire—Abingdon's girl next door. "As I live and breathe." I was speechless. I couldn't move. I knew there must've been a smile on my face, but I wasn't sure, I could only hope. Jolene Wire had been one of my closest

45

friends in Abingdon. Growing up, she was always one step ahead of me and the guys. That's where she liked to be—one step ahead. A tomboy unlike any I'd ever seen, Jolene held her own with all of us. I wasn't surprised to see that she was a police officer, now. I suppose I was more surprised to see that she never left.

Her hair was wavy and looked as if it probably were long enough to bypass her shoulders, but she wore it in a ponytail. It was a chestnut color, too—like always. Her eyes were deep and dark, before I could notice another thing about my old friend, she had both arms around my neck, throwing professionalism out the window. I hugged her back and felt her cold nose dig into my shoulder.

Jolene Wire was a Korean American, adopted by a country family, Ned and Gina. The Wires relocated to Abingdon after a string of racial threats that were made to them for adopting someone from South Korea. In the political warfare of today—it made me wonder if that experience, and a thousand more like it, were some of the reasons Jolene decided to become a police officer. Or maybe—she just loved being on the opposite side of the bad guys.

"It's been a long time," I said, as I gently patted her shoulder blade.

"A lot longer than you think, Egg," she said.

"Oh no," I said, as I broke up the hug. "No one calls me Egg anymore."

"They better not," she started with a smile. "I was the only one who ever did."

I laughed. I actually laughed. I laughed for release, and pleasure, but also nervousness. Jolene was the opposite of me in almost every way. I might be crooked at best, but on Jolene's worst day, she was still straight as an arrow. Justice and purity went hand in hand with Jolene Wire. She always knew the right thing to do and never seemed to struggle with doing it. At least that's what she was back then. As I stood in the police station, however, and saw her decked in the colors of the law, I knew she hadn't changed—not like me. Perhaps that's why I hadn't come back for her in ten years. Perhaps that's why she never went looking for me.

I found myself, an hour later, sitting in a dark bar and grill somewhere in the midst of town, with Jolene on the opposite side of the booth.

"A couple of beers for a couple of old friends," Jolene said in a cheesy way.

"Actually, just make mine a coffee," I said to the waitress, a twenty-something with a pierced lip who looked at me like the pretentious snob in which I sounded. "I don't drink," I added, as Jolene eyed me carefully. "Sugar," I said to the waitress, who remained silent, and walked away, jotting down on her pad.

"A coffee man," Jolene said in fake amusement. Small talk wasn't her thing.

"It keeps the monsters away."

"How? Keeps your eyes open?" She asked.

"The withdrawal headaches—those are the monsters I fear," I said, half-jokingly.

She shook her head. "You still talk like that, huh?" she asked.

"Talk like what?"

"Like everyone else in the room is holding their breath."

I snorted a petty laugh and shook my head. "I don't know what you're talking about, Jo."

She grimaced. "You know I hate to be called Jo. No one calls me Jo. I don't let them."

"You let me."

"You are a part of an elite group," she teased.

"What kind of group is that?" I asked, laughing.

"The kind that has seen my bedroom," she said, smiling, but quickly recoiled.

The waitress silently approached, sat a cup of coffee in front of me and a cold beer in front of Jolene. I shifted nervously in my seat, sipped my coffee and glared at an area of the table where a small chunk of wood was missing.

"At least tell me why you've graced our humble presence again, after all these years, Detective Grant," she asked in a playful manner but I knew she was eager to change the subject and to sink her teeth into why I was really home.

"Ugh," I grimaced at the word detective. "Don't call me that. I've heard that there has been a recent murder in your part of the world," I said. "Same M.O. as—"

"—As the Shoestring Killer," Jolene finished my sentence. "And you are investigating, Mr. Grayson Grant, P.I?"

"You know I'm a private investigator?" I questioned.

"Your dad is a proud man," she said with a hint of a smile cooking. I sighed and sipped my coffee again, only to give myself reason to pause. "In fact, he has been an active eye in the town since it happened."

"Has anything come of it?" I asked, eagerly.

Jolene raised an eyebrow to me as she sipped her drink. "Come of it?" she said as she swallowed, bitterly.

"Since the recent murder?" I repeated.

"We're trying to keep a tight lid on it, we don't want the public to lose their minds in fear. Your dad knows, only because he knows everything that happens here," Jolene said.

"Of course he does," I sighed.

"I'm assuming it wasn't your dad that got you back here?" She asked. She twisted the beer bottle, slowly, in circles on the table—an old habit of hers. She was nervous. I knew her when she was nervous.

"A girl, lady—woman," I tripped over my words. "Sister of the victim, Lexi Keats lives in Springfield. Her sister was here visiting Emory and Henry and never made it home. She contacted me," I explained. "My dad got to her, gave her the whole conspiracy theory rundown. Now I'm here."

"You don't believe it is the same guy from—well, before?" Jolene tiptoed around the words.

I shrugged. "The wrist, Jolene, the knot, no one knew about the wrists or that knot."

"That's been twenty years, Grayson," she stated. I nodded my head.

"I don't know. I haven't had enough to go on to come up with any kind of decision. What about you? You guys don't have anything? Word of this gets out in town, the people will panic, whether it is a copycat or the real deal. Either way, there's a dead girl."

Jolene rotated her bottle around the wood, playing with the water ring it left.

"Who is asking me? Egg? Or Grayson Grant, Private investigator?" she questioned.

"Does it really matter?" I asked.

"It matters. Because if it is Egg asking me these questions, I would say: The department is working on several leads to figure out this situation. We're doing everything we can to keep the people of Abingdon safe."

I nodded, playfully. "And say it is the other guy asking," I stated.

"We got nothing and if we did I wouldn't tell you, anyway," she blurted out. I snort-laughed again. "Sorry," she started with a smile. "I can't share my entire hand to a private investigator, those are the rules. Should have joined the force and become a real detective," she teased.

"And have the opportunity to boss you around? I don't think you'd stand for that," I replied. The laughing erupted from both of us, but ceased just as quickly.

"Don't do this, Grayson. Don't get mixed up in this just let the police do their job," she said.

"I have to try, Jo," I said. "You know I have to try."

Jolene rolled her eyes and looked downward. "You're so stubborn," she said. "But I know."

"Can you do me a favor, though, Jolene? For old times' sake?" I said. It felt fabricated, asking so politely when it was so obvious I was only being polite to get what I wanted.

"What, Grayson?" she said in a soothing voice. "What could you possibly want from me?" Her smile was different this time.

"Can you find out what they had back then? In '95? Who they were looking at or leads or something?"

"You know, your dad probably already has a lot of that information," she stated with a relaxed shrug.

"I'd rather keep him out of it."

"Have you seen him, yet?" she asked

"I just got into town."

"Are you going to see him?"

"I have a lot of stuff to do. I am on the clock, after all."

"It would mean the world to him."

"Jolene..."

"I know, it isn't any of my business, I'm just the lowly lady-cop who sees him sitting alone on his front porch everyday on patrol, who has a bleeding heart for a man who had so much and ended up with so little. It's one thing to be a mountain range or two away, but to be down the road from him, Grayson..." Jolene's voice trailed off.

"I get it. I need to see my dad. I need to be a good son. Or just a son, for that matter. I will. I'm here, though, because I have a case. And I wouldn't be on this case if it wasn't for him. And assuming by the monthly mail I get from him, my visit from Lexi Keats, and just knowing who he has been for the last twenty years, I'd say he's more concerned with me doing my job rather than me wasting time to see him," I said, sternly.

There was a pause. Jolene cleared her throat and nodded. She looked neither hurt, alarmed nor upset, which told me she was scary-furious. "Okay. You're right. Far be it from me to try to tell a Grant boy what to do, right?" she said. I sighed, dug my hand into my jeans and dumped a wad of ones on the table.

"How much time do you think I'll get before the boys in blue kick me off the case?" I said as I stood up.

"About as much time as we will until the state takes it away from us."

"Jack still around here?" I asked, changing the subject, quickly.

"Believe it or not, he is."

I nodded, and forced a smile to my face as I walked away from the booth. "I'll see you soon, Jolene."

"Hey wait," she called out. I hated to admit to myself the thrill that surged through me in that moment.

"You said not to call you a detective?" she asked.

"Yeah?" I said while turning to her.

"Why not? If you're not a detective then what are you?"

53

"I'm whatever is left when you realize you're not one."

I turned, without waiting for a reaction, and moved my way through the dimly lit bar. I wondered if Jolene was just as happy to see me as I was to see her or if there was a lingering wonder on her end about why I looked uncomfortable in my own skin just being within the city limits. Jolene never wanted to leave. When she looked at Abingdon, she saw a healing town, twenty years in the making. When I see it, however, it is still bleeding.

It took the rest of the day, four cups of coffee, and a self-help pep talk to do it, but I finally decided to stop by my old homestead. After passing the house seven or eight times, slithering up and down Main Street like the snake I was, I pulled the SUV into Alan's driveway. Of course I was faced with an onslaught of memories that triggered even my most forgotten thoughts: Playing basketball on our broken net in the driveway; sneaking out the bathroom window, which was the only one that didn't lock and burying a time capsule in the backyard.

The house was big for us, two stories, and four bedrooms. It was old, too. Not the kind of old that looks pathetic sitting on a patch of brown grass. The kind of old that people paid good money to live in—that made you look like you were worth something. It was a family home that was left to us, but that didn't stop my parents from letting it make them feel like they were worth something. I couldn't say that I blamed them—who doesn't want to be worth something?

In the backyard, sitting adjacent and askew, was the barn from my nightmares. Once I stopped being afraid of it as a teenager, I made the top floor of it mine. A place that was for me and my friends, or more accurately, Jolene and me.

I walked the stone steps to the porch, falling leaves lay nearly perfect on the walk up. It was easy to forget in all the darkness that engulfed my memory, Abingdon was a beautiful town and in the autumn it proved even more gorgeous. The front porch had a green tint to it, with brick columns that held up the old structure. A white porch swing was located on the right side—complete with chipped paint. There were memories on the porch too, but in all my hindsight, it was exceedingly bigger.

I took a deep breath, cursing myself, and Jolene, for allowing me to get to this place. The oak door had a glass center, so while it wasn't too late to turn back, I could already see into the house. I could see the staircase that broke off to the right, the french doors leading to the living room on the left, and in the center a long narrow hallway that eventually lead to the dining room and the kitchen. I was already here, where my father called the homestead, where my mother called her favorite place, where the locals called Killer-House, and the place where I called home.

I knocked twice, and was ready to turn around when I saw a figure emerge in the hallway. It was large—he was large. Muscular, strong, stocky—the gene pool must certainly have skipped a generation. As he approached, I saw him pause for a moment. It must've been when he realized who was on the other side of the oak and glass. It felt like it did in the movies, when someone is in prison and a loved one comes a-calling. They stared at each other with a narrow sheet of glass between the two of them. The feeling felt a little too natural for the two of us. I guess he was the prisoner, and I was the poor sap still willing to visit.

"Grayson," Alan said, the moment he opened the door. He looked tired. Too tired to be shocked, but too tired to hide his excitement. His eyes were a deep brown, almost black. He hadn't shaved in a couple of weeks, almost a full graying beard covered his face, and he was easily twenty pounds heavier than the last time I saw him. He wore a sloppy t-shirt, one with worn-holes, oil stains, and a stretched collar. I imagined it being a shirt he probably wore when I was a kid. Below his bulbous stomach was a pair of cargo shorts. A different look for him. A little more relaxed, but the man was retired these days.

"Hey Pop," I said. Despite not seeing him in ten years, and always referring to him as dad or pop, I wanted to call him Alan, as I did these days when I thought of him. A small part of me reverted, though, to the seven-year old Grayson. An even bigger part of me hated myself for it. Without another word he wrapped his arms around my neck, pulling me inside. He smelt like aftershave and sweat.

"I didn't expect you," he said, passive-aggressively, as he released me from his firm embrace and stretched me out to arm's length. He stared in my eyes for a moment, surveying me, as if he were unconvinced I was real. I understood the feeling. "You got my packages, then?" he asked. He looked like a boy on Christmas morning.

"I got all your packages, Alan. I've always gotten your packages. That's not why I'm here, though."

"You're not here for the case?" His eyes widened, his mouth shrunk. I could crush the man's soul with a single *no.*

"I'm happy to see you too," I said, sarcastically. "I'm here for the case, you're just not my client. Miranda Keats' sister sought me out, thanks to you."

Alan looked offended now. He straightened up his posture, his eyes pointed downward at me now. "We have to remain united, son. A concept I'm not sure you understand." A silence broke out between us. I hadn't been home five minutes before the tension started to suffocate us both. He lead me through the house, attempting to be a proper host, as if I weren't a son, but rather an onlooker ready to buy all of this away from him. Though he was eager to reintroduce me to home, nothing had changed—not a thing.

"Are you going to canvas the families from the '95 murders? Everything you need should be in the notes I sent you," Alan said, matter-of-factly. Though he was passionate for personal reasons, he almost sounded professional— unattached. I knew it was a facade, though. For Alan, this is all there was...no present, no future, just the past and how to fix it.

"Miranda Keats is a dead end. Her sister told me she was here touring a college. Wrong place wrong time. If he's here, though, if he's back..." my voice trailed off.

Alan glanced at me, there was something in his eyes. Fear? Intrigue? Excitement?

"I wish I knew you were coming," Alan started, shaking the gaze and moving toward the staircase. "I would've gotten your old room ready." I stopped quickly when I realized where he was going, and remained in the hall.

"Actually, I got a room at the Martha Washington."

"Why?" he asked, confused.

"I didn't want to impose," I lied. I shrugged, and moved to the living room, opening the French doors. Alan came off the bottom stair, following me.

"You know, despite everything I'm still your father, Grayson," he said sternly.

"I'm not denying that."

"Then where do you get off coming here, acting like a stranger that I happened to bother?" I scoffed at his words and rolled my eyes. "Tell me, son. I'm intrigued. I really am." I had almost forgotten the boom that his voice had—almost.

"Why wouldn't I be bothered, Alan? Do you not find all of this...bothersome? A killer...*Mom's* killer is back."

"Yes, yes it is terrible, but son think about it—now we have a chance for justice, vengeance, closure." Alan spat back. I sighed. "Son," Alan's voice calmed. "I know this is a tragedy. A horrible tragedy that I wish I could prevent but I can't. I feel for these victims, their families, no one knows their hurt like we do, son. It is our chance, though, to do something for Elizabeth...to give her justice." His voice nearly broke when he said her name.

I plopped down on the yellow sofa that sat in front of the picture window, facing a blank television. "Then why me?" I asked. Alan cocked his head to the side, like he didn't understand the question. "You could hire any private investigator. You could give all of this to the police. You could do any of it yourself. Why me?"

"You're a private investigator," he said simply.

"Barely," I shrugged.

"It's your mother. You are good enough."

I buried my head in the palms of my hands. The weight of the situation was finally catching up to me. Grayson Grant, playing detective, playing son, playing friend, oh how I missed out on an acting career. I thought of Jolene, who all but warned me I shouldn't be on the case in the capacity in which I was—smart girl.

I wanted to scream at Alan. I wanted to ask him why I was good enough to handle this investigation, but not good enough to call and check up on. I wanted to know why I got piles of notes, possible clues, written testimonies from eye-witnesses, but never a birthday card. I could chalk it up to Alan being a different kind of a parent. The kind that shows love through respect and not affection, or the kind of parent that expects you to already understand decent things like love and kindness. That wasn't Alan though, not in his DNA. Once upon a time, when Elizabeth, my mother, his wife, was alive and well, Alan was a gentle man. A cool, reflective, collected man. If the years had made him hardened, rough around the edges, cynical, somewhat like me, I could understand. That didn't seem to be the case, either, though. Alan was just obsessed. That's all he was now. Alan had an obsession I didn't understand. The difference between him and me— when we put my mother in the ground, I let her lie there, and he has tried ceaselessly to dig her up ever since.

A few small words and half-hearted promises later, I left my father's home, with the agreement I'd settle in, catch up on sleep, and speak with him the next day. It was difficult to admit but I found myself appeasing him because it was easier that way. It had always been that way, after the murders. I checked my cell phone for the first time in hours, forgetting I had a contact to the outside world. A text message response from Kiddy awaited, telling me not only was I not getting a raise, but I would probably be getting a pay decrease. Kiddy was a better detective than comedian.

I sipped my coffee, which had settled into a state of luke warmness as I gazed outside my hotel window. One of those ghost stories, the ones that you'd find on the Abingdon haunt tour, was in the very hotel I'd chosen over my parents' home. The story goes that before it was a hotel, it was a woman's college. During the Civil War, however, it was transformed into a hospital for wounded soldiers. Apparently a young Yankee captain was brought to the hospital with injuries, and a nurse fell in love with him—playing the violin for him as he died. When a Confederate soldier came looking to transfer the prisoner, the young nurse informed him that the Yankee captain died. The nurse, ironically named Beth, died soon after from a fever or maybe a broken heart. Guests have reported seeing Beth's lonely ghost roam the halls, and the room in which her and her captain died, along with a puddle of blood that has never seemed to be washed out of the carpet. It has also been said one can still hear her violin, as she's still trying to make a sweet sound for her sweet soldier.

My cell phone rang once more, and I was sure it was Kiddy, wanting a full report. It wasn't his name across the caller I.D, though, but a number I didn't recognize.

"Hello?"

"Egg, it's me," Jolene's voice whispered on the other end.

"Jolene," I said, a little surprised. I suddenly glanced at the mirror in my room, to double check my appearance.

"I'm breaking more than one rule with this phone call," she started. "We've found another body."

"What?" I said, as soon as I could comprehend what she said to me.

"The Shoestring Killer, Grayson," she stated. "It's him. It has to be him. He's home."

Things like the Martha Washington Inn hauntings didn't obtain a rise out of me. Violins and forever blood soaked carpets, broken hearts and dying love. What bothered me wasn't old Civil War stomping grounds where soldiers died. It was places like the upstairs rooms of my childhood home, where I found my mother's lifeless body before anyone else. What bothers me isn't the ghosts, but the demons that make them.

Extraordinary Secrets

Elizabeth's Work Journal
October 3rd, 1993.

I am somebody here. An important person, a doctor, a colleague and people respect me. I'm not just some bubbly pretty face with a pair of tits and a smile. I'm valued. And beyond that...I'm adored. Dr Liam Walker brought each and every member of his staff onboard because of their different strengths. We work and breathe as a unit, but each of us have something remarkable to bring to the table. My charges, the band of patients that are relying on me to make a difference in their lives, are growing. Just last week, Dr. Walker saw to it that two more patients join my roaster. It is difficult, and taxing, but I've risen to the challenge. Some patients, like Tony, continue to be resentful and violent. Other patients, like Marvin and Franklin, continue to impress me. Marvin never wants to eat his lunch (he says he had the same thing for breakfast, which is an obvious lie). And sweet Franklin refuses to wear his shoes, but he listens to me and opens up when I ask him to talk about his thoughts and feelings.

Dr. Walker's Tomorrow's Minds, program is going well: Three patients in the past four months, who entered into our care as outrageously violent individuals with severe mental disabilities, have calmed. They're far from being independent citizens, but Dr. Walker is able to make violent cases mild and civil. It's truly a work of wonder.

Jody is continuing to work hard. He's helped the patients artistic juices flow. The Asylum has more color because of him. He smiles at me, perhaps a little too much. It isn't bothersome, or even inappropriate. I wonder, sometimes though, when I'm working late, doing paperwork, writing notes about my patients, catching up on my continued education, why he still roams the halls, playing guitar for the patients and finding small, nearly insignificant jobs to do, until I'm ready to leave. I'm not sure if there just isn't more in his life or if he is looking to add more to it.

His eyes are kind. His voice is lovely, and I can't help but wonder what he sees in a place like Old Dominion. I see purpose, I see cases, and people who need help. But what draws the artistic? Is it purpose for him, too? Is it compassion? Boredom? Love? Love is a complicated subject. I've learned, in my time here, that it takes many shapes. I take care of Grayson. I feed him, clothe him, tuck him in bed. I wash his clothes and give him hugs and kisses. That's how he knows I love him. He draws me pictures, calls me mommy, meets me at the door, or at least he used to before he started growing up. This is how I know he loves me.

My patients do the same: Marcy shows love by letting Marvin have the apple she gets for lunch, because Marvin only gets one apple, and it is the only thing he'll eat. Walter will show love by helping clean up the recreational room. He says it is his first step back to society. (He was a custodian before he was admitted to Old Dominion). And Franklin shows his love by sitting quietly when told, despite the fact he'd rather be doing something else. He'll just sit, quietly, patiently, when I know he doesn't want to. And Tony doesn't really act like he loves anything. Which is a shame, we all need love.

Chapter Four

Bedroom Window

That feeling returned to Abingdon. That feeling of not only fear, and awareness, but pity. It didn't take long for the whole town to find out that Kathy Collins, an elementary school teacher had been found strangled in her home. One girl, a passerby, can go unnoticed, but when you have an Abington original in the morgue, that's something else. What Jolene told me was the heart wrenching details.

"There was a shoelace tied around her wrist," I could hear the uneasiness in her voice over the phone. That eerie feeling that this is real...the past had returned. I kicked myself for letting something like this happen right under my nose, when I was in Abingdon for the sole purpose of catching this before it went bad. I realized, in that moment, while I sat on the edge of the hotel bed, that Jolene wasn't the only one who felt in over their head.

"The knot was a perfect match, just like crime scenes from 1995. You were right, I think it really is him" she said, like it was a consolation prize.

"A lot of good it did Kathy Collins," I replied.

Jolene hung up soon after; she had just arrived at the scene. Over the course of the next few hours, the word had spread like wildfire, and suddenly being back in Abingdon made everyone seem all the more awkward.

"Hey, you're the Grant boy," a lone voice at the bar said as I entered the diner. Eyes from across the restaurant cast their gaze in my direction. The response was mixed, there was pity, but there was speculation, too. I didn't blame them. A forgotten son returns home the same time the Shoestring Killer does? The town stopped believing in coincidence, at least they should—I did. I nodded at the man at the bar and took my seat in a corner booth, avoiding eye contact with him. My phone vibrated on the table, just in the nick of time.

"Talk to me, Kiddy. Give me some good news."

"I was hoping you could give me some."

"There's a new body."

"I'm running some background checks on the families from '95, even yours. Hope to get that back soon. You gonna talk to the new family?"

"That's the plan."

The diner's door open and the *ding* of the bell alerted the entire restaurant which was otherwise pretty quiet—it was Tuesday morning, after all. Jolene, head to toe in police uniform, stepped into the diner.

"I gotta go, Kiddy. I'll call you soon." I hung up as Jolene made eye contact with me. I watched her, as she walked through the diner. Not in an idolizing way or even a sexual way. No, I watched her as a public figure, she was more than a cop, but a cop would've been enough. Two waitresses waved at her, the cook yelled her order from the kitchen before Jolene had a chance to open her mouth, and the glaring eyed man at the bar turned a smile her way, until he saw her sit down with me.

"You're too classy for a place like this," I said as she sat across from me.

"Is that your idea of a joke, Egg? I traded class for a badge years ago," she said. The waitress brought us two cups of coffee and confirmed with Jolene her standing order of two eggs over-easy. I told the waitress again that I would stick to the coffee. "We're going to have to get right to it, I don't have a lot of time," Jolene started. "I shouldn't be stopping to eat. We're trying to get as much done on this case as we can before the feds swoop in."

"What are the police doing?"

"Searching the entire town, every nook and cranny, road blocks at all the county lines. Canvasing the neighborhoods, just a bunch of desperate attempts," she said as she sipped her coffee. Watching her, I could see her brand of authority, she wasn't the seventeen year-old girl that use to sneak out her bedroom window at night to hang out with Jack and myself. She was strong, it was something I always admired about her. I sighed.

"No strong leads then, huh?" I added another pack of sugar to the cup.

"I wouldn't say that," she said, and a hopeful heartbeat pumped hard in my chest.

"Yeah?"

"That favor you asked of me, who the department was looking at in '95? I pulled some old files, most of those were in hard copies so you are welcome for that unpaid grunt work, by the way. It looks like, just before the case was handed over to the state, the department was looking at a Walt Rodgers. He was questioned several times, but never arrested."

"That name sounds familiar," I said, letting my voice trail off because I hadn't any fact or memory to back up the otherwise meaningless statement. "Why did it stop there?"

Jolene shrugged. The waitress approached again, laying the plate of eggs in front of Jolene. She smiled brightly at the waitress, and thanked her. "I don't know," she went on, eyes focused on the eggs. "The report says that he was suspicious and Detective Wilson said he liked him for it, but that's it. Nothing ever came of it. The case was handed to state police and they followed up on him I'm sure," she said, matter-of-factly. "But then I did some digging to see where our Walt Rodgers is today. Do you know?" she said, eagerly.

The excitement in her voice triggered a realization that wasn't ever-present before. Jolene was involved in a high-profile case, it was the first of her career, and if she stayed in Abingdon, it might be the only one. She was thrilled to be a part of it, in some small way. I couldn't blame her. It wasn't her mother's killer. "No, where?" I answered, playing along.

"That's just it, no one knows. He *dropped* off the face of the Earth, it seems."

"What?"

"He moved to Abingdon in, get this, '94, and then around 2007, just disappears. His bank account cleaned out, insurance cancelled, everything. He's a ghost to the world," Jolene said.

"Well how does that help us? He could literally be anywhere, if he's even still alive."

"He's alive, and he's here—in Abingdon."

"How do you know?"

"I've seen him before, Egg. I know he's still around here somewhere. He's just a whacko that lives somewhere secluded. No one knows for sure where, but Egg—this could be him. This could be the guy," she said, chewing the last bite of her second egg. "I've pointed it out to Detective McCoy, he's going to look into it."

"This is good," I nodded.

Jolene let out a subtle sigh. "Grayson, I know you want this, but you can't. You know that, right?" She looked at me with sulking eyes. I knew the look well, she'd been giving it to me for years. It angered me. Despite her involvement in my life, despite the relationship that was always present, she still looked at me like the rest of them did—with pity. "You don't want to do this, your father wants you to do this. I don't know, Grayson, pick a reason."

"This doesn't have anything to do with Alan," I barked.

"Oh please," she said, rolling her eyes and crossing her arms. "This has everything to do with Alan and you know it. Do I think you want your mother's murderer brought to justice? Yes, I do. I think you want that and I even think that a small part of you is eager to be one of the people that brings that person to justice but I know you, Grayson. You left without looking back. You were ready to move on, weren't you? Your dad, wasn't and still isn't. He isn't a secret, Egg."

There was an uncomfortable silence that I didn't know how to process. It was my turn to say something, to breathe words into a conversation that I wanted to die. I wasn't use to silence between Jolene and I...not the bad kind, anyway.

Jolene rose from the table, laid a crisp ten-dollar bill by her plate and waved a goodbye to the cook. Before leaving, she turned to me, I only glanced up for a moment.

"You know, when you left, it hurt a lot of people. A lot of them missed you. I missed you, but you know what? I was happy for you, because you got out." She paused, maybe waiting for me to say something. Maybe waiting for me to do something impressive. Maybe none of those things—just waiting for me to absorb it. "Don't let that be in vain," she said sharply, and exited the diner.

When I collected my cool and a second cup of coffee, I decided to go by the Collins house. A feeling of panic stirred in my stomach—vomit and coffee beans. The house sat on the North end of town, away from the old confederate streets. It was a beautiful home, white picket fence, bright red door, your typical homemaker magazine spread. Kathy Collins was an elementary teacher but she still lived with her parents. Out of college only a couple of years, and a six year old daughter that was now an orphan, considering the father was so far out-of-state he might as well be six-feet under, too.

The house had a wrap-around porch and I could feel the wood of the steps creaking, almost breaking when I walked up them. It was a beautifully old home—beautifully broken. The doorbell chimed and a small, yapping dog barked, suddenly. It took several seconds for a response, but soon the red door broke open. A woman, no taller than five foot, stood half behind the door, weary of my arrival. She had short, brown hair. A fifty-something grieving mother was looking at me.

"Mrs. Collins?" I asked.

She nodded. She trembled behind the door. She'd talked to cops all day. She was waiting for me to be another detective delivering some kind of horrible news or make her go through some sort of painful ordeal. She was half right. "My name is Grayson Grant, I'm a private investigator and I'm working on the Shoe—I'm working on a case very similar to...l," I was terrible with people.

"Mrs. Collins, I'm very sorry about your daughter," but my sentence was interrupted. The door opened wider, and a slightly taller man appeared. He was box shaped with a square torso and large, uncomfortable arms that looked like they never rested. "Enough," he said, in a raspy voice.

"Excuse me?"

"I said enough. We're mourning, right now. We've told the police everything we need to tell. Who do you think you are?" he shouted. I could hear the faint cry of a small child, deep in the house somewhere.

"I don't want to disrupt this time of grief...I'm just trying to help. I'm Grayson Grant, I'm a private investigator."

"Grant, Huh?" He eyed me. "We're not talking to any more of you people today. We've had enough. Stop asking us questions. We don't know anything. Please, just let the police do their jobs. Abingdon has already had one Grant ruin an investigation. We don't need another one!" His words were as loud as the door when he slammed it shut. I couldn't blame him. How does one survive the aftermath of losing a child, if not by letting a little bit of themselves go with them?

I pressed onward to the next stop. I called Kiddy and asked him to run Walt Rodgers through our databases, while I grasped at straws by canvasing the victims' families of ninety-five. The second victim, after my mother, was Carol Hanna, but I knew knocking on the door of the Hanna house was futile. Too much past to knock on that door.

I decided I would try the Lassiter home. In '95, Rebecca Lassiter was a nursing student, lived with her parents, and two younger siblings: Charlie and Anne. Rebecca was found six blocks away from her own home, in a dumpster—a shoestring tied around her wrist. She was, of course, strangled. Since then, the parents divorced. Her mother, Karen Lassiter moved out west—she just couldn't bear the pain of Abingdon any more. She was gone a year after her daughter's death—took the two kids with her. Her father, Reuben Lassiter now lived in an apartment on Valley Street.

"Mr. Lassiter," I said, when Reuben Lassiter opened the door.

"Can I help you?" He looked tired—like he just woke up or hadn't seen the sunlight all day. He wore a pair of sweatpants and a white t-shirt with a ripped collar. I could smell vodka on his breath—hard, unforgiving liquor, the kind that burns your throat and, if you're not careful, your mind. My mind hadn't gone without a scorch or two.

"I'm Grayson Grant. I'm a private investigator working on a homicide investigation that I, and the department believes to be the work of the same person responsible for—well, for your daughter's death," I pushed the words out. His eyes grew a little, and his clenched eyebrows relaxed.

"The body they found, the one on Stonewall Drive," he connected his own dots.

"Yes, sir," I replied.

He opened the door wider and allowed me to come inside. "Do you want something to drink?" he asked. I politely declined, and took a seat on the sofa that he gestured towards. His living room was dark. Curtains covered all the windows, the lights were off, and by the looks of the dust collecting on the shades, didn't appear to be used very often. The only source of light in the apartment was the glowing of the television.

"We thought, at first, it was some kind of race crime," Reuben started. "Black violence. There wasn't a Black Lives Matter movement in the 1990s. So why come knocking on my door, Mr. Grant?" he asked, as he sat down in an easy chair across from me. The room wasn't clean either. Pizza boxes and empty soda cans were in a variety of places over the living room, and of what I could see of the kitchen—it wasn't much better.

"I'm looking to get your statement, the department has a lead or two they're looking at but I want to get a closer look at his victims. I'm looking for a pattern," I told him earnestly.

"I don't know what I can tell you. Rebecca was going to be working late the night she went missing, so her mother or I didn't even expect to see her until the next morning. When we got up we realized she didn't come home. We called the hospital, found out she left at ten. We called her boyfriend's house, a few of her friends, even the homeless shelter she volunteered at, to see if they'd seen her at all. No one knew where she was or hadn't talked to her since before she left for work. We were worried sick." Reuben picked up a seemingly dirty glass, smelled its clear contents, and took a quick swig. His recoil told me he found the vodka he was looking for—and swigged again.

"Did you ever have hunches? Feelings about who might have been behind her attack?" I asked, making up questions as I went along. I stole the line from a police drama on television. I hoped he couldn't tell how fabricated my line of questions were.

"Everyone loved Rebecca," his voice trailed off as he glared at the last swig of vodka left in his cup. "Don't I know that name? Grant?" he asked, eyeing me, suddenly trying to figure me out. I didn't move, just sort of smirked and shrugged, like the idea of anyone in Abingdon knowing me was ridiculous. "Elizabeth Grant," he finally said, the truth had just dawned on Reuben Lassiter. "You've grown up."

"Apparently not enough if you still recognize me," I joked.

"Son, we were all over the place back then. Our faces were all over national television, our pictures were on every street corner. We put those Cindy Parker campaign ads to shame," Reuben said, as he stood from his chair and eased into the kitchen. "It's impossible to forget a face that has been horror-struck into the worst parts of your mind. No offense kid but, I see you in my nightmares."

"None taken," I started. "Nightmares are our meeting place." This registered with Reuben, somehow, as he finished pouring himself a new glass of vodka, he held it up, as if to toast the words I just said.

"Here, here," he said, and he downed the rest. "I can't help you, though, kid. I don't know anything. I didn't...I didn't do what your old man did—devote his life to the case. I couldn't. I tried for a little while. Lost my family out of it. My wife, Rebecca's mother, she's gone. My other kids are gone. I can't keep sinking my life into 1995, I just can't."

I found his words ironic, because he spoke as if he had moved on with his life but, as far as I was concerned, pay-per-view and pizza wasn't a life. It was just an existence.

"I know it is difficult, I know it isn't fair, what has happened to you, what has happened to me...I'm just trying to comb over every detail...there has to be some kind of connection between these girls, these murders. I'm just looking—"

"How old were you when it happened? When you found your momma face up in a pool of blood?" Reuben spat out, quickly and bitterly. I was taken aback by the sudden change in attitude. The scent of alcohol was strong in the room now. A primary scent that was coating the conversation like an angry bar scene. "Eight? Nine?"

"I was eleven," I finally said.

"Ah," Reuben said, nodding, and collapsing back in his chair. "I was forty. I lost my baby. I'm not saying what you experienced wasn't heart breaking—it was, I'm sure of it. But when everyone's kid was graduating college and walking down the aisle, I was putting flowers by a headstone. Don't talk to me about what is fair."

I nodded, and stood from the sofa. I was wasting my time on a drunk who was blaming the world for his misfortune. It is one thing when the world pity's you, but you reach the bottom of the barrel when you start pitying yourself. "Thanks for your time, Mr. Lassiter." I walked to the door but paused before I left. I couldn't help my curiosity. The bitterly drunk is like a teenager's diary—open book and full of squeals. "Why did you stay, Mr. Lassiter?"

"What?" he asked, almost offended.

"You lost your life, here. You lost your daughter and your family. Why do you stay?"

He took a swig of vodka and made a sigh as it slid down his throat. I could almost feel its burn from the other side of the room. "I thought maybe if I stuck around, he'd come back and finish the job."

Soon after I left Reuben Lassiter to drown in his cocktail of tears and vodka—I went to Lauren Kelley's address, hoping to find luck with the next victim's family. In short, I didn't. There was no one there by the Kelley name— or even knew the Kelley's. Jolene confirmed that the only known relatives alive were her mother and aunt. The former moved to Richland and the latter died six years prior due to cancer. I called Lauren's mother, but I was met with hostility and curse words.

On top of hitting dead ends with the victim families of '95, I had another issue to deal with—Lexi Keats. My phone buzzed in my pocket. Lexi was ringing and I had already missed two calls from her whilst sleeping. I couldn't talk to her now, not while I was coming up short on new leads, and not while the Shoestring Killer had claimed another life. My last thread of hope was that Jolene would come around with some information on Walt Rodgers. I was tempted to go looking for him myself, but hadn't a clue where to begin.

I decided to revisit Alan, taking a shot in the dark that he might know something about Rodgers, or how to find him. When I arrived, I found the house empty.

"Alan?" my voice echoed throughout the house. I looked up the staircase, thinking he'd somehow appear. I slowly stepped on the bottom step, but felt my feet grow heavy the moment I did so. I backed off back onto the landing. "Dad?" I called again. I continued calling out for him for the next several minutes until I heard a faint thud erupt from the backyard. The closer I followed the noise, the quicker I realized it wasn't coming from the backyard—but the barn.

I hadn't been in the barn since I left Abingdon, something was stopping me. Too much good, too much bad. Oddly enough, from the moment I stepped inside, the memories flooded the forefront of my brain. Alan hadn't changed that much, at least from the bottom floor. It was still stockpiled with belongings we never figured out what to do with, so we just let it sit. I could hear Alan loud and clear now. He was upstairs. He was in my oasis, my home when I didn't feel at home. When I reached the top stair, I could see him—sweaty and heavy breathed. He was on his hands and knees, nailing a board violently between the pool table and the torn and tattered couch.

"Alan?" Alan jumped backwards, turning pale for a second. His eyes relaxed when he saw me.

"You almost gave me a heart attack," he said, putting his hand on his chest. He was nothing of a dramatic actor. His brow was sweat-ridden, the result of a man full of frustration and private haunts.

"What are you doing?" I asked.

"This board had a loose end. I was in here putting a box away, nearly tripped over the thing."

"You come up here often?" I asked, looking around at a room that spoke the opposite.

"Not hardly, but now that the investigation is hotter than ever, I thought I'd make some room in the spare bedroom, and bring some of the crap that's piling up in there, out here. Until I get a chance to go through it. Some of it is your stuff from grade school, if you want a peek at it."

I waved my hand causally. "No thanks. I don't need it. Why do you need more room?" I asked eagerly.

"Come up and see the room and you'll see," he said, cocking a smile.

"Hello?" A third voice interrupted the conversation. It echoed from the doorway. I eyeballed Alan, who seemed just as surprised as myself.

"Expecting company?" I asked.

"I don't get company, son," Alan replied.

"Yeah, I believe that."

I began descending the staircase until I could see the doorframe, and the man standing in it, causally leaned against its left side. For a few seconds the face didn't register with me. Blonde hair, shiny blue eyes, a rough beard covering up a rather pale face, a v neck t-shirt, ripped jeans and tattoos ranging from his collar bone to the edge of his wrists. Jack Hanna, my childhood best friend, was staring at me in the eyes.

"And here I thought the rumors were false," he said, when I failed to find words.

"Jack?" I had to ask it like a question, because I was still expecting to see the eighteen year old version of him, struggling with his band and still bragging about that first tattoo he got on his birthday.

"In the sexy flesh," he said, and reached for a hug when I offered a hand. I hugged him back, awkwardly. Alan noticed who it was and went back to nailing the floorboard.

"I had...I'm sorry I didn't contact you. I—I guess I didn't expect you to still be living in Abingdon," I said.

Jack nodded as he reached in his back pocket and pulled out a hard pack of cigarettes—Camels, to be exact. He slid one between his lips and lit the end with his Marilyn Monroe lighter.

"Not many people would, man," he said. Jack always knew what to say. His demeanor was a flowing cool I could never emulate. Jack Hanna, the essence of cool. At least, that's how he came across to most. Seeing Jack reminded me how unique a person could be and still remain genuine.

We sat on Alan's front porch. I made a cup of coffee from Alan's kitchen. It was terrible coffee, but I shouldn't have expected better—not from a 90's coffee pot. Jack puffed a second cigarette, whilst leaned against the railing.

"I lived in Johnson City for a while. My band and I worked a few venues at a few spots nearby—played Asheville for a while."

"What happened?" I asked.

"Same thing that always happens, Grayson. It fell apart," Jack said without conviction. A cloud of smoke passed through his pale, thin lips as his eyes darted down main street. I felt my phone buzzing in my pocket—it was Lexi again. She was relentless.

"You live next door?" I asked, nodding to the light blue house beside us—the one he grew up in, the one he spent a childhood, like me, trying to forget. He laughed and without looking at the house, shook his head.

"I'd have to be crazy to live there," he said, tossing his cigarette onto the porch floor while he reached into his pack for another. "Besides, my old man is so long gone—he drank a bottle of gin to wash down the gun that he ate soon after."

"Jack," I stated. "I had no idea, I'm so sorry." There was a silence that erupted after the sentence. We couldn't help, even at this state of adulthood, but to succumb to the awkwardness of my leaving Abingdon in my rearview mirror.

When I left for St. Louis, I didn't hesitate. I'd saved the money I needed to, I had a working car, somewhat of one, anyway—so I left. I didn't wait around to tell anyone, not even Jack, not even Jolene. I think that's around the time my ethics started to fade. Leaving them behind, that was the first bend in my straw, my first sin on a path to being the careless investigator I grew up to be. It wasn't a recent realization. I think part of me, a big part, knew it even back then, as I burnt rubber leaving. I knew it was a crooked thing to do, but it was a small price to pay for getting out.

"I'm sorry I kinda disappeared on you," I finally said, looking away—like a boy who is forced to apologize for hitting a home run ball through a living room window.

Jack inhaled a large drag of smoke. "That was what—ten years ago?" he started. "I'm sure you have plenty of story and plenty of regret that's built up inside of you between then and now. Don't let something like getting out of this place be one of them."

I nodded. "This coffee is terrible," I said after another sip, and Jack actually laughed. Before I could help it, I found myself smiling, too. There was a bitterness in the air, a tangy aftertaste that stayed on my tongue. There was something amiss between Jack and I, and what else should I have expected for over a decade of not speaking to my best friend? There was still our friendship, however, that found its way through the uncomfortable tension, at least long enough for us to share a laugh.

"So, private investigator, I hear?" Jack said, taking a seat on Alan's porch swing. I took my seat on the top stair of the porch and glared down the walkway that lead to main street.

"It isn't as glamorous as it sounds," I admitted.

"Well, that sucks, Grayson, because it doesn't sound glamorous at all so it must be really bad," Jack replied.

"It's mostly cheaters. That's the stuff that comes across my desk," I said, shrugging.

"Not this time," Jack's voice was almost singing.

I looked back at him, his foot was gently guiding the swing back and forth. He was proud of his knowledge. He wore a smile that told me so. Jack was always cocky, that hadn't changed.

"Nothing stays quiet in this stupid town," I muttered.

"So it is really him? He's back?" Jack asked, his sing-song voice dropped and now he was serious. A victim's boy wanting a victim's answer and I couldn't give it to him. I looked to him. His hand was steady, he pulled the cigarette from his mouth and a puff of smoke covered up any expression of anxiousness or interest. He stayed calm and cool behind his smoke and mirrors. Jack couldn't fool me, though. Not only were we best friends, and not only had I spent a childhood learning his body language, his emotions, his reactions, but we lost our mothers the same day, the same way. We literally knew what the other one was feeling. He was the only one to which I could relate.

"It's him. As best as we can assume, it is him." I replied as coolly as possible. Jack took another drag and tilted his head.

"Well, what do you know?"

I let him ease the information in, slowly. He knew the truth, he just needed me to say it. It's hard to say how I could walk away from someone who so easily connected to who I was and what had happened to me—and sometimes, times I don't like to admit, I wonder if that wasn't one of the reasons I had to leave in the first place.

A car horn honked, as an out of town taxi cab pulled up in front of the house. I half expected Kiddy to come flopping out of the car, mustard stains on his shirt and a half-zipped suitcase in one hand. I actually crossed my fingers, hoping it was him. Perhaps he'd realized how unprofessional and stupid it was to send someone out to investigate a murder case that involved his own mother.

It wasn't Flynn Kiddy, though, who stepped out of the taxi cab, handed a wad of cash to the cabby, and proceeded up the walk with a fine walk and a suitcase in hand. No, it was Lexi Keats. "Hi y'all," she said, her southern twang escaping her mouth.

"Lexi? What are you doing here?"

"I tried calling you to tell you," she said as she parked her suitcase on the bottom step. "I took a flight from Nashville. I'm here to help you." She glanced over to Jack for a moment, then back to me.

"You can't be here right now," I stated. Though it should go without saying, Lexi looked at me like I had just ruined the ending to a good book.

"Look, I hired you, Grant. And when I call, I expect you to answer or at least call me back. I deserve to know an update. I finally got ahold of Mr. Kiddy, and he told me where to find you here."

"What's a Mr. Kiddy?" Jack's voice trailed off in the background.

I sighed, hung my head and shook it. "That wasn't an invitation to come out here and stick your nose in this investigation."

"Was it true?" she jolted the question into the conversation before I could get my next sentence out.

"Was what true?"

"Do you have a lead?"

"I don't know. Sort of."

"Sort of?" Her nose wrinkled up at the reply.

"Sort of?" I heard Jack's voice again.

I lead Lexi by the arm to the sidewalk, away from Jack's earshot. "Listen," I started as I hushed my voice. "I'm going to level with you Lexi. I'm trying here, but I don't have much to work with. I have a lead, a guy that was in the right place, both now and in '95, but it's a slow process."

"Why?" Lexi's voice was soft, muffled like mine, but stern. Her eyes were wide, her lips were tight. I hadn't recognized the beauty of her face until it was boiling with anger. I wondered what that said about myself.

"No one is letting me in this case. I tried talking to Collins' family, they wouldn't talk, and although I have a friend in the department, she's riding my back pretty hard when it comes to this—she wants me to keep out of it."

"We can work around them, right?" Lexi said, shrugging.

"Work around the police? No. I don't know what you think this is but this isn't some TV drama where we just go around and do what we want to and the stupid police forgive us when we win. Life doesn't work that way. And the department is the least of our problems, the state will be all over this any minute. I'm surprised they haven't planted themselves in this stupid town yet. And there isn't any *we!*"

I exhaled quickly. My face was hot. I could feel the stress bubbling up underneath my skin, little pricks like needles charging at my skin. Lexi looked to the sun for a moment, she closed one eye, squinted the other, and I wondered just what she thought she was doing.

"The Collins' family," she started. "Why wouldn't they talk to you? I was thrilled to talk to someone else that this happened to. How many people can say they've been through the same thing you have when someone you love was strangled to death by a lunatic with a shoestring?"

I looked away, back towards the house. Jack was back on the porch, smoking his cigarette. He seemed content. I envied him, when it came to that kind of thing. I don't remember a moment when Jack wasn't calm—not even in ninety-five.

"I didn't tell them anything about me," I admitted. Lexi jerked her head to me, I could almost hear the southern snap out of her mouth before she spoke.

"What do you mean?"

"What do you *think* I mean, Lexi?"

Lexi rolled her eyes, and eyed the driveway. "Is that your car?" she asked, pointing at the only car in the driveway with Missouri plates.

"Obviously," I snapped.

"Let's go."

"No," I said, but I found myself following her to my car.

"I flew all the way here, Grant and I had a layover in *Kentucky,* of all places. I'm not leaving, or giving up that easily. So the quickest way to handle this is to just go with it, okay, P.I?" Lexi opened the passenger door to my car and hopped in, slamming it shut once she was inside. I sighed and looked to Jack, who was tossing his cigarette onto the porch, and stepping on its flamed end.

"You sure do have a way with the ladies, Grayson. Still just as sharp as ever," he said—a smile on his face.

"Well, we can't all be like you, Hanna," I said.

"I guess we'll play catch up later?" He said, there was a serious tone in his voice now.

"Yeah, sure, I'd like that," I said, taken aback. "I'm sorry about this."

Jack waved his hand, as if he were slapping my pathetic words back into my throat. "Hey, I lost a mother too, alright?" he said, as he slid another cigarette between his lips.

"So go play detective."

I parked my car in front of the Collins' house, against my better judgement. I didn't budge. Instead, I fixated on their neighbor's lawn. A beautiful redhead was on a sign by the walkway. *Vote Cindy Parker for Mayor.* I heard Lexi sigh. She looked nervous. She did from the moment I pulled out of Alan's drive way. She was tough, with a mouth that could fire faster than any handgun, but there was a stillness in her now that told me how much of it was determination, not stubbornness. Lexi wanted the ends but could barely justify the means.

"Well, let's go," I said, half bluffing.

"Yeah, let's go," she called me on it, and opened the door with force. We walked to the house, and this time I was prepared to have the police handcuff me and drag me to jail. Every bit of this investigation felt uncomfortable—every bit felt like a dirty trick. Lexi, calmly, and semi-collectedly, rang the doorbell and I stood a couple of feet back.

The door opened, the stocky man from before was standing behind a screen door that looked flimsy and small compared to him. His eyes lingered on Lexi for a minute. Kind eyes, the man probably thought she was a friend of Kathy's. After all, the ages weren't too far apart. Then, his eyes raised to me at the end of the stoop. He frowned, I could see his teeth clinch through the screen. "I told you people to stay away," he barked. His raspy voice was terribly uninviting.

"Mr. Collins? I'm not with the police. I'm not a detective," Lexi interjected. Her southern drag had a charm to it.

"I'm not so sure he is either," the man said, nodding towards me.

"The truth is, Mr. Collins, we are trying to figure out who killed your daughter," Lexi said, attempting to bring his attention back on her and away from me. It was a good plan.

"Then go down to the police department," Collins' said.

"And hopefully they'll be able to find who did this but we have some leads that the police aren't looking at," Lexi started, but the man shook his head vigorously.

"Then maybe it ain't worth looking at, you ever think about that?" he spat.

"Mr. Collins, my sister was killed by the same person who killed your daughter," Lexi started, bluntly. "And as much as I hate that you lost your daughter, I'm sort of thinking about me right now. I'm thinking about my family. So I am here, to find out as much as I can, so I can do as much as I can, to help the police or even this guy here, find the one responsible. There is a lot of evil going on right now, Mr. Collins. We're on the same side of it," Lexi finished.

I was impressed. There was a disturbing silence in Mr. Collins. He'd fixated on her. I thought he was going to start yelling, or rip the screen door in half like cardboard, but instead, he opened the door and ushered us both inside. Lexi stepped inside with purpose, with belonging. She was strong, like Jolene but in a different way. She can hold her own—I'm just not sure I want her to mess with all this ugliness.

The house was old and resembled something of a Victorian theme. Like most of the houses in Abingdon, you'd think that the Collins' home was a historical landmark. We entered into the kitchen first, which looked like it had been remodeled recently—marble countertops didn't exactly have their place in the Victorian era. A small girl, Kathy's daughter I assumed, sat at a beautiful dark wooden table off from the kitchen. She held a coloring book in hand, and vigorously coated the page in bright, vivid colors.

Mr. Collins lead us past her, and into a living room where Mrs. Collins sat near a phone, glaring at the television. She hardly looked away from the screen when we approached. She forced a smile on her face but her eyes stayed flat. Mr. Collins wrapped her in a blanket that had fallen to her waist, before taking a seat across from her, by the television.

"You'll have to excuse my wife, she's taken the past few days very hard," he said in a hushed voice, looking over her shoulder towards Kathy's daughter.

"I understand," I said, trying to interject some sympathy into the room.

"I couldn't imagine the pain it would be to lose a child," Lexi said.

"More than losing a child, but losing one to such violent...Olive is who I worry about now," gesturing towards the kitchen table at Kathy's daughter. "She's only six. Martha and I...Well, we have each other...we'll make it alright. How do you explain to a child, though? How do you grow up like that?" Mr. Collins said, shaking his head. Lexi's eyes slowly glanced at me. I felt my heart hit the pit of my stomach.

"It won't be easy for her," I said as calmly as I could.

"Mr. Collins, can you tell us what happened?" Lexi stated.

He sighed and pushed his glasses up the bridge of his nose. "Not really. Kathy was a school teacher at the elementary school. She came home late that night because of a parent teacher meeting. Olive was already in bed. I heard her come in, but I was already in bed myself...I was just going to see her in the morning. But, I don't know, sometime later, we heard a lot of movement coming from her side of the house—where her and Olive's rooms are located. That's when we found her..." His voice trailed off as his bottom lip quivered.

"And no one saw anything?" I asked. I tried to remain sympathetic, but I was growing impatient with the little information we were getting on the Shoestring Killer.

"Rain," Mrs. Collins finally said. The three of us looked to her, as if the family dog just spoke his first words.

"What, honey?" Mr. Collins asked.

"It was raining that night," she said.

"Yes...honey it was raining," Collins said in that demeaning voice one has when speaking down to a child.

"No...it was *raining.*" She said again.

"Yes, raining—oh!" Mr. Collins' eyes lit up, but quickly dimmed. He glanced at Olive, who was still coloring, and then turned to me. "Olive has a fear of thunderstorms. Anytime it starts to rain, she usually crawls in bed with Kathy, or Martha. She wasn't in bed with Martha so she must've been in bed with Kathy."

"Unless she was already asleep," Lexi interjected.

"That kid will wake up at the sound of a pin dropping," Mr. Collins fussed. "She heard it, and she was scared."

"Are you saying that Olive might have seen something?" I asked, not tempting to hold my breath.

"It is possible—but if she did, she didn't say anything to the police," Mr. Collins said.

"May I try?" I asked. I could see that Mr. Collins didn't like the idea of it. I didn't blame him, protecting the innocence of a child is futile, but noble. "Mr. Collins...this happened to me, too. My mother was...well, I wish I could've stopped this before he got to Kathy, but he's still out there, and if Olive knows something that could help us," but my forced speech, which felt bitter and cheesy, was interrupted by a soft and small voice behind me.

"I can help," Olive said, climbing down from the chair on which she sat.

"Olive, sweetie, go play in your room, it's okay," Mr. Collins said, shooing her away with his hand. Olive, however, continued to walk forward.

"You're policemen aren't you?" she asked, looking at me and then to Lexi.

"Something like that," I said with a small smile.

"Where is your badge, and where are your policeman clothes?"

"I'm a different kind of policeman, I guess," I was terrible with children, too.

"You want to know about the man who hurt my mom?"

"Randall," Mrs. Collins said in a nervous voice, looking to Mr. Collins.

"Did you see him?" I asked.

"She's just a child," Collins interjected.

"I was laying in momma's bed when she came in from work. She laid down with me. We cuddled. She asked me about my day. I told her what I did, but she stopped me. She got really nervous and told me to go get in bed with Granny and Grandpa. I asked her why. She started pushing me out the door. I looked back and that's when I saw him, through the bedroom window," Olive stated. Her voice raised an octave and began to shake.

"Olive, sweetie, you don't have to tell this if you don't want to," Mr. Collins said—his voice was shaking, too.

"He started beating on the window," Olive's voice broke and tears began to flood her face. "He looked so scary. There was something on his arm! A big sign. And his face...." Her voice was failing. She cried so hard now she had hiccups in her breath.

"What about his face?" I pressed.

"Grayson," Lexi said, trying her best to pull me back.

"His eyes...and there was a triangle on him."

"A triangle?" I asked. "What did he look like, Olive?"

"Leave her alone. Get out!" Mr. Collins yelled.

"I just saw eyes. Big, scary eyes glaring at me. And his face...his was different. His eyes! Just eyes glaring at me!" Olive belted out as Mr. Collins scooped her up in his arms and began carrying her away. "His eyes saw me!" Olive yelled one last time. We heard her cry until she was deep enough into the house that the walls and doors muffled her pain.

"Let's go," Lexi said, disturbed and angry. "We're very sorry, Mrs. Collins." Martha didn't respond, she only glared at the television, as a tear ran down her face.

"You shouldn't have pushed her," Lexi said, bitterly.

"We got what we needed," I stated. "That's what you do in the private investigation business. You get what you need. At least we got the description."

"Which tells us what? Did you hear what she said? Breaking news, the shoestring killer has eyes."

"I know what she's talking about though, Lexi," I stated. "I saw the same thing the night my mother was killed. I saw pale eyes staring at me. They were haunting."

"You've seen him? You saw what Olive did?"

I nodded. "Back in '95. I thought it was a dream, a nightmare I got mixed up with the reality of that night.

"Did you get a look at his face?" Lexi pressed.

I just shook my head. "I could only see the eyes, I think the rest was some kind of mask or something. I really thought it was a dream," chills covered my arms.

The ride back to town was fairly quiet, and I could tell Lexi was still judging me from my behavior in the Collins' home.

"You know, I wasn't being insensitive back there," I stated.

"Could have fooled me, Grant," she snapped.

"I was eleven when my mother was murdered. I found her body. I saw the face as the man fled the scene. Do you know how badly I wished someone would've listened to me?"

"She was crying," Lexi said.

"She'd be crying either way. At least she got to help. At least she feels like she did something. That's all she has right now—the feeling of doing something. It is the same reason you are here. It is the same reason I took your case. We can't change what happened. No matter how phony we get with it, we really just want to be able to say we did something—that we made some kind of difference."

Lexi nodded, but didn't say anything. She knew, on some level, that I was right, even if she was too stubborn to admit it. Lexi's mistake is thinking that my twenty-year-old wound isn't as fresh or as painful as her recent loss or Olive's loss. Years don't take away the tragedy, though. Losing a mother is unlike any other feeling, like a warm blanket being ripped off cold bones. The rest of the world becomes a blistering wind a-blowing, and one is reduced to a shiver.

Elizabeth's Work Journal
April 12th, 1994

It's been too long since I last wrote. The hospital has been like a child. A living, breathing, infant that needs constant care and supervision. I, along with several other staff and locals are petitioning to change the name from Old Dominion Asylum, to East Bristol Psychiatric Hospital. There's something about the word asylum that leaves an uncomfortable response in people. This is supposed to be a place of learning, of healing, of recovery—that message is not getting through. Liam—Dr. Walker, finally admitted to changing the name.

My patients are becoming extensions to my own family, it seems. I've taught Marcy how to knit. She's only allowed when there are enough authority figures present. She loves it so much. There is so little she can comprehend, and even less that she actually wants to comprehend. Knitting, though, that's something she can lose herself in—for hours, if she could. Franklin is even letting me put on his shoes for him, although he refuses to attach the velcro straps. His personality is so vibrant, so energetic. It is so cute, his little personality. He's come a long way from the quiet loner he once was when I met him almost a year ago.

103

Walter, unfortunately, is no longer my patient. I will miss Walter. He was making such strides and so handsome! A real ladies man, if he could just work up the courage to socialize. I wish I could say he left Old Dominion under better circumstances, but his care became too costly for the family that admitted him. They had to seek alternative treatment. It saddens me that Tom's mind may now be in jeopardy because his family didn't have the means to cover the bill. Tony is still a handful. He shows little growth and continues to act out against authority. I've taken his case file to the board more than once, explaining that Tony needs care from a maximum-security institution, but my notes and requests continue to get overlooked and overruled.

"Tony is in the best of hands, I'm sure of it," Dr. Walker told me personally. It's nice to have such a successful doctor trust me the way he does—but I'm beginning to disagree with him on more than one issue. His Tomorrow's Minds project is growing, but it is still ambiguous to the rest of the staff. Only those few select doctors are allowed to visit the bottom two floors. This is where Dr. Walker works closely with the most advanced patients. The ones that struggle the hardest. The ones that make Tony look like a cakewalk.

I've lost a bit of my professionalism, I'm afraid. The Elizabeth that started working here is fading. That Elizabeth looked at these patients as people, like any good doctor. Now, this Elizabeth is starting to see them as friends. Friends who don't want to take medicine that they don't understand. Friends that shake and cry when word gets to them that they've been selected for Dr. Walker's elite program. Friends that need more in their lives than board games and doctors. Friends need people. Friends need love.

I try to express it to Alan, but he's a hands on man, a dirt digger. He understands what I do, but he can't fix it, and that's all he'd try to do. Besides, when I get home, after a long day, when I can feel the tears behind my eyes and the ache in my bones, I see Grayson's smiling face. And I smile. I can't talk shop when I'm spending time with him. I'd never want Grayson mixed up in a world stripped of so much innocence.

Chapter Five

Irusan

I drove Lexi and myself back to The Martha Washington. Lexi rented herself a room at the Inn, as well. She was at the end of the same hallway. I still didn't approve of her sudden presence in Abingdon but I would be lying if I said I didn't enjoy, at least on some level, her fiery personality. I tried desperately to sleep, but instead I stared at the patterns on the walls, which were covered in a faintly pale-yellow wallpaper. The room was certainly unlike average hotels. The Martha Washington had a class all on its own—historical with a hint of posh.

My eyes were tired but my brain wasn't. It was lost in a sea of reverted memories that daren't cease. My first kiss, my first heartbreak, my short but intense relationship with Jolene, my friendship with Jack. People might say that I'm a pessimist—that I find the underlining bad, and find it to be overpowering the inherent good of life. It isn't that, not exactly. It isn't the ultimate bad verses the ultimate good—it is the impact that it has on the constant. I'm the constant. The impact that Abingdon had on me, ultimately was unfathomably negative. It is just factual. A first kiss doesn't outweigh the boulder that is the deconstruction of one's family.

My body finally allowed me to drift off to sleep, only to be awaken sharply at 5:45 the next morning.

"What?" I said, answering my cell phone incoherently— and a little angrily, too.

"Get over here," Alan's voice demanded on the other end.

"Why?"

"Just do it." There is no arguing with a man who still sees you as the fourteen year old boy absentmindedly raised.

I made it to Alan's house, sans shower or morning coffee, to find a black sedan sitting in the driveway. I entered the house to find a man and woman in sharp suits, each with a badge on the hip. Just past the French doors, my father sat in an easy chair by the television.

"Grayson," Alan muttered.

"Mr. Grant," the female officer said.

"Yes?" My father and I both answered. She was looking towards me, though.

"I'm Agent Strout and this is Agent Killian," she said promptly. "We're with the state, just came in from Bristol."

"What brings you to my childhood?" I followed up.

There was a glance that was shared between the two agents. I knew the look. I'd shared the same eye dance with

Kiddy a thousand times, when some poor sap stumbled into our office. Someone we didn't believe. Someone we would ultimately reject. Someone we considered a liability.

"May I have a word with you?" She said in a most politely rehearsed voice. "Is there a room we can speak, privately?" I looked to Alan, we shared a similar look, concerned thoughts behind identical eyes.

"Is that really necessary?" I asked. Agent Strout's lips stretched, a very plastered smile.

"I'm afraid it is, Mr. Grant," she said, collectively. I nodded my head and without gesture, walked to the kitchen. The Grant kitchen was small, it was the last room at the end of the house's bottom floor, save for the laundry room tacked on the end, just past the kitchen sink. Against the inside wall, by the doorway, was a wooden table—yellow, with bits of paint chipped off here and there. It had been in the family longer than myself.

"Have a seat, I guess," I said as I walked to the coffee maker on the kitchen counter.

"I'll stand, thank you," she said. She was professional. A slick navy pant suit—her long hair tied tightly in a ponytail. Her badge on one hip and her gun on the other. "What brings you to Abingdon, Mr. Grant?" she asked, passive aggressively.

"Family, of course," I said.

"Really? Family?"

"It's been a while, thought I would pop in." She studied for a moment. She wanted the truth, even though she already had it. "Would you like some coffee?" I asked, as I poured what was probably old coffee into a mug. "Fair warning—not sure it is coffee."

"Mr. Grant, I really don't have time for the witty back-and-forth, nor do I have time for pretenses. You're here because your..." she hesitated and rolled her eyes, "The Shoestring Killer is here and now so are you—working the case." Her voice was strong, unwavering, unapologetic.

"Excuse me," I replied. "I came here because the Shoestring Killer murdered my mother—my father's wife. My father is in his sixties and his heart isn't in the beset condition. I came here to make sure the excitement wasn't too much for him."

"This is the same father that has spent the better part of twenty years asking questions, tracking down information, trying to bribe police and medical officials for inmate and patient records everywhere from here to Bristol?" Strout said, tossing a thick file onto the yellow table, which wobbled under the file's weight.

"He's, well, eccentric," I sighed, admittedly, taking a sip of coffee, "but now that things are getting real, and violent, the man is breaking. He needs me here. And last I checked, visiting your broken-hearted, lonely father wasn't a crime," I snapped.

"You're not in trouble, Mr. Grant," she said, lowering her voice. She took a step closer to me, almost as if she were going to whisper something in my ear. She stopped just in front of me, and looked back towards the door for a moment. "Is there the slightest chance I can persuade you to stop this right now?" She asked.

I considered for a moment, because I wasn't sure if she was right. Every bit of me wanted to say yes. It might not be noble, but neither was I if I were being honest. I sighed. "In this moment, standing in my mother's kitchen? No. There isn't," I finally said. It felt like an oath I was unwilling to take, a pledge I mouthed the words to but if I didn't take this oath, which one was I taking?"

"I didn't think so," she said. "But this is the deal. I can't and won't tell you any official police business and if you get any kind of lead at all, you bring it to us. If we can agree to that I don't mind keeping you on a short leash," she stated.

"I'm sorry, 'leash?'" I asked.

"Your father's a different story," she said, ignoring me. I paused, and looked at her suspiciously. "Mr. Grant," she started after a brief sigh. "Your father has been a liability in this case. The locals we've spoken with upon arrival, along with the police department, have mentioned your father by name as someone who is heavily emotionally tied to this case. We understand the situation, and I know this is difficult to hear, but your father's involvement could jeopardize this investigation." After an unsettling lull in exchange, I realized the detective was looking at me, waiting for me to say something.

"I don't know what you expect out of me?" I questioned.

. "Frankly, Mr. Grant, I need you to keep your father away from this, okay?" She directed. I nodded.

"If you find something," her voice trailed off. "You bring it to me. Remember, the best way to help in this investigation is to keep your father out of it." The agent exited the kitchen, and a few faux pleasantries later, Agent Strout and Killian left. I remained in the kitchen. I don't do well with pleasantries, real or fake. Not a moment later, Alan entered.

"What was that about?" He asked.

"Same crap they spoon-fed you, I'm sure," I said. "I told them you had a heart condition."

"I don't have a heart condition."

"I know."

"She ask you to babysit me?"

"I don't think those were the words she used."

"But something like that, huh?"

"Something like that, maybe."

"Well, you know what we're going to do?" He said. I looked at him strangely, pouring out the bad coffee. "We're going to have a meeting."

Within the next hour, Alan had made a few phone calls, and I found myself sitting at the kitchen table, surrounded by familiar faces. Alan, Lexi, Jack, and Jolene, squeezed around a table barely big enough for four people let alone five. It was an unusual and awkward meeting: Jack showed up first, with little to say but apparent energy for whatever he spoke to Alan about previously. Lexi was next, with undisputed eagerness, and lastly was Jolene, who entered regretful and seemingly uninterested. Upon sitting down at the table, I was faced with a myriad of forgotten memories—morning breakfasts, where I would see my mother before she left for work, evening dinners when it would be Alan and myself, wondering if mom's dish would go cold, single meals had after my mother's passing, and when my father sobbed too much for food.

"Let's get this show on the road, Alan," Jack said, the first to break the silence when my father entered the kitchen.

"What is going on?" I asked—realizing I was the one left out of the loop. Lexi eyed me, carefully. I could tell she felt out of place. The only non-Abingdon citizen mixed in someone else's nightmare.

"It's obvious what is going on isn't it, son?" my father asked me. Eyes were on me, then, waiting to confirm—waiting to agree. I glanced around for a moment, sighed to myself, contemplating how all of this looked to me—pitiful.

"What is this? A killer hunting party?" I said, half joking. The room remained silent. "You've got to me kidding me," I added, when the room avoided to make eye contact with me.

"We're just trying to help. That's why we came here in the first place, Grayson," Lexi said.

"Where do we start that the police department or the state don't already have covered?" I blurted out, fearing that I was the only one in the room that had a logical stance.

"I have to agree with Egg on this one," Jolene came to my rescue. "Between the department and the state detectives there's little else anyone else could do. We are combing through the county, provided that the Shoestring Killer is even still in the county."

"Egg?" Lexi asked, but no one answered her.

"And what if he is?" Alan asked.

"We're keeping a tight watch on the county lines," Jolene stated.

"I'm sorry, why did you call him Egg?" Lexi said again.

"If you're so eager to hand this case off, why did you even come back?" Jack asked me. He looked discouraged, maybe even disappointed. I felt a twist in my stomach—maybe because I wasn't sure how to answer him.

"I'm here to help, you're right," I admitted. "All I'm saying is I don't know what to do now. Don't mistake me for a brilliant investigator. I'm a petty investigator who handles petty cases. I don't exactly bring harden criminals to justice," I said, feeling a wave of relief rush through my chest.

Jack pulled out his pack of Camel cigarettes, placed one between his thin lips and reached for his lighter. "Not yet you haven't," he said with confidence.

"The truth is, this case needs all the help it can get. There is a monster running around *killing* this town," Alan started. His voice broke somewhere around *killing*. "Jolene says we might have a lead, right Jolene?"

She sighed, but nodded and looked at me. "Walt Rodgers, the man I told you about before. He was a prime suspect in '95, but it ran out of steam, or they couldn't find enough evidence or something. Anyway, I looked through his

records again, after what you told me happened at the Collins'
home. There's something," she stated, her voice trailing off
for a moment. "You said Kathy's daughter said something
about a triangle? Rodgers has a triangle on his forearm. Not
a tattoo, but markings, almost a symbol, carved on his arm. It
was assumed it was some kind of self-abuse but it matches
what the Collins kid saw."

I could feel Alan's excitement, anxiousness, and
sickness. I felt it too, a sickness that swelled inside me.
Suddenly my mother's death was all-the-more real, and all-
the-more painful.

"Are the cops going to bring him in?" Lexi asked, but
Jolene shook her head.

"Nobody knows where Rodgers lives. He's off the grid—
has been for years."

"I can find him," Jack said, inhaling a drag of his cigarette.

"Do you have to smoke that in here?" Jolene asked.

"Sorry, Jo," he said, smashing the tobacco ridden ash into
a glass plate on the table. My eyes darted to Jolene, when Jack
called her Jo, but she was sure to avoid me.

"Anyway, I can find him. I know a few people in town that
might know where he is—the kind of people that wouldn't give
it up for a badge."

"Fine," Jolene said, nodding.

"Is Detective Wilson still in Abingdon?" I asked, doing my best to ignore whatever just happened. "

"Does a lot of fishing," Alan interjected.

"I'd like to talk to him about the case, and about Rodgers," I said.

"Good luck," Jolene started. "I hear he doesn't talk about the old days."

"Well, that's the thing, Jo," I started, automatically feeling Jack's eyes on me. "The old days are back." There was another silence that lingered in the room a little too long, and wasn't broken until moments later, by Alan.

"Okay then. Jack will do what he can to find out where Rodgers likes to set up camp. Grayson will see what he can get out of Wilson, and whatever we find out we'll give to Jolene. Is that straight-arrowed enough for you, darling?" he said, looking to Jolene. She sighed and nodded.

"No one does anything without notifying me first, though. I'm serious," she ordered.

"And what am I supposed to do? Sit here and look pretty?" Lexi said, insulted.

"You and I can canvas the grounds, Miss Keats," Alan stated. "We may not know where Rodgers is but I know this town like the back of my hand. There aren't too many places he could hide that I wouldn't know about."

"Be careful," Jolene and I said in unison. With that, Jolene rose from the table and made her way to the kitchen door.

"My captain can't find out about this," she stated. "Any tips you guys give me have to stay under the radar." The door closed behind her and the silence returned.

"Is someone going to tell me what Egg is all about?" Lexi asked, again. Jack let out a snort.

"It is his initials," he said.

"Initials?"

"Edmund Grayson Grant," I said, regretfully.

There was actually a laugh at the table. If anyone had entered the kitchen in that moment, they might have assumed we were some kind of happy family. There wouldn't be so much pity. That's something I found solace in, and it helped me understand why each of us had sat down at that table in the first place. We had all been plagued with pity. Pity had been stuck in my brain since I arrived in Abingdon once again, just as it had years prior. It all went back to the people who looked on to us mournfully, pathetically. There's a cautionary glance that has come my way since my mother died. Heavy irises peel through the first layer of tragedy. The layer that is pity. Pity is why I left, because nothing kills the dead faster than pity.

I called Jolene later and asked for Detective Bill Wilson's address. She didn't give it to me, but she did tell me where I could find him. Damascus is a place you might find your average Abingdon fisherman, but with a record like Detective Wilson had, solidarity is a medal that can't be pinned to your chest; which is why I found him in Alvarado, a quiet little piece of nature where the former detective sat off a riverbank. Back in his prime, Bill Wilson was an A list investigator who rallied the police department to find the Shoestring Killer. Soon into the investigation, however, the case was handed to the state.

I approached a white-bearded man, who sat peacefully, by himself, on the riverbank. His beard was long, narrow, and came to a point that reached mid-chest. He wore a tight blue t-shirt that had a faded logo across the front, and off-white shorts.

"Detective Wilson?" I asked, as I got closer. He looked to me with a look of disdain. Whether it was because I wasn't just a fellow fisherman, or because I was calling out to him specifically, I wasn't sure.

"There's no more 'detective' to it, son," he said, as he turned back to the water. "I left that garbage behind a long time ago." The sun was beating off his hard skin. Old tattoos faded into what was a crisp darkened tan. The opposite of

Jack, I thought, who sported pale skin with fresh, bleeding ink. The former detective flicked his wrist—his line now deep into the river.

"She's angry, today," he said, suddenly.

"Who?"

"The river, son, she's not giving me anything."

"Maybe she doesn't have anything to give."

"Everyone has something to give."

"Can I speak to you about something, Mr. Wilson?"

"Is it about police work? I'm assuming it is because you called me detective," he said, sighing. I couldn't tell what his tattoos were supposed to be, they were faded memories of an old past. Old tattoos for an old man.

"It's about the Shoestring Killer case," I answered.

"I wished they hadn't given him that stupid nickname," Wilson blurted out before I could finish my sentence. "When you give someone a nickname, especially when it is someone dangerous, you give them an immortality—you give what they do an immortality. It's been twenty years and he's still the Shoestring Killer." Wilson just shook his head.

"It's more than just his name—you know he's back, right?" I said, sharply. I caught Wilson's glance, from the corner of his eye.

"It's probably a copycat. Sick freaks these days want to leave some kind of lasting impression. One nut job starts choking women to death with shoestrings, twenty years later someone gets inspired. Disgusting," he shrugged.

"It's not," I said, losing my patience. "A copycat, I mean. The shoestring tied to the wrist. That was a detail that was never released." Wilson cocked his head as he looked into the reflecting waters, casting his fishing rod in once more.

"What's your name?"

"I'm a private investigator," I said, in lieu of giving my own name.

"You do a lot of fishing, Mr. Investigator?"

"Can't say that I do, sir."

"I like it. I do a little catch and release. Keeps my mind at ease. You know what's funny? I don't even like the taste of them."

"Walt Rodgers," I interrupted his stream of consciousness, annoyed that I wasn't getting easier cooperation from the once-detective. He sat down his rod—safely secured against a leaning tree. "He was your number one suspect, wasn't he?" Wilson pulled a ratty bandana from his back pocket and wiped his hands with it. I could see cracks in his hands—old hands that have worked too hard for too long. I'd never have those hands.

"You ever hear of Irusan?" Wilson asked the question as if I hadn't just asked him one.

I paused, for two reasons. Firstly, I hadn't the first clue what Irusan had to do with the case-at-hand, and secondly, I was hoping the answer was nothing.

"I've heard a thing or two," I said, coolly. It was during my sheepish answer that Wilson removed a pocket knife from somewhere on his person and flicked open a scratched, metallic blade. My heart rattled in a chest a little harder than it should have—a natural reaction when you're talking about horror stories.

"What have you heard?" he asked. There was a sense of pleasure in it somewhere for him. Maybe because he hadn't gotten to play in a while, or maybe because he just loved the game.

"Rumors, mostly, stories we told as kids. The Irusan is going to find you, trap you, torture you, and feed your body to his cats and if you're lucky you'll be dead long before they start feeding. I heard once that some people—a couple of guys, high school seniors—found a path off of the Appalachian Trail. They traveled down it, pretty soon they started smelling this terrible stench. They followed it—thinking it has to be a dying animal or something. Instead they found a decaying body—human—being fed on by the Irusan's cats, and Irusan himself."

Wilson picked up his fishing pole and ran the exposed knife right through the line—the sound of the taut line snapping could be heard in the silence between us. "Never buy cheap fishing line. That's the number one rule I can tell you about fishing," he said, as if I hadn't just relayed a terrible story. "What do you think of that?"

"Cheap fishing line? I honestly didn't know there was such a thing as cheap and expensive fishing line," I said, dryly.

"No, I mean about your Irusan story."

"I never really thought too much about it. Sounds like a ghost story to me."

Wilson glanced at me, eye to eye, if only for a moment. "I didn't hear any ghosts in that story." He closed the knife and put it back in his pocket as he bent down to access his tackle box—a rusty gray metal container that sat only a couple of feet from the fishing rod. "You see what I mean about nicknames, though? Give a guy like ours a name like the 'Shoestring Killer' you've all the sudden added so much power and persona to someone who is just—honestly—a nut job. Take Irusan. He's nasty, yet almost magical in his ability to lure in subjects for his torture. He's a local legends, him and his fleet of cats. Do you know what the word Irusan means? The name comes from British folklore—means King of the Cats. Of course the Abingdon version and perverted whatever it was originally. Take away that name, though, and he's just a crazy guy in the woods eating people and feeding some to his felines."

"The difference is the Shoestring Killer is real," I blurted out.

"So is Irusan," Wilson scoffed.

"Thought he was *local legend?*"

"Legends can be real, Grant." He caught my attention. I never gave him my name. If I've learned one lesson from myself, as an investigator, you can't trust anyone—even the detectives. "I recognize you, if that's what you're wondering." Bill Wilson pulled the rod back over his shoulder, jolted his wrist forward, and sent a long line out into the river, sinking beautifully beneath the water's surface. "I remember interviewing you and your dad back when, well, all this started."

"That was twenty years ago," I said, perplexed. I'd done the private instigating thing for a while, and there weren't many names I remembered, or faces. The faces are faceless to me.

"You don't forget a case like that, son," he said as he began reeling. "Biggest thing that ever blew through this town—at least for me. They pulled it out from under me too quickly."

"You were pretty sure it was Rodgers, though?" I asked, maybe a little too eagerly.

Wilson scoffed, again. "Nothing," he said as he finished reeling in his line, which happened to catch a plastic bag instead of a beautiful flapping fish. "Are you one of the investigators, or are you just obsessed with the case?" He asked, bluntly.

"I'm not my father, if that's what you're asking," I matched his forwardness.

"Never said you were, son," he shook his head. "I just thought I would warn you, if you're investigating, be prepared for disappointment. This case—It's too much for any one man. The state will have it in their pocket if they don't have their greedy little hands on it already. Or some other son-of-a-gun will have a bullet between the guy's eyes for trying to snatch his daughter. Honestly, this guy's luck has to be running out at some point."

"I just want to know if you really thought your man was Rodgers." My impatience started to tremble through my voice. There was a long silence before he answered. He pulled the plastic bag off his line. An empty beer can fell out of it.

"He was my man," Wilson finally agreed. "Now, let that be the end of it. I left that stuff with my badge," he finished.

I nodded my head, thanked him, and turned back for my vehicle. I had more questions I wanted to ask: *What, if he speculated, was Rodger's inspiration?; How did he pick his victims?; Where, if anywhere in Abingdon, would he start looking for him after all his time?; Why didn't they get him then?* I knew it was pointless, though. I barely got the information he gave me. It wasn't a total failure. I knew that Rodgers was a solid lead. "But I would be careful, if I were you, Grant," he called out to me. I turned back to him, gesturing inquisitively. "Because Walt Rodgers and Irusan, the cat king, are one and the same."

As I drove back into Abingdon proper, I contemplated what Detective Wilson had told me. There was a crazy man, somewhere within the town lines who feasts on flesh, who could be responsible for my mother's death. I tried calling Jolene but couldn't reach her. Never a cop around when you need one. I found Jack, and we traded notes. I told him that Walt Rodgers might not only be the Shoestring Killer, but also a local legend known as Irusan. Jack didn't believe me, but checked with a few of his less-than-reputable sources, and found a possible location of where one might find Irusan, the king of the cats.

Immediately, Jack and I decided to investigate the area. Neither of us trusted the source very much, assuming that even if he had been honest about Rodger's location, he might be stupid enough to warn our suspect before we arrived. So, eagerly looking for justice, Jack and I drove up White Top Mountain, without notifying my father, Lexi, or Jolene —the latter against my suggestion.

"She's a blue shirt, Grayson," Jack said, flatly, after he placed something in my car trunk and slammed the hatch. "She'd just slow us down." We made it up to the top of White Top Mountain, a beautiful peak that looked over Abingdon and nearly the rest of the state. The mountain top was mostly uninhabited. There were few residents and the ones that lived there didn't have what you'd call neighbors. It was a leafy, dirt road kind of existence. An existence I wasn't use to, having gotten use to the city life in Saint Louis. I parked the car on the side of the road where Jack had told me to do so. He'd spent time on the mountain before. In fact, Jack was exactly the kind of person you'd want beside you in the woods—a mountaineer that loved to mingle above the pines.

"What did you put in my trunk?" I asked, as we stepped out of the car. The pines wafted straight into my nostrils and gave me a cleansed feeling, as if I were smelling nature for the first time. The hatch to my trunk popped open and Jack reached inside.

"You ever hear the phrase 'speak softly and carry a big stick?'" he asked. I nodded. He pulled out a dark wooden baseball bat, and slammed the lid once more. "Well, carry a big stick, hombre." I scoffed, until I realized that Jack was completely serious. He gripped the handle of the bat in his right hand and slapped the other end into the palm of his left hand—some thug from a gangster flick. I was seeing something else, in Jack, something that wasn't there when we were ten years old. Jack had grown up, and the more up he went, the further away he got from the Jack I knew. "You have a gun?" He asked, refusing to break eye contact with me.

"A gun?"

"You're a private investigator, aren't you?"

"Yes?"

"Then shouldn't you have a gun?"

"Not necessarily, no,"

"But you do, don't you?"

"I don't like guns."

"But you have one," Jack's words were solid, thick—he was drowning me in his demand.

"Yes, in the glove compartment," I sighed in defeat.

He picked it from my compartment and handed it to me. The heavy pistol weighed down my palm. I wasn't a man of guns. I only had the firearm because Kiddy insisted. In fact, I was almost certain that legally the gun belonged to him. I stuck the pistol between my lower back and the band of my jeans—a baller move I saw in movies. This man-hunt, however, didn't feel like a movie. It felt like something else, something worse—something you wouldn't want to turn into a movie.

I followed Jack, who walked seemingly aimlessly through the woods, breaking down the twig-like beginnings of future great pines and oaks, and snapping the branches of trees that have long since become elderly. I would've appreciated the beauty of White Top Mountain, if I had time to pull my brain away from the fact I was hunting for the man who might have terrorized the entire town.

Jack took us to a path in the woods that was unbeknown to me, or probably anyone else. Several locals, and not-so-locals, flock to Abingdon for the infamous Creeper trail, which runs through the great Appalachian. It's a trail for walkers, runners, bikers, and lovers. The trail that I found myself on, in the middle of the woods, far from any road I knew, far from Abingdon, was unmistakably a more proper *creeper* trail than the one in which held the name. I had heard about trails like the one we were on, small walkways that zigzagged throughout the trees, over water and under caves, and each of them were accompanied by a tale too horror-struck to be anything short of terrifying.

It was scarier to me, a man who had just entered his thirties, than it was for me as a kid—who use to wander the woods without a fear-gag rumbling in the pit of my stomach. Age either brings wisdom, or the fear of it, I'm not sure which.

"Do you remember exploring these woods when we were kids?" I asked, remembering a time when Jack and I had still had our childhood.

"I remember," Jack started. "Our parents use to get so mad."

"You know why, don't you?" I said, bending back a branch of a tree that Jack seemed to avoid effortlessly. Jack shook his head. "There were rumors about some of the out-of-townspeople that moved up here in the woods. Said they hanged dogs and cats on the trees. Some sort of demonic sacrifice. I don't know—devil possession or something."

"Sounds like a load," Jack scoffed.

"It seemed silly then, but nowadays— I wouldn't put it past people." As we walked the trail, Jack and I saw a flock of birds—crows, actually, as they feasted upon the carcass of a decaying cat.

"Well, that's the thing, Grayson. The devil doesn't need to possess people anymore—they are evil enough on their own."

We wandered the wilderness, for what felt like hours. Jack eagerly clamped onto the baseball bat, sometimes swinging it against unsuspecting trees. A cold chill found me beneath the scorch of a boiling sun. The kind of chill that wakes you up. The kind of chill that bothers you, that finds you in the heat of the day when you have to realize the terribly important—something was wrong, very wrong.

"Do you really think it's this guy?" Jack asked, as if he expected it to be some sort of joke.

"The timeline fits. Detective Wilson had his eye on him, thought he was the killer. Rodgers is a weirdo maniac that lives off the grid that, somehow, has earned himself the nickname Irsuan. By the way, I think that dead cat back there is a good indication we're getting close."

"I don't know," Jack shrugged in a way that made me think he did, in fact, know. "I just always thought it was someone closer."

"Someone we know?"

"Someone that at least knew our mothers. In twenty years I've never heard my dad or anyone else mention Rodgers, or Irusan or anything like that."

"Maybe that's why he's gotten away with it for twenty years," I said, smartly.

"Maybe so," Jack replied, but it was evident that he had deeper issues on his mind.

"Did you have someone in mind, Jack, or is all of this just thoughts?" I asked, pausing in the last word, unsure of what to call it. He shook his head, slightly, but kept his eyes away from mine: A subtle habit he'd always had, since we were kids. He doesn't look you in the eye when he lies—not if he cares about you. I didn't press him. If Jack was going to lie, he was too stubborn to tell the truth.

We treaded forward, further from our common town and deeper into an unmanned wood, and it wasn't until the trail began to lose its depth, obvious ridges, that we began to wander away from it. I began to wonder about Jack's tip, but daren't bring it up to him. Jack was a passive man, at least he used to be, but something that had remained constant with him: If Jack were on a mission, he was focused, aggressive, and pursuant.

"There!" He suddenly said, in his most excited whisper. We pushed through the woods and entered a vast opening— a field of grass uncovered by trees, and in the distance, where Jack was pointing, stood a small stand of trees. They cluttered together—huddled, as if they were whispering secrets they didn't want the rest of the woods to know.

"What do you mean?" I asked.

"Rodgers lives there," Jack replied.

I brought my eyes back to the stand. The stand stood almost in the center of the field, as if it were the main attraction—center ring, under the big top. The woods we emerged from lined around the edge of the field like scared limbs ruffling in the breeze, their eyes gazed on the stand and what it might do next. The grass around the stand stood tall, too, a natural gate to announce to curious parties that this was no place to be curious. Message received.

"He lives in the stand," I said. I meant it to be more of a question, but as I said it I realized how true it must've been.

I could sense Jack's grip tightening around the bat. "I don't know if this is your guy, Grayson, but you don't live out in the middle of nowhere, like this, without having a secret or two you don't want anyone to know about." We approached the stand slowly, and quietly. I expected something dramatic to happen—a detective in the midst of an evil uprising. I watched too many movies, I guess. I felt the tall grass bend and snap against my shins. I prayed there weren't snakes near.

"We should call the police," I stated.

"And say what? 'Hey we know where this guy lives?'"

"We should at least call Jolene," I stated.

That's when Jack stopped, his heel digging into the Earth before he turned to me. His eyes were inches from mine. I could smell his sweat in the wilderness.

"I just gotta know something man," his voice was somber— as he was past exhaustion with me. He probably was, to be honest. To be honest, I was past exhaustion with myself. "You really think this guy, Rodgers, Irusan, whatever you want to call him is our man?"

I nodded more assuredly than I felt on the subject. "Yeah, I do."

"Then you're talking about the person who killed our mothers." There was a twinkle in Jack's eyes, a seven year old on Christmas morning. "We've talked about this since we were kids. Since we were pissed off teenagers. Since we tried to survive their absences by crying into our pillows and punching holes into walls. And you want to call the cops? Are you freakin' kidding me?"

I let a pause arise between the two of us. He deserved it, and I needed it. He was kind of right, in a way. Of course he was right, not on a moral level—on a personal one. I didn't respond, but moved forward. I marched into the bleak meadow, toward the stand of trees, knowing that within the twigs and branches a boogey man could be waiting for me.

As we approached the stand, I suddenly felt the heavy weighted presence of the handgun rubbing against the small of my back and the rim of my jeans. I tried to remember the last time I fired it. Months ago, at a shooting range, and that was just to make sure the stupid thing still worked. I tried to walk, shoulder to shoulder, beside Jack, but I found myself hanging back half a step, as if there was something he knew about hunting potential serial killers that I didn't. We entered in through the stand, and as soon as we made it past a half-dozen row of trees, we entered into a large, open circle where a house stood at its center.

A chill, ripe with bitter-frost ran across my shoulders, up my neck and settled somewhere in my teeth. "This is it," I muttered. The house was a makeshift house old, broken, settled. It had two stories, from the looks of it, and a pointed roof. The warped wooden panel siding, which was rotting away, was a faded gray, with a strip of tan across the top, which had been weathered by the overhang. A large square, which neither resembled a door or a window, which was about three feet off from the ground, was boarded up.

I jumped, slightly, when I felt a sly tickle run across my shin. A gray and black cat purred, whilst rubbing against my leg. "Well, I guess we're at the right place."

"I hate cats," Jack said.

"Pets, statistically, lengthen a person's life."

"Statistics are statistically wrong."

"Jackie...that doesn't make any sense."

"Let's go," he said, ignoring me.

The gray and black cat, lightly and practically, pranced away from me and toward the bleak house. Jack moved toward the house, unapologetically, without waiting for me to join him. I followed suit, as I tended to do, however, as we approached the house we were suddenly taken aback. Just past the house, beside a weary rotting stump, sat a shirtless man, his back to us, legs folded, and his arms stretched out far and high—as if the canopies were dropping their leaves into his invisible basket. He seemed to be a tall, lanky man—thin with chapped, white, almost wrinkling skin and a very thin coat of hair atop his head that appeared to be platinum blond. He could be heard, even from our distance—murmuring something nonsensical.

The cat, which had darted from me to the house, now was by his master—who was clearly entrapped in some form of meditation—and wasn't the only one. An orange tabby cat had literally come out of the woodworks as well, followed by two more black cats, and a white, almost albino cat—with pink eyes.

"Living up to his name," Jack's voice trailed off and I was afraid it was enough for our suspect to hear us but it wasn't. Irusan continued to mutter unintelligible words and phrases. We moved forward quietly, on tipped toes, praying the dead leaves and broken twigs beneath our feet wouldn't give our presence away. The woods, save for the excessive mumbling, was quiet—still. My breathing suddenly sounded loud and veracious, not to mention shaky. I tried to steady myself, breathing deep, slow, through my nose. It didn't work. We didn't even have a plan for this point—what were we going to do? What was Jack going to do?

There was, of course, an overwhelming anger present. I was glaring at the back of the head of who might be my mother's killer. It was slowly settling to the back burner, though. As if I knew I had to be objective and that if my emotions were to get the better of me—now wasn't the time.

Jack didn't feel the same.

136

"Irusan!" Jack called out. My heart jumped. The lanky man jumped from his relaxed position and turned around. His face just as pale and droopy as his torso's skin, his lips thin, stretched, and his eyes small and hollow. I wanted a piece of him now, too.

"The gun, Grayson," Jack muttered to me. Irusan stood still for a moment, eyeing Jack with his bat. He looked afraid, but kept his heels still. "Grayson, the gun!" Jack said louder. Irusan, arms and legs bouncing and waving, sprinted off into the stand of trees, and before I knew it, I was chasing a potential madman through the woods.

Extraordinary Secrets

Today was a sad day at Old Dominion. There was some sort of security compromise in the wee hours of the morning and several patients from the bottom floors were accidentally released from their rooms after-hours, and a large fight ensued. Several of the security guards, nurses and orderlies were inadvertently involved and were hurt in the process. As I arrived to work this morning, I saw one of the nurses, Bri, I believe is her name, tending to a large wound on Jody's shoulder. My dear, sweet Jody was sadder than I'd ever seen him before. The usual bubbly exterior had faded. Jody—the man who entertained every soul in this building with his guitar or theatre performance, was left in shambles. When I comforted him, asked him about what happened—he told me that he had come into work early to check on one of his patients from the bottom floors, as they had been having a particular rough time as of late. Jody had only showed up just before the break-out ensued and was caught in the fight by mistake. He was only trying to protect himself and some of the weaker patients. His compassion is remarkable—as wonderful as his talent.

Unfortunately, the very patient he was there to see, to give a little extra cheering up, was one of the ones that escape. Jody is unlike any man I've ever met—he doesn't get paid much, doing what he does for the patients. It's sad, he's worth so much because what he does is just as important as what we do. He doesn't complain, though. He doesn't fret. The only moments you ever see him down are the moments like the one in which I saw him today. Where he feels he has let his patients down. There is so much to admire about him.

Because of the security breach I was asked to take the day off. I hesitated, of course, because my work is too important—and Jody—what would he do? I did, though. I came home, persuaded Alan to take off work as well and we had a lovely day together. It was much needed. Things have been tense, lately. He has accepted my long hours at Old Dominion, but I know he doesn't like it. And Grayson—that boy is growing up before my very eyes. He's going to be a man before I even realize it. I wish I could split myself into two pieces,—equal parts mother and doctor.

Even now, at this moment, as pen hits paper, Grayson's asleep, his head resting on the opposite end of the couch I'm sitting on, and Alan is asleep in the armchair next to me. I'm halfway watching a movie Alan and I started, but it doesn't hold my attention. I know this is supposed to be a work journal. But how do you have work without a little personal thrown in there somewhere? Alan doesn't see it that way, not like I do, not like Jody does. Alan thinks work is work and personal is personal. I suppose for his line of work that's true.

I hope Grayson finds a calling that allows him to get personal with his work. Like Jody and his missing patient, like me and mine. I hope Grayson finds passion in work and takes it personally—that's the best kind of work. The work that leaves you emotional. The work that leaves you open.

Chapter Six

The Matches Red

I wasn't the runner that Jack or Irusan were, apparently, because after several minutes of breaking through twigs and dodging trees, I lost them in the stand. Panicked, I broke out from the trees and into the meadow that me and Jack started in—hoping to see one of them, or both of them, in hot pursuit of the other. There was nothing. I heard the faint songs of birds and the remainder was a resting silence.

I returned to the stand of trees, darting my eyes between every bark and leaf, looking, listening for any hint of either my friend or the stranger we were hunting. I could feel the cold steel of the gun dig into my sweaty back and it suddenly felt twice as heavy—as if it needed to be in my hand or else it would be lost. I resisted the temptation and was reminded how Jack cornered me into pulling a gun on an unarmed man who may or may not have had anything to do with the killing of my mother.

I made it back to the clearing, suddenly feeling exposed, vulnerable, and regrettably drew the firearm from the back of my jeans. There was still no sign of Jack or Rodgers—and I was growing increasingly uncomfortable in the silence. Investigating the house, in its rotted and broken state,

141

was my best contribution now. A mountain of evidence could have been awaiting anyone—me—to find. Or worse, another victim, or what would be left of one.

The door squeaked open—my hand jittering on the door handle, my other hand firmly holding the pistol. The house was seemingly unlivable—Rodgers was a hoarder. A cat jumped from the top of an armchair and scurried into another room. Another one meowed by my feet somewhere beneath the stacks of garbage and storage that lined the walls and covered the hardwood floor which had started to rot. On the walls, at least in the places that weren't hidden by stacks of boxes and other assorted junk, were a collection of strange pictures. Some were of his cats, candid shots but in frames.

I found myself looking around the room for any signs of evidences—shoestrings, weapons, something that would give me the slightest indication that Walt Rodgers was The Shoestring Killer. I even looked around for a mask. A hollow mask with wide eye-slits, which would explain what Kathy Collins' daughter saw—what I saw years ago. Something to explain the wide eyes and mysterious, almost none present face. On one space of wall, which was above a broken couch, was a map that drew me in close. A map of the state, with red lines, permeate marker lines, drawn in various places. One on the mountain, one on Abingdon, and a large blood red circle drawn on the border of Virginia and Tennessee— with Bristol in the center of the red ring.

In that moment, my gut flipped upside down, my intestines twisting in a knot. I was sure it would never unravel, in the cusp of realizing that this entire investigation had dark tunnels deeper than my flashlight could shine. I heard a howling in the clearing outside the house. I turned around, aiming the firearm at the door, shaking. I wondered if the safety was even off. I would find out soon enough. I could hear a voice echoing in the trees—Jack's voice. Through the broken window I could see Jack, standing—bat in hand, while Rodgers lay at his feet, covering his head. This was where the howling came from.

As quickly as I could, I made it out of the house and across the clearing to the two of them. Jack held out his hand, as if to tell me that he had this under control. My patience with my old friend was wearing thin. I tried to remind myself that it was his mother too, and I hadn't any more right to be here than he did. Still, by the look of Rodger's face, which was covered in blood and one eye that was already beginning to swell, I had a feeling that he'd already become acquainted with the end of Jack's bat.

"Jack," I said in an inquisitive but harsh tone. Rodgers looked up at me, he shook and I almost heard a whimper, if he was our guy, he was doing a heck of a job at playing the coward.

"This is the other guy I was telling you about, Rodgers. The other boy who had to see his mother die." Rodgers looked up at me, the eye he could see out of teared and wouldn't break contact from mine.

"It isn't me," Rodgers said, his bottom-lip quivering.

"Don't lie, you'll get the bat again," Jack said. Something changed in Rodgers, he stopped shaking. His eyes ticked back and forth, a grin emerged, and his head slowly cocked towards my friend. It was unsettling—chills and shivers.

"I sometimes hear it. Trumpets from the sky. I hear them calling. The voices command the past. It is 1994 and we are all *dead*." Before I could process the dialogue, Jack swung the bat, pegging Rodgers in the rib cage.

"Jack!" He ignored me. Rodgers fell, bent over—I thought he would vomit.

"Walt," I started.

"That is not my name!" he yelled back, through the gritted teeth of baseball bat-related pain.

"Irusan," I corrected. "The Shoestring Killer is back. You know what I'm talking about. Right now all of our signs point to you. You were in the right places at the right time, you're out here, all alone, and a senior detective has believed you to be guilty for the past twenty years," I said firmly. Rodgers—Irusan—didn't respond. Jack swung the bat once more. I heard a crack—the rib was surely broken now. He yelped. I stopped trying to stop Jack. You couldn't stop Jack, though. I couldn't stop Jack, at least.

"The fortunate thing for you, Irusan, is that we aren't police. We can't arrest you for this—but we want our answers," I said.

"The unfortunate thing for you, Irusan, is that we aren't police, so we can beat the blood out of you without compromising the case or our jobs," Jack said, slyly. He pressed the round edge of the bat against Rodger's lips. A trickle of blood from his nose cascaded down his lip and onto the rim of the bat.

"Show us your arms" I demanded. Rodgers hesitated at first, but did as I told him. He was shaking again, but lifted his arms and stretched them forward. A symbol, a triangle like Jolene said, was carved into Rodger's left forearm—a triangle with the vertical lines extending past the top point, forming an X, while three horizontal straight lines remain in the center of the shape.

"That's our symbol," I said, my blood pumping.

145

"This is our guy, then?" Jack asked, almost surprised. "Working alone, or have help?" Jack swung once more, but I managed to grasp the bat before he made contact.

"Wait, I have questions."

"Quicker ways to get a confession," Jack said, furiously impatient.

"What is this?" I asked, motioning toward the scar. Jack mumbled curses at me. Rodgers didn't answer—his head downward.

"Tell him or I swear I'll kill you," Jack said through gritted teeth.

"It was a bond— a brotherhood." Rodger's voice boomed suddenly, with energy. A few cats started to nose around the scene—at a safe distance, of course. "We were all we had. We tried to stick together. I'm not the only one with this mark."

"How many?" Jack asked.

"I don't know!" Rodgers exclaimed. "I don't know how many were a part of the movement. We had to be careful—or else they'd see!"

"Who?"

"The voices," Rodgers said.

"So you had accomplices?" Jack questioned in tempered laughter.

"Where were you, Irusan?" I asked, suspiciously—hoping my gut feeling was wrong. He eyed me, with his one good eye and then back to the bat. "Answer me." He fell silent. Jack was about to wind up for another swing. I reached into my pocket, pulled out, and unfolded the map he had tacked to his wall above the broken couch. He was obviously taken aback, and even tried to stand—Jack forced him back to the ground. I pointed to Bristol on the Virginia-Tennessee line.

"Was it here? Was it Old Dominion Asylum?" I asked, nervously. Jack shot his eyes to me. Yes, we were starting to realize how far the rabbit hole goes. Rodgers nodded. He looked to me, as if his personality were completely changing once more, no longer the shaky, nervous Walt Rodgers, but a sly, calm, almost scary grinning Irusan.

"You have your mother's eyes," he said to me through that cheeky smile. I wanted to leap at his throat and beat him myself, but as Jack began to pull the bat back for another swing, he was interrupted by a new voice.

"Put the bat down, Hanna!" Jolene said as she emerged from the stand and into the clearing. She pointed her firearm at Jack, who dropped the bat in disgust.

"How did you find us?" he asked.

"I texted her when we arrived," I admitted. Jack turned to me. His eyes shook. I knew what he was thinking. He thought I betrayed him. I suppose I did—Justice over vengeance.

"Do you even want to catch the guy? He *murdered* your mother, right?" Jack grimaced.

"We have him, Jack. He isn't going anywhere." Jolene lowered her gun. "I don't even want to ask what is going on here."

"The questioning got a little carried away," I said to her. "There's a warrant out for him, right?"

"That's none of your business," Jolene snapped at me.

"You can hold him long enough for us to get evidence," I stated.

"I *know* how to do my job. I'm a freaking cop. You won't be getting any evidence. This is a police investigation. You two could get in a lot of trouble for being here—and doing this. Get out of here."

"Jolene," I started, but she wouldn't have it.

"I said I would help you as much as I could but you've left me no choice, Grayson. Get out of my sight—both of you. I'll cover for you. But I don't want to see your face right now and I don't want to see either one of you in this, again. You were never here. Go."

Jack and I hesitated for a moment, but it was clear Jolene wouldn't have it any other way. We slowly, defeated, walked away from the clearing and into the thick stand of trees.

"Old Dominion," Jack said. "Isn't that where your mom worked?"

"Yeah," I said, in some sort of hushed voice.

"You know I meant what I said," Jack started. I looked to him, inquisitively. "I would have killed him."

"I know all signs point to him, Jack," I started. "But you heard him say a lot of people have that scar, and we don't even know if this is the same triangle Kathy's daughter was talking about—we're grasping at straws here."

Jack shook his head and picked up his pace and walked without me. There was a path Jack was on that I knew I couldn't follow. It twisted and turned—and lost its pavement ages ago. It was kicking up dirt now and my shoes were dirty enough.

That evening I kept to myself. A couple of cups of coffee to keep me company. The walls of the Martha Washington were closing in—fast. I started looking for the ghosts, even. I decided, against better judgement, to creep over to my father's house. I would have to tell Alan what happened in the woods, and that hopefully as we spoke, the police were questioning Rodgers in an interrogation room. Alan wasn't around though, and I was relieved. I, subconsciously, held my breath every time I entered the house. I wasn't sure that was my— Alan, or my mother's fault.

Instead of hanging around near bad memories, I retreated to my old stomping ground—the top floor of the barn. I kept forgetting how it made me feel when I reached the top step—an overload of nostalgia. Over by the pool table sat a radio that played cassette tapes and CDs. I tried to remember the last time I'd actually bought music from a store.

I opened a window, the only window in the barn. It was just a couple of feet from the pool table, and it led out onto a slanted section of the barn's roof. I crawled out onto the course, black shingles, and found a spot to sit, my back against the siding. I could see Virginian sky through patches of the oak tree leaves. I thought about Rodgers—Old Dominion Asylum, and wondered if this case was worth it anymore. Since my return home I'd felt little like a private investigator and more like a lost boy playing *Eye Spy*.

The afternoon passed quickly. The evening sky, with brush marks of pinks and oranges. I sat on the roof, as if to attempt a rekindling of my childlike habitat, and listened to the blistering silence of Abingdon as the sun went down. A knock on the window sent a cool surge of fear through my veins. Jolene stuck her head out the window, a half smile arising—probably because she knew she'd scared me.

"You're so predictable," she said, as she climbed out onto the roof with me. She was in civilian clothes now, a flannel shirt and worn jeans—a standard mountain ensemble. I hadn't seen her in such since I came back. It reminded me of the Jolene I knew—seemingly a million years ago. Her hair was down, too, instead of being pulled up in a tight pony tail when she was decked out in her blues. Her wavy hair sat beautifully on her shoulders. "Of course this is the place you're going to be—brooding." Her joke was sharp but true.

"I have to admit, I didn't expect to see you," I said. "I thought you would still be mad."

"Oh, I am," she retorted, quickly.

"Am I under arrest?" I said, dryly, hiding any kind of excitement that she was on the roof with me, again.

"No—not this time," she said. "But you can't go play cops and robbers like that, again. And what was with Jack?" she asked.

I shrugged an "I don't know." I didn't have words for Jack's behavior. He had turned into a hunter. A vengeful spirit. Maybe there was something wrong with him. Maybe there was something wrong with me—after all, the passion for his mother is what drove him to near-murder. "What happened after we left?" I asked.

"I brought Rodgers in because there was a warrant out for him. Tax evasion. He's in lock-up right now."

"Is he going to be investigated for the murders?"

"I don't know, Grayson."

"What do you mean you don't know?" I was beginning to get infuriated.

"It's out of my hands, Grayson. I don't get to make that call. I'm not officially on the case," she snapped.

I sighed and retracted my argument, leaning my head against the siding—giving into defeat.

"I'm sorry," I muttered. "I shouldn't have snapped at you. I shouldn't have gotten you involved at all."

"I'm not going to say it is okay that you snapped at me," Jolene started with a shrug. "But you know me. I would've gotten involved, anyway." A red pick-up truck drove by, on the back road from my parents' home. A large sign reading *Elect Cindy Parker for Mayor* sat upright in the truck's bed.

"Wasn't Cindy Parker the redheaded girl that Jack took to prom?" I asked.

"If you mean took to prom and left to go get high, yes," Jolene said with a quick laugh.

"Speaking of Jack," I started, now double-thinking my sentence. "You and him, huh?" She looked at me, nervous, skeptical. Big doe eyes in front of my words—booming bright headlights. "I'm not the world's greatest detective, but I'm not stupid," I said.

"It was a long time ago, she explained, nodding.

"How long?"

"It isn't any of your business."

"I was just curious."

"Not long after you left. A year, maybe two," she admitted, with eyes rolled. "It was a weird time for the both of us— harder for him, I think. Then Jack's dad killed himself. He didn't seem to want to come around much after that and I guess I didn't, either. "

"Did it last a long time?"

"It lasted long enough."

"You didn't have to hide it from me."

"You've never been around to tell," she said. "Besides, there isn't anything to hide. It didn't last long, and it happened almost ten years ago. It is ancient history.

"Not to him," I said.

"How do you know?" She said. I looked over to her. Bright eyes, fixated on me.

"He still calls you Jo."

"So do you," she smiled. She almost laughed but shook her head, rolled her eyes—a universal sign that Jack was one-of-a-kind. "He's not still in love with me. Jack just likes to remind people about the past." I studied her, wondering whether or not she believed what she had just said, was trying to believe it, or just wanted me to believe it. Either way, it didn't matter. Neither Jack nor myself weren't good enough—put together—to be on Jolene's radar after all these years.

"Maybe that's how you see it," I replied.

"What is that supposed to mean?" she asked, her Virginian accent peeking out behind its curtain. I realized, coming home, that my tongue had turned Missourian.

"I mean the winner gets to write history, right?" I jabbed, lightly. "So who was the winner between you two?" Jolene shook her head.

"There's no winner, there. Jack doesn't let anyone win—not even himself." There was a pause. I'd traveled to unchartered waters. I wasn't welcome here.

"Who was the winner between you and me?" I asked, taking a large bet whether or not this was a safer topic to approach. She scoffed, like I just told her favorite *Guy walks into a bar,* joke.

"I guess you did," she said. Now it was my turn to scoff.

"How do you figure?"

"You left."

"You left me."

"But you *left.*" She moved a stray hair away from her parted lips as she sighed.

"Would it have made a difference?" I asked, trying to hold my ground. She didn't answer me. Whether she thought it was rhetorical or literal, I'm sure she wasn't willing to answer such a loaded question. That's what I did, with my questions—it was handing her a loaded gun and daring her to shoot.

"If this guy is our man—our Shoestring, I wonder what it is going to do to your old man," she said.

"What do you mean?" I asked. Her eyes drifted to me, slowly.

"What do you do with yourself when your life for the last twenty years is suddenly over?" She asked.

We sat, in a comfortable silence for a while longer, until one of us would think of a memory we could laugh at or debate about its authenticity. Just two friends trying to remember an easier time. When the sun was obviously down for the night, we decided to slip back in the barn, through the window. Jolene stumbled in the darkness—too clumsy for an officer, I thought.

"Hold on," I said, almost laughing. I felt around in the black, remembering where the light switch was—old reflexes are like habits, they don't go away without a fight. A small fixture over the pool table flickered on. It was an old lamp—something out of the seventies. A brown-yellow colored glass monstrosity that I loved, despite one of the glass panels missing.

"No way," I heard Jolene's voice break away into a whisper-breath. She moved toward my stack of music next to the CD and cassette player. Atop the giant stack lay a CD case I hadn't seen since I left. I held my breath for a moment.

"Our band," she said, popping open the case. I could hear the plastic hesitate, after being left alone for too long. She placed the CD into the player, hit play, and crossed her fingers. "Here's hoping you took care of your collection, Egg," she said, playfully.

"It wasn't our band," I protested. She rolled her eyes.

"You are full of it."

The CD successfully played, and Jolene almost squeaked in excitement. She pressed her finger against the forward button and skipped the song to track 8. I was officially uncomfortable, as she moved toward me. I was uncomfortable when she looked into my eyes, and refused to blink. And as 'our band' *The Matches Red* began to play the song she and I had our first kiss to, two-weeks after graduating high-school, Jolene leaned into me. One hand behind my neck, the other on my back. I instantly found my hand on the back of her neck, and my other hand on her hip—those reflexes, again. Jolene had transported me to a different place. I was eighteen years old, again. I'd escape my father and crawled out from underneath the murders. She leaned as I leaned, and somehow, in some way, we allowed our lips to touch once more. I knew it wouldn't last. It couldn't last. Jolene didn't care and she made me not care, either. That's what she did. It wasn't fair. It was irresponsible, messy, and it drove me crazy—and I loved her for it.

"This coffee is terrible," I told a police officer who sat at the front desk of the Abingdon Police Station as I added more sugar, and cream this time, to the cup. Jan, the officer, gave me one look that told me exactly where I could go. I smiled politely and began to pace the area once more.

"This way," another officer called out to me a few minutes later. I sipped the—what I'm assuming is dirt based—coffee and followed the rookie cop to a private room. "You'll only have a few minutes," he said, sounding annoyed with the prospect that I'd get any minutes at all. To which he had every right. I had no grounds for talking to Rodgers, but since no one had charged him with anything relating to the murders, and was only there for tax evasion, I talked Jolene into letting me have a few minutes alone with him. How I pulled that off, I don't know. Jolene was still mad about what happened in the woods but some part of her allowed herself to trust me. I just had to get in and out before Strout or Killian found out about my visit.

"Thanks," I said, earnestly—at least, earnestly enough. The room was just a table and two plastic orange chairs. My chair had a wobbly leg. I always got the chairs with the wobbly leg. It had to be some kind of omen. A few moments later, the door opened and two officers escorted Walt Rodgers into the room. He looked malnourished. He appeared this way in the woods, too, only I was just now truly recognizing how pitiful the human begin in front of me was—but it didn't make me feel sorry for him. The officer closed the door, and remained just on the other side of it. I could see the shadows from the officer's boots, slithering into the room with me and the infamous Irusan.

"Let's talk, cat man," I said, breaking the silence. Rodger's lips were small and chapped, and I wondered how that could happen in the warm weather that Abingdon was having. He almost smiled, and his thin lips stretched even further, cracking before my eyes.

"I'm glad you mentioned my felines," he started—his voice a velvet somber. "I wasn't expecting to be detained and I didn't make arrangements for my cats to be fed and watered. I'm worried sick about them. Since you know where I live, obviously, could you please make sure they're taken care of?" He asked, completely serious. I looked at him for a few seconds, half expecting him to laugh or tell me he was kidding—neither, of course, happened.

"Listen, Rodgers, I don't have much time with you so we need to cut to the chase. All signs point to you as The Shoestring Killer"

"But I'm not him," he interjected.

"Yeah, I'm not surprised to hear you say that," I sighed. "But that doesn't change facts. You were in Abingdon at the right times for the murders, both the ones from '95 and the present, and a witness identified the markings on your wrist."

"But I told you—I'm not the only one who had these. A lot of us did, back then—in the asylum." I knew he would say it, just as he did in the woods, just as the map showed me. It didn't make hearing it again sound any easier. Old Dominion Asylum, where my mother worked as a psychiatrist, shut down around the same time my mother died. Apparently, after a small mishap with a few of the patients and staff, it caused a police investigation that uncovered some, not-so-

159

legal practices. Then there was a small fire that burned down half the building. It just added to the situation. Just another rumor to float around town: *What were they doing in that creepy asylum? Is that what got Elizabeth Grant killed?*

Of course it wasn't—this was the work of a serial killer. None of the other victims had anything to do with the asylum, but hearing now that this somehow connects to that place, put a hole in my stomach that I didn't know how to fill.

"I'm sorry to be a bother," he interrupted my thought. "But where do we stand on the cat situation?"

"Rodgers, the light at the end of your tunnel is fading. You better talk fast or I'll march out into that murky garbage you call a house and snap the necks of every one of those cats, myself," I bluffed and he bought. His eyes sunk into his skull, and his pale skin almost turned blood red.

"You know there was a fire," he said, softly, brokenly.

"I know." I replied. "A lot of people thought there was foul play."

"Most of the brotherhood died in that fire. They couldn't get out of their cells—I'm sorry, rooms."

"Doesn't bode well for you then."

"Not everyone from the brotherhood was a patient. There was one gentleman, lived nearby—worked part time."

"What's his name?" I asked.

"I don't know his last name," Rodgers said, his delicate hand scratching his balding scalp. "He was one of those caregiver types. The ones who didn't have medical degrees but still wanted to feel important. One of those that never tells you his last name, just adds mister in front of his first. We all called him Mr. Jody." A knock on the door told me my time with Walt Rodgers had come to a close.

"Anything else you can tell me? Your life depends on it," I said, coldly, but he just shook his head. I stood from my seat and walked toward my exit, but hesitated as I cracked the door. I turned back to find Rodgers running a lanky thumb over his scar.

"What does it mean, Rodgers—the scar?" I asked.

"Its literal translation means Temporary Home. It was a reminder that one day we'd get out of that place and..." his voice trailed off—a hand caught in the cookie jar.

"And what?"

"And that we'd burn that place to the ground."

"Is that what happened?" I questioned. Rodgers sighed and leaned his head against the wall.

"No," he stated. "Someone beat us to it."

Extraordinary Secrets

Elizabeth's Work Journal
October 30th, 1994

I'm beginning to despise Dr. Walker. I, against authorization, snuck down to the bottom floor—The Tomorrow's Minds wing. I did not see exactly what goes on down there, but the sounds I heard were ghastly, to say the least. Screams, wretched, wretched screams echoed from every corner of the floor. My skin crawled. My eyes watered, and before a security guard asked for my identification card, I caught a glimpse of a former patient of mine, as he was being escorted down the hall. He was half the weight I'd saw him a year ago, at least, and his eyes looked like round black marbles, instead of the beautiful eyes I'd seen upon meeting him.

I left, and barely made it to the restroom before vomiting all over the floor. There I sat, vomit bleeding onto my blue flats and into the black cracks between the floor's white tiles. I leaned my back against the wall and let out a cry. It was humbling, in the most embarrassing of ways. My first day at Old Dominion—I felt like a queen. A ruler among pitiful souls who needed my guiding hand. And now, what was I? What was I part of? And what have I allowed to happen?

When I got the strength to pick my pathetic self off of the floor, I continued my rounds. Franklin has been distant lately, yet I haven't been able to pinpoint it. I tried to sit with him and talk. He wouldn't listen. Instead I combed his hair gently. He seemed to like it. I played with the curls and it reminded me of Grayson's hair—Alan's when he was younger. My stomach turned when I made the connection that Dr. Walker had recently inducted Franklin into a short trial of his program but ultimately decided he was better left in my care. What did Franklin go through down there?

Tony hasn't improved. I have continued to suggest Dr. Walker evaluate him but he has steadfastly refused. Now that I've glimpsed inside the monster that Dr. Walker is, I wouldn't dream of sending poor Tony to him. It does worry me, though. Where do you send someone who can't be cured?

I had to get some fresh, Bristol air. When I finished my rounds, I stepped outside, just long enough to let the sunbeams graze my face. He found me there: Jody. All smiles and his long blonde hair pulled tight into a ponytail. Now he had a silver stud pierced in his right ear. "It's cool, Lizzie," he told me once, when I mocked his style. Not even Jody could make me laugh today, though—or so I thought. What can I say? Jody has a way...with me.

163

After Jody comforted me, I made my way back into my office and I caught Marcy trying to sneak out of her room. Marcy, sweet sweet, Marcy. She's become an expert knitter, but her family has abandoned her, it seems. She hasn't had a visitor in months. Which is a tragedy all in itself. After all, if you can't count on family...

Who can you count on?

Chapter Seven

Arrested Guilt

"Don't count on it," Alan said, after I told him my conversation with Rodgers at the police station. He was hosing off his work boots, which were caked in a brown, murky mud.

"I know he's crazy, but it can't be a coincidence, the connection to Old Dominion and mom?"

"Don't make your mother the center of this. She wasn't the only one" Alan's tone was sharp. A go-to-your-room, sharp. I took another glance at his boots, cracked and worn— a decade of hard work, but my old man was retired.

"What have you been doing?" I asked. He motioned toward the barn.

"Clearing out some junk in the bottom floor."

"Throwing away my childhood?" I joked, attempting to lighten the mood. The joke repelled, though. Which was expected—my childhood was thrown away years ago.

"That's your mess to clean up," he said.

"EDMUND GRAYSON GRANT!" My name echoed in a shout behind me. Lexi, in a raging stomp, crossed the street in front of my childhood home, to the back yard where I stood with Alan.

165

"Speaking of mess," my father murmured, satisfyingly.

"Hi Lexi," I said, with held breath.

"Don't 'Hi Lexi' me, Grant," her southern twang was more apparent when she was mad, apparently. She pushed her blonde strands out of her face.

"What's wrong?" I asked, playing dumb.

"I heard you found him. That *IRA-SU-AN* guy," she spat.

"Rodgers, yeah, we found him in the woods."

"And why did I hear about it *afterwards?* Why weren't I there with you?"

"It was a spur of the moment thing, we weren't even sure our lead was a good one," I said, wondering why I was defending myself against my own client.

"I didn't drag my beautiful self out here just to sit in a fancy hotel room and wonder if anyone *died* in my bed," She was furious, in a cute kind of way.

"Weren't you supposed to canvas the town?" I asked. I could hear Alan behind me, sighing. Lexi crossed her arms.

"You mean busy work? Your father wouldn't let me anywhere near anyone who might be helpful."

"That true, Alan?" I asked.

"Would you *stop* calling me Alan? I'm your father."

"I'm not some wall ornament here for the ride along. I hired you, Grant. That means I'm your boss. I'm here to be a part of this investigation. I'm *sorry* you lost your mom. That's tough, Sugar, it really is—but I lost my sister, too. And not that long ago, by the way. So don't treat me like I don't have a right to be here. I may not be a detective, but if all you are doing is chasing rednecks in the woods and beating the crap out of them—hand me a freakin' bat," Lexi's words were strong and her eyes were stronger. Piercing—a freshly sharpened knife.

"I get it, okay." I replied. "But if you think you're my boss, you have another thing coming. You hired me, so that means I call the shots."

And at that moment, as if a cosmic reminder of how I was absolutely wrong, Agent Strout's car parked in front of the house.

"Of course," I muttered.

"Mr. Grant," Strout said, as she opened her door, stepped out, and adjusted the sunglasses that sat on her pale, boney face.

"Yes?" Alan and I said, in unison.

"The younger one," she pointed to me. I walked towards her, meeting her several feet away from Alan and Lexi, hoping to contain whatever disaster stood on either side of me.

"What can I do for you, Agent Strout?" I asked, kindly—like she was a neighbor hunting for a cup of sugar.

"We can drop pretenses, Mr. Grant," she stated, I couldn't see her eyes through the thick black shades. A tactical move—it was a cloudy day. "I told you to come to me if you had anything. And I trusted you, despite your father's reputation around here. Maybe because you're a P.I, maybe because you just seemed like a good man. So imagine my surprise when I find out Grayson Grant is in the woods with his pal, beating up suspects."

"Is he a suspect?" I asked, dodging her lecture.

"That's not the point," she said.

"Of course it's the point."

"We were supposed to work together, Grayson."

"I didn't know I was going to find him, okay? It was just a wild lead."

"Doesn't matter, you should have told me, and you shouldn't have pursued, you could've jeopardized the case. Luckily Officer Wire was there."

"Who I *called*," I stressed.

"It should've been me, you called. Officer Wire isn't leading this investigation. The Chief of Abingdon police isn't, either. Agent Killian and myself are, is that clear?" She scolded like I was a schoolboy. I nodded—with gritted teeth.

The Agent sighed, and tilted her head, slightly. Her blonde ponytail dangled—a pendulum ticking away at my grasp in this investigation.

"I understand your heart, Mr. Grant," she stated. "But unfortunately crimes aren't solved with the heart. I took a chance on you and that was a poor judgement on my part. You're too close to this case. You're out."

That is where Agent Strout made her first mistake with me. She assumed I was a good man.

"Listen, I get that what happened—"

"No Mr. Grant, you're done," she said, as she began to walk back towards her car. It was hard to identify what it was I was feeling. This wasn't a case I particularly wanted, but now that I had it, I didn't want to let it go. A kid with a ball he didn't want to play with, but didn't want to give it to the other kid, either. That's what I was, a kid with a ball.

"Just tell me if Rodgers is legitimately being considered as a suspect," I called out, hoping she'd throw me at least that much scrap. She paused and I held my breath.

"Not really," she said, as she turned back to me. My blood was on fire.

"Why not?"

"Because there's been another woman victimized, Mr. Grant, and as far as we can tell Mr. Rodgers was in our custody during that time. He's been released," she said, nonchalantly. She grazed over telling me there was a new victim, as if it were just a name on a page. A Jane Doe to add to a collection of Jane Does.

"Who? Who was it?" I called out—an urgency in my voice that demanded respect.

"Cindy Parker," she stated, opening her car door. "And if you're caught sniffing around her family, work, or any known associates, I'll arrest you myself." With that, the detective entered her car and spun quick wheels to escape the Grant house.

"Cindy Parker," Lexi said, approaching me. "That name sounds familiar, why does it sound familiar?"

"Because the name is plastered all over every other house or business in town. She was running for mayor," I said, refusing to break my vision from the agent's car as it drove off into the distance. Lexi squinted her eyes, blinking in the sun. A dissatisfied look came over her as she looked at me.

"So does that mean it is over? We're packing it in?" she asked, as if she was expecting me to disappoint her. I looked back at Alan, who had just dropped the hose onto the ground and stared out into the same direction I had been.

"No, not yet we're not."

"We might have a break, Gray," Kiddy's voice sounded relieved and tired on the other end of the telephone.

"I could use one, Kiddy," I said, realizing my voice sounded the same. Despite the lecture I got from Agent Strout, I reached out to the Parker family. Holt Parker, Cindy's spouse, spoke to me for a brief moment on the telephone but there was nothing he could really offer. Cindy's body was found in a dumpster near her campaign headquarters. She was working late—no one else was in the office but her.

"I got your message about what Rodgers' said—about the Asylum."

"Tell me you have something good," I started. "There's been another murder and Rodgers is looking pretty clean."

I could hear Kiddy's husky voice rumble in a cataclysm of mumbles. He called with good news and I hit him in the face with bad—usually how our partnership worked, I wasn't sure why he wasn't use to it, yet.

"Here's what I have on the asylum," Kiddy said, seemingly ignoring everything I had just said. I was pacing my hotel room at the Martha Washington. I could hear the chimes of excited tourist just outside my door, no doubt settling up for a cozy weekend of historical site seeing, lucky them. "Old Dominion was a privatized business, set up through grants and donations. Dr. Liam Walker, he was running the show back then, apparently impressed the owners with some unorthodox methods."

"Unorthodox?" I interrupted.

"Yeah, good luck finding out what that means," Kiddy started. "I've been trying to figure out what *Tomorrow's Minds* was all about but I'm coming up empty. That's what he called it, Walker. *Tomorrow's Minds* was his own little program on the bottom floor of the hospital. Only him, his small staff, and his patients were allowed down there, and I can't find anyone to tell me what that is exactly. Anyway, the hospital was losing money. People started checking their family members out, and weird rumors started circling nearby, which kept most people from coming inside. There was an investigation as to the standards of the hospital and it looked like it was going to get shut down but, well, that's when it happened."

"The fire," I replied. There was just enough of a fire to deem the place unsalvageable. "I knew it shut down—or was— around the time of the fire. This only backs up what Rodgers was saying about how awful it was there and how so many died in that fire."

"Whole place was just an eyesore, now—no money to save it, no one fooled with putting it out of its misery," Kiddy stated.

"Didn't you say you had some good news? Tell me something I don't know," I said.

"Dr. Walker didn't stop practicing when he left the asylum. In fact, he didn't retire until about five years ago. I don't know where he is now but I'm trying to find out. He has no social media presence and it seems like he is trying to keep a low profile. I have a stack of names I have to go through—patients, to see if any of them are clean, coherent, and able to talk, but your little triangle symbol doesn't stop with Rodgers and your killer, Grayson. Remember Joseph Farmer?" The name shot through me, a silent victim left abandoned.

"Our only male victim," I said.

"Coroner's report says he had an identical mark on his forearm, too." There was a pause on the phone.

"He wasn't a patient," I stated, in a half-question.

"No, he wasn't. At least not as far as we know." Kiddy confirmed. I sighed into the phone and flopped down on my bed. The house-keeping at the Martha Washington left tight, new, rose-smelling sheets on my bed. It was lovely and I hated it.

"And we have nothing on him? No family? Employer?" I asked.

"Nothing like that yet," Kiddy said. "But it's something."

"If Rodgers isn't our man, I don't know where to go, Kiddy," I stated. "What about this Mr. Jody? Anything on him?"

"I can't find a Jody anywhere in patients or staff records at Old Dominion," Kiddy replied quickly. "It's like he's a ghost." And the tragedy that lingered in Kiddy's words, was the unfortunate truth that he might be right.

I must've given in to the warm welcome brought on by the housekeeping staff at the Martha Washington, because as soon as I hung up with Kiddy I drifted off into a deep nap. It wasn't so surprising. It's hard to sleep when you're hunting a killer. Yet when I gave into the sandman, I gave in hard. A knock on my door erupted me from my sleep, drool trickling down the corners of my mouth, my eyes feeling dry and unwilling to open, my skin feeling patchy, hot, sweaty. I stayed still, listened, attempting to understand my surroundings. The knock occurred again.

"Wake up, Inspector," Jolene said on the other side of the door. And as quickly as I could, I opened that door for her. My hair was disheveled, hers was tied tightly into a ponytail.

Drool has damped the collar of my shirt, Jolene wore her uniform, perfectly pressed cloth with a shiny hostler. She smiled apologetically, which didn't make sense at the time, and handed me a paper cup with a flimsy plastic lid. "From my favorite coffee shop, I go there at least once while on patrol," she said. I nodded and took the cup from her.

"I think they call this enabling," I sipped the coffee. It was bad, but I smiled like it wasn't.

"You're a little more pleasant when you have it in your system, I'm just being selfish," she joked.

"Come in," I said. It was confusing, now. Jolene and I had let our guard down while in the barn, but hadn't spoken about it since. I didn't know what Jolene was thinking, nor did I have a clue as to what she wanted, but then again, neither did I— Abingdon wasn't going to dig its nails into me that quickly. Jolene stepped inside. She surveyed the hotel room more like an officer than a friend.

"You're a slob, Egg."

"Then I guess I haven't changed that much, have I?" I retorted. She smirked and shook her head as she lingered near the door. The not-so-subtle suggestion that this wasn't a sequel to our evening in the barn. "Is everything okay?" I said before I realized what I was saying. Of course it wasn't. Things were already not okay.

"Egg, I need you to stay calm," she said—the ironic intention of the phrase is ridiculous.

"What?" My word was sharp, and quick.

"We got an anonymous tip at the station. Agent Killian and Strout are on their way to your dad's place with a warrant to search the grounds," she said, her eyes darted to me, but away just as quickly—a school girl trying to talk to a boy. She wasn't a cop, not in that moment. And I—whatever I was—wasn't any longer, either. I had been changed—reduced, when I no longer thought that was possible.

"What kind of tip, Jo?" Her arms folded this time—the cop in her tried desperately to make a reappearance.

"I'm not sure, Grayson."

"Then why are you here?" I snapped.

"Because I wanted you to hear it from me," she replied, quickly. "I didn't want you to show up and see lights."

"Or are you trying to keep me distant?" I could feel my molars grind together. My eyes went dry from a refusal to blink. "Excuse me, officer," I said as I reached for my keys and brushed passed her on my way out the hotel door.

"Grayson," she said, stopping me before I could get into the hall. Her hand around my arm. "The department doesn't want you near the case, you know that—this could be trouble for you, real trouble."

"This isn't a case this is my family, Jolene," I shrugged my arm free and marched down the hallway. "You're welcome to come, too, if you want," I said—my voice echoing throughout the Martha Washington.

Jolene followed me to my father's house. In that moment it was almost easy to believe her that she wanted to save me from something. It felt excessive, the amount of police cars that were lined in front of the house, packed in the drive, and intruded upon the lawn. Forensic teams were clearing out the barn and digging in the yard. I parked on the street down from the house and jogged my way up to the driveway, Jolene close on my tail.

"Hold up," I heard an officer call out to me as I approached. He held his hand out and I stopped.

"He's with me, Jim," Jolene called out behind me.

"Where's Alan?" I asked the officer, ignoring Jolene's voucher.

"Are you his son?" Jim asked. I nodded.

"Your father is inside answering some questions we'd both love some answers to," A voice behind me boomed. Agent Killian stood, almost smirking, in front of me. Strout was to his side, though she seemed far less pleased. "Maybe you can help us out with that, Mr. Grant."

"I don't know, two Grants don't make a right," I said, annoyed. I looked to Strout, making it obvious I was finished speaking to Agent Killian. "Where is my father and what is going on here?"

"Mr. Grant," Strout started. "Abingdon PD received a very disturbing tip earlier about some evidence pertaining to our case could be found in or around your father's barn. Know anything about that?"

I sighed and almost laughed. "Oh yeah, how could I forget the mound of evidence we found and buried in the backyard? Are you kidding me with this? You get a tip and you are ready to call in the troops? Take a look in the town you're in," I said, gesturing outwards. "Do you really think people aren't going to get bored or interested enough to make a prank call? This case brought fame here. Do you have any idea what this might be doing to my father?" As the words spewed out of my mouth, I suddenly found my own self wondering what this was doing to Alan—and I was shocked how much I seemingly cared.

"Obviously we take everything into account but we must take these calls serious. We can't afford to ignore any possible leads," Strout said.

"And let us be honest, Mr. Grant, I've uncovered just about every rock in this town. The more I search for the

178

Shoestring Killer the more I have people cast a cold shoulder towards the Grant house," Killian added.

"What does that mean?"

"It means," he started, getting close to my face— I could smell the Five n' Dime aftershave above his white collar. "Your daddy isn't exactly Mr. Popular."

"We've got something," an officer yelled out, near the barn. Killian smiled

"And maybe there's a reason," he said, brushed passed me and went in the direction of the barn. I could feel my heartbeat between my ears as I followed the agents, and Jolene, to the barn. An officer emerged from the doorframe, with gloved hands, carrying an old, grungy box.

"We found this under some floorboards upstairs in the barn," the officer said.

"What do we have, Officer?" Killian asked—a boy on Christmas morning. The officer flipped open the box to show the detectives, Jolene, and myself. I subconsciously held my breath upon the removal of the box's lid. Inside were a few items that the officer slowly pulled out. An old, gray, wadded t-shirt and the most gut-wrenching of items, a long black shoelace. Both items were coated in a dry, dark ruby colored substance—most likely blood.

"THIS IS RIDICULOUS!" I heard Alan's call as he stormed out of the house. The door flapping against the wall so hard it bounced back—shutting itself. Two officers from the house followed him. "That barn is full of junk from thirty years of living here. You can't possibly be serious as to think I'm a part of this! I'm trying to stop this!" He directed his yelling at anyone with a badge, including the agents and Jolene, who stood awkwardly on the side. His eyes were wide, panicked—afraid. I'd never seen that look in his eyes before—not even after we lost my mother. Those eyes darted to me now, and his lip quivered before he spoke, in a much softer volume this time.

"Tell them, son," he started. "Tell them about how I've been working so hard all these years." I nodded at him, as if to tell him that I believed him and that I understood, that I knew he threw his life away because mom lost hers.

"There's a room upstairs completely devoted to the victims," one of the officers said to Agent Killian.

"That's for the investigation!" Alan blurted out.

"What exactly is up there?" Agent Strout asked, coolly. The officer sort of shrugged.

"Pictures of the victims. Lines drawn from face to face. There's a map of Virginia and Abingdon. There are words written all over the walls.

"It's my thinking space!" Alan spat. Agent Killian glanced at my father, then to Strout, and then to the officer.

"Okay, let's take him in, I have a lot of questions I want to ask. And someone get in there and take pictures of that room. Don't touch anything though, just sweep it for any more evidence. I'll be back later to check it out."

"You can't do this!" Alan yelled, almost laughing. "This is insane. What motive would I have?"

"The first victim was your own wife, Mr. Grant, there's plenty of motive from where I'm standing," Killian said.

"Then I feel sorry for whatever poor woman gets in bed with you every night," Alan said. Agent Strout stepped behind my father and removed her pair of handcuffs. I was in shock. Silence had taken over. I wanted to leap forward and stand in the way of her and Alan but I couldn't. I couldn't move. I couldn't think—not while I was still processing the bloody shoelace found in the flooring of the barn. Strout started reading his Miranda rights, and all sound seemed to drown away from my ears.

The scene started to clear away. My father had long left the house in the back of a police car. He was probably being booked at the exact moment that I watched Jolene walk across the yard, to where I stood, by my car on the street.

181

"Go back to the hotel, Grayson," she said in a soft, pity-filled voice. "There's nothing you can do, not right now."

"Who?" I asked, folding my arms and leaning against my car's hood.

"Excuse me?" she asked, taken aback.

"Who called in the tip?" I snapped. She sighed and looked down for a moment.

"I don't know, I'm not exactly kept close to this investigation. It's not my case."

"Who?"

"As far as I know, Grayson, it really was anonymous. But I will be honest, it wasn't a surprise to any of us" Jolene said, the words slipped out quick, painful for me to hear, and just as much for her to say. "The more the detectives asked the victims' families from ninety-five, asked people around town who might remember a thing or two. All the bad vibes kept coming back here, I guess," she tried to explain.

"Bad vibes, huh?" I tried to brush it off. "Everyone really thinks my dad is the monster?"

"They're just afraid he might be," she started. "And now with this evidence and the room upstairs. Did you know about that, by the way? The room upstairs?" she asked. I shook my head.

"No," I said, quickly. "I mean, I knew he kept a twenty year investigation going, so I knew he had a bunch of stuff up there but I didn't see it. I don't know what it looks like."

"Why not? If you're here to solve this case and everything," Jolene said.

"It's in the bedroom," I interrupted. There was a pause. A lull between us both before Jolene sprang into an apology.

"I'm sorry, Grayson." I waved my hand at her to stop.

"It's okay. It's childish, I know. I can't go in my father's bedroom because the last time I did I found mommy dead. It's stupid."

"It's okay," she said. Another silence erupted—if I had a dime.

"Do you really think he did it?" I asked, breaking the silence.

"Honestly? I don't know," Jolene admitted. I nodded, silently. It hurt to hear Jolene admit her confusion but I couldn't blame her. The shoestring itself bout be enough to convince a jury and if I were being honest with myself, it made me uneasy just thinking about it. There was no excuse I could think of for why my father would have a shoestring coated in blood, or why he would hide it.

"But they're going to come tear that room apart, looking for anything to suggest that he is the Shoestring Killer,

Grayson. And if there's a chance your dad has some kind of lead it might be in there."

"Alan told me what he had, he sent me crap in the mail all the time. He only had suspicions. This guy, or that guy. Honestly, Walt Rodgers is the closest we ever got, and that really wasn't much of Alan's work."

"Well, maybe Alan didn't get it, but another pair of eyes wouldn't hurt."

"It's too late. Remember, I can't do anything now," I sighed and flung my head back, staring up at the sun through the tree branches. Abingdon was a beautiful place but I forgot how to enjoy it.

"Unless you had a connection with a very cool, smart, beautiful police officer that can get you in the room," she said—a smirk on her face. I brought my head down, eyed her for a moment.

"Jolene Wire is willing to bend the law?" I mocked. She sighed.

"Egg, look around," she started," who isn't bending the law?"

Elizabeth's Work Journal
January 17th, 1995

It's cold today. Winter has been rough. Alan blisters in the winter, his hands are covered....covered in dry cracks that bleed if he works outside for too long. And he works outside for too long. Every day, all day, I think on purpose. I think to avoid me. Yesterday, my off day, my only day away from the hospital, I watched him work outside all day. Which, by the way, is his off day, too. He shoveled snow off of the sidewalks, not just in front of our house but the Hanna's house as well, and the Newmar's, two doors down. I watched him and I could see the reflection in the window of a pitiful wife waiting impatiently for her husband to come inside, to pay attention, to wrap his arms around her. I stood there, with a cup of warm coffee in my hand, wearing a purple turtle neck—I'd become quite accustomed to turtle necks as of late—and a warm afghan blanket his mother made us, wrapped around my shivering body.

Of course, he blames me too, for ignoring him. He blames me for pushing him away, for putting my work, my career, ahead of the family. I argue with him but not very hard. Not as much as I use to. I know, deep down, I've let him hit the back burner. And poor Grayson, I see him pulling

185

away from me a little bit. He tells his father about the game at school, and the girl in his math class. He thinks of me second. I suppose that's how it is. The parent that puts bread on the table is the last one to get any dinner talk.

But this journal is supposed to be about my patients, my work, my studies. Despite consistent consideration to leave Old Dominion, I cannot bring myself to abandon my patients. I'm fully convinced that Dr. Walker and his program are an ill-fit for this kind of psychiatric treatment that is provided at Old Dominion. He is, however, the captain of our ship and to rise against him would be little less than mutiny. My patient load has also increased, as I was recently promoted. Several patients and a team of doctors are now under my supervision. It makes less time for me to spend quality time with patients, but I still manage to see my long-term cases. The ones grandfathered into my time here. Franklin experiences several different mental illnesses, including Schizoaffective Disorder, and a serious Impulse Control problem. I often wonder if there is some kind of trauma induced disorder, but much of his history before coming to us is unknown. He, through proper medication and care, has become a very excellent patient. I'm very proud of the progress he's made. He's actually quite adorable. Sometimes in our sessions, he will hold onto me—like

Grayson did when he was a small child. He holds onto me like Alan did when we started dating. It's nice to be needed in that way, again.

Marcy, on top of a dangerous eating disorder, also suffers from violent mood disorders that cause her to be a danger to herself and people around her. A history of rape abuse has also caused trauma, and has skewed an already weak mind. I've been able to work with her on her eating disorder (she's gained ten pounds since last year!) the rest, I'm afraid, is much more of an uphill battle.

Tony, poor Tony, he desperately wants to get better...but it has been a difficult road for him. Tony has a dissociative disorder, leaving his identity completely unchecked. Often times he doesn't even identify as Tony, but other, often more violent, personalities. Despite the promotion, despite the increase in pay, despite it all—Old Dominion Asylum is falling apart. Dr. Walker is losing his grip on reality when it comes to patient care. The hospital's funding is barely in the black, and our efforts as a beacon of light are more of an A for Effort attempt, than actually a productive practice. I look at my husband, as he shovels snow and salts the sidewalk, and wonder how much more he is contributing to life, by clearing one sidewalk, than I am in my own career. I ran my hand across the fabric over my throat—my fingertips hovering just below my chin.

It's easy to feel pity for yourself, when everything feels like it is crumbling. Sweet Jody saw something like that in me. He listens, he pays attention, there's not a wall of bitterness there, with him. My stomach turns as I think about how close I let him, that day after he was assaulted. I feel my cold fingers gently grip even through the turtle neck, grimacing at the memory of Jody, as he leaned in and unapologetically kissed me, with full lips. I pulled away, of course, but it was too late. It was already a crime.

Chapter Eight

Rumors

Consistently within my detecting career, I have been able to be *bought.* The bigger dollar wins. It isn't right, but it is the truth. The way I see it, my reasoning, or my excuse, is simple: If you're going to a private investigator, you have a private reason. People, in my own experience, fall short somewhere between the good intended and up holding stamina for decency. There aren't too many people that walk through my door that I would call decent. If you need a P.I, chances are you have a reason to keep it private. People spend so much time righting old wrongs—and not enough time trying to avoid wrongs in the first place.

As I stood in my parents' old bedroom, which had mutated into a room full of pictures of the dead and theories scrambled on the walls, I wondered what we were doing, trying to right old wrongs, or stop new ones. I'm a lousy detective, so I hadn't a clue. The space around me was mapped similar to the one Kiddy and I had constructed back in St. Louis, except where Kiddy and I used a cork board and push-pens, Alan used wallpaper, a staple gun, and permanent markers.

189

"This is a little unsettling," Jolene stated, introducing us to the elephant in the room.

"Well, it isn't like he's playing fantasy football, Jo."

A young picture of my mother hung above where my parents' headboard use to be and beside her was a picture of Carol Hanna. Another young picture, long brown hair. A little further away, near the window seal was Rebecca Lassiter's picture, along with Lauren Kelley's. Beneath the window was a large map of Abingdon, four permanent marker lines crossed from the four pictures, to various places on the map. On the other side of the window were three other photos: Miranda Keats, Lexi's sister, in her graduation cap and gown, Kathy Collins, and Cindy Parker, the young red headed woman running for mayor.

"Seven women," Jolene sighed. I frowned—because she was right. I looked around the room, but there were no more pictures of anyone other than these seven women. Various pictures of my mother, Carol Hanna, and the rest of the women coated the other three walls, but only these women.

"Wait a minute," I stated, turning to Jolene. "Where's Joseph Farmer?" It puzzled me. Even if Farmer was the victim of a copycat, he should be somewhere on the wall.

Jolene looked around as I did. "Your dad knows everything there is to know about this case, right?" I nodded.

"Trust me, he knows that Farmer exists. He knows the victim list frontwards and backwards. So why isn't Farmer up here like the rest of them?" I questioned. Jolene walked closer, examining the map.

"Maybe he had an idea of how Farmer fit into it all," she said.

"Then shouldn't that be here? Sketched out like the rest of it?"

"Maybe," Jolene's sigh was tiresome. She was exhausted from the beginning. Lexi is driven by passion. Jack, by revenge, Alan, by obsession, and me by obligation. Jolene, though—Jolene's reason is justice. She just doesn't want to see anyone else get hurt. As noble as it is to be driven by logic, it sometimes can be the most draining. "Either way, we need to talk to him about it. Those agents have an idea your daddy's a killer and we need a better idea."

I shook my head towards her. "The world is not short of ideas. We are swimming in them. Action, that's what we lack. We're hallowed. Guns without bullets," I replied.

"Okay, so stop swimming in circles and tell me what you think?" she asked. "Where do we go from here?" I looked over to a corner of the room, where Alan had pushed my mother's desk to, and stacked towers of what looked like paperwork on top of it.

"You know where," I said, subtly, as I walked towards the desk.

"What is all of this?" Lexi said, loud and drawn-out as she walked into the room. I quickly looked over to see her and Jack stepping into my parents former bedroom, then back to Jolene.

"What are they doing here?" I asked.

Jolene looked to me, earnestly. "What happened to the team Alan assembled? If I'm sneaking you into the underbelly of this case I might as well sneak these guys in, too. Besides, we need all the help we can get if we're going to prove your father is innocent," she explained. Lexi walked through the room silently—almost gliding in a catlike fashion.

"Your dad was really in deep wasn't he, sweetheart?" Lexi said, eyeing over at me. I caught a look from Jolene. Lexi reached up and gently ran a finger across the picture of her sister. "You know Miranda hated this picture? Said she thought the gown made her look fat. Can you believe that?" Lexi's voice broke for a moment—attempting to evade tears. "That dumb slut thought she looked fat in a graduation gown."

"Your pop was arrested?" Jack said, leaning on the door frame. I nodded towards him.

"They found some apparent evidence. Bloody shirt and shoelace, in a floorboard in the barn." I said. Lexi turned around when she heard it.

"You think he had something to do with it?"

"No", I said, picking up a stack of papers from the desk. I said it with confidence despite the fact that I couldn't stop thinking of the bloody shoestring that was found under the floorboards of the barn attic.

"I don't know," Jack said, at nearly the same time as I denied it. I turned around again, glaring at my best friend.

"What?" I said, more exclaiming than asking. "Are you kidding me, Jack?" He just shrugged. He wore a black tank top with the name of some indie band no one has ever heard of on the front. The sleeveless shirt exposed the tattoos that ran up his arms and onto his shoulders, ranging from everything to guitars to dragons.

"I'm just being honest with you, Gray," he said, nonchalantly. "You can't say he didn't—you have no evidence to prove he isn't." I gestured my hands so he could see the room we were standing in.

"What does this look like to you, Jack? Maybe the most depressing collage ever?"

"This is so like you, Grayson," he started, raising his voice a little and moving into the room. "Your thought process is an inch deep and a mile wide. You're afraid to dig to a real place and you're afraid to see what is there. Don't you get it man, whatever this is—it is deep and it's scary. You were uneasy about going into the woods even if it meant finding your mother's killer and when we found a weirdo who you totally believed was the killer by the way, you still hesitated to pull the trigger—literally or metaphorically. Well, here you are again, Grayson. You're standing in the woods. This could be your dear old daddy trying to find the person who took his wife from him, or it could be a sick serial killer who is obsessed with his victims," Jack spat off.

The room grew silent for a moment. I watched the wall for probably too long. It didn't matter—no one was going to speak after that spill. Not until I would.

"I grew up with the man, Jack. I think I would know if I grew up with a killer. Alan lived and breathed this case. He wouldn't spend his time looking for the person responsible if he knew that person was him, would he?"

"You're too close to it man," Jack said.

"Then what are you?" I snapped.

"Logical," he stepped closer to me. "He makes the most sense, Grayson. Let's look at it. Evidence was found in the barn? The entire town hates him. He's harassed the victims' families, mine included. He's been notoriously mean and closed off. He doesn't let anyone in the house. And then there's the other thing, the rumor," he said.

"What rumor? Jack?" I asked. His eyes shifted at that part. He didn't look so angry anymore, but he looked just as serious.

"This town does a lot of talking, we both know that, but rumor has it him and your mom, well," Jack's voice drifted.

"Jack," Jolene intervened, quickly.

"Him and my mom what?" I asked, angrily. He sighed and looked over at Jolene, who shook her head subtly—just not subtle enough for me to not catch her.

"What's he talking about, Jo?" I asked. There was an awkward pause again—a stalemate of speech.

"I think I'm just gonna step out for a second, y'all," Lexi whispered as she tiptoed between Jack and me.

"Alan and mom WHAT?" I asked—the last word with a loud voice.

"She was going to leave him," Jack said quickly—like ripping off a Band-Aid. I shook my head as I turned to him.

"No, there was nothing like that going on," I said.

"It's just a stupid rumor that's floated around town for twenty years, Egg. There's been plenty of stupid rumors, Jack," Jolene stressed. Jack nodded.

"But this one is true. My mom knew. She told my dad. It makes sense, doesn't it Grayson? Just pretend you're not his son," Jack said, approaching me, opened armed, almost excited with his theory. "Alan kills Elizabeth, but he knows my mom knows Lizze's secrets because they were best friends. So he kills her, too. And by that point, he's unraveled this whole thing," Jack said.

"Except for our moms, there is no other real connection between the women, Jack. My mother wasn't friends with any of them, or even knew any of them."

"That's not the thing he unraveled," Jack stated. "He unraveled that he liked killing people." Before I could *logically* react to his statement, I *impulsively* reacted, with a strong right hook to the jaw. Jack fell to the ground in a second, flat. My knuckles were throbbing with pain—I bit my lip to keep quiet.

Jolene rushed between us as Jack rebounded to his feet.

"You son of a—"

"WHAT DID I MISS?!" Lexi yelled as she ran back up the stairs. Jolene pushed Jack and I away from each other.

"I swear if one of you moves a freaking muscle I will arrest you. Don't even tempt me. Don't," Jolene said. Jack stared, wiping the blood away from the lip he bit.

"Looks like your emotions are in check, Detective Grant," Jack murmured as he turned and walked out the door.

"What was that?" Jolene asked. Her tone was sharp and unforgiving.

"Nothing," I snapped. Lexi walked into the room, slowly, cautiously, as if I were handing out jabs. Jolene wiped her forehead and looked down.

"Stay here, Grayson," she demanded, and stormed out the door. "Jack!" I heard her call out

"You clocked him pretty good," Lexi said, her words drew my attention out of the hallway after Jolene and Jack, and back to her.

"He was being a douchebag," I muttered, turning back to the stack of papers on my mother's old desk. Flipping through them, it didn't take long for me to realize they were patient files, from the asylum my mother worked in before she died.

"Hmm," I hummed, to myself.

"What is it, Sugar?" Lexi asked. It was hard to tell if her demeanor towards me was flirtation or just part of her southern friendliness. I hadn't heard her call anyone else sugar or sweetheart.

"Just my mom's old patient notes from her days at the hospital."

"Workaholic?"

"I guess," I shrugged. "Although to be honest I don't really remember." There were stacks of papers on various patients, notes on their rehabilitation, their attitude, medication, personalities, backgrounds—both medical and personal. "Rodgers said I needed to focus on the asylum and the inmates there," I said, thinking aloud. I'd flipped through nearly twenty files so far and hadn't come across a single Jody. Franklin Butler, Marcy Springs, Tony Sanderson, DJ Cassidy, Selina Albright, the list went on and on. No sign of Jody. "All these years I never thought to connect it back to Old Dominion Asylum," I said. "Not until Rodgers mentioned it, and again when Kiddy brought up Dr. Walker," I said.

"Old Dominion Asylum?" Lexi asked, surprised. I frowned at her.

"What do you know?"

"Well, even though your old man said no, I canvased some of the victims' families. In fact, I straight up stalked most of them on various social media sites. I've talked to friends, and friends of friends, and friends of friends of friends," she went on.

"Lexi, focus," I said.

"Kathy Collins, you remember her?" she pointed to the picture on the wall.

"Of course I do, we were thrown out of their house, remember?" I said.

"I talked to one of her ex-boyfriends, whom she was still on good terms with. Isn't that sweet? I always think it's nice when two people can put aside their failed relationship and still be friendly with one another."

"Lexi," I stressed.

"Sorry—anyway, ex-boyfriend said he talked to Kathy about two and a half weeks before she was killed, and one of the last things they talked about was this new ghost hunt."

"Ghost hunt?"

"Sorry, yeah, okay so you know how you told me that this town is full of ghost stories? Well, apparently there is this ghost hunting club. Or a ghost enthusiast club? I'm not sure hunting is the right word. Anyway, they investigate old and new ghost haunts. The last one she mentioned to her ex-boyfriend, who is apparently into this thing too, was one she was going to at Old Dominion."

"What's the story?" I asked, eagerly. Lexi shrugged.

"Don't know. All the ex knew was that there had been reports of a figure moving within the old grounds of the asylum. Some locals even called the cops a few times but every time they looked through the place they couldn't find anything. The figure was always back, though. And the place apparently has enough history of terrible endings—ghosts are just bound to pop up. That's what the ex said. I don't believe in ghosts," Lexi finished.

"Why are you just now telling me this?" I asked. Lexi shrugged again.

"I just figured it was a ghost story. I had no idea the asylum was connected to any of it!" Jolene reentered the room, looking just as mad as she did when she left.

"Well, is he downstairs waiting with a baseball bat?" I asked, sharply.

"No—what is wrong with you? You're just going to punch your best friend in the face over his stupid mouth?"

"No, he's always had a stupid mouth. I punched him because my father who has been a terrible excuse for the term, is still nowhere near a murderer. I don't care if he hated my mother, which, by the way, he didn't." And again, like some sort of recurring nightmare, I saw the bloody shoestring, being carried out of the barn with the blood soaked t-shirt. I suddenly remembered seeing Alan board up something in the barn attic. It was a terrible realization that he was hammering the board in order to cover up the shoestring and t-shirt.

"Egg, you have to remember you're not the only one who lost a mother. Jack may not show a lot of emotion but he's eaten up on the inside too."

"You don't have to defend your boyfriend to me, alright?" I said—the words slipping out before I could stop them. Jolene's eyes changed in front of me. I hit a nerve she didn't expect for me to hit. "I'm sorry, Jo. I didn't mean that."

"Let's go," she said, quickly. I can't keep you guys here all day. Killian will be here soon enough," Jolene said, ignoring my apology.

"Awkward," Lexi whispered as she left the room the same manner she did before. I picked up the stack of papers, and moved to follow Lexi.

"What are you doing? I didn't say you could take anything," Jolene snapped.

"Jo, these are my mother's patient files. Maybe there is something here we could use. You said it yourself the agents want to close in on Alan. They're not going to give this the fine tooth comb it deserves," I argued. Jolene hesitated for a moment but then nodded her head. "Besides," I started. "We'll need it for where we are going."

It took nearly an hour to turn Jolene's mind around about my idea to visit the emptied, half-burnt building that use to be Old Dominion Asylum. *After I'm off duty. I can't go as Officer Wire*, she stressed when she finally agreed. She was still angry but not so much at me. I waited anxiously for Jolene's call in the family living room, curtains drawn and lights out—a mob of reporters and nosey townspeople gathered in a large flock outside the house. They muttered and glared and tried to peek through the windows. Too many news outlets had already called for a statement. *The Shoestring Killer is back and he could be your father. How do you feel about the possibility that the man who raised you might be responsible for the death of your mother?*

I had only answered one phone call from them—and laughed when they pitched me their top question. Laughed, thinking that my father could possibly be behind this, and laughed because they think he raised me.

I paced the dark, empty living room back and forth. The sun was going to go down soon and I felt uneasy about investigating the asylum at night, not to mention how much more difficult that would be to look for anything useful. A knock on the back door jumpstarted my heart, but by the time I ran to the kitchen, Lexi had already let herself in.

"Oh," I said. "It's you."

"Wow," Lexi said, smiling, but obviously hurt.

"I didn't mean it like that," I replied.

"Most men are happy to see me, you know," Lexi added. "If you haven't noticed, I'm cute."

"Of course you are," I said, waving off her self-handed compliment. "It's just—"

"Jolene? Miss hot cop?"

"We're going to check out the asylum. It is for the case," I said, annoyed.

"Relax, sweetheart, I'm teasing. When are we leaving?" She crossed the kitchen, matter-of-factly, and sat down at the yellow kitchen table. "And don't even sass me about not coming along. I'm the one that gave you the idea about the asylum."

"No, you weren't, it was Rodgers," I corrected.

"Still," she argued.

"I'm too stressed to argue with you anyway," I replied.

"Aw, so sweet," she said, dryly. Beside Lexi was the stack of patient files I'd taken from my parents' former bedroom. She ran her finger across the edges of the papers—a fake eye scan over what looked like seemingly boring paperwork.

"Grayson, can I ask you a question?" she said, drawing out the last word.

"What is it?"

"If it isn't your dad—and don't punch me because I don't think it is either—who is the most likely person? I mean it's not that cat man either, right?" I shook my head slowly.

"I don't think so, no. I don't know who it is, to be honest with you. Those files, it could be any of them or none of them."

"Rodgers is connecting the scars to the asylum, are the police looking at it?" Lexi asked. I shrugged and sat down across from her.

"Not really, the only people who have mentioned the triangle scars are the Collins girl, Olive, and Walt Rodgers. Olive didn't tell the police what she told me, and even if she did I don't know how seriously they're taking her—and *no one* takes Rodgers seriously."

"No one but you, apparently," Lexi pointed out.

"Apparently," I sighed. Lexi ran her fingers through her blonde hair, and shook her locks to either side of her face. At this point I was almost positive she was flirting with me.

"Besides, they really want Alan for this one, it seems"

"He can't be as bad as they say," she stated—almost a half question. My eyes connected with Lexi's for longer than they should have without one of us speaking.

"Depends on what they say."

Unsuspectedly, she reached across the table and clasped my hand in hers.

"Listen," she started, in a soft tone. "I know this isn't easy for you. I'm really sorry, sweetheart, and I'm going to do what I can to help." Her sensitivity was random, but heartfelt. I smiled slightly, unsure of what to say back to her.

Three gentle rings from my cell phone broke the soft, cold hand that was around my fingers.

"Must be Jolene," she said, bringing herself back to reality.

"Jo," I answered my phone quickly.

"Let's go," she said on the other end, quick and sharp. I hung up a second later, feeling Jolene's chill from the phone and looked to Lexi.

"Let's catch a bad guy, sweetheart," she smirked and moved to the door faster than me.

The drive to Bristol was quiet. Jolene drove, I sat in the passenger seat looking over my mother's patient files, and Lexi sat in the back, occasionally saying something to which Jolene nor I had a response.

"Franklin Butler," I mumbled aloud as I looked over some notes my mother made. There was only one picture of him, just like the rest of the patients. He had dark, thin hair and a pale face, his face was drooping and looked hunched over. "Camera shy," I read my mother's scribble—a doctor's handwriting, for sure. "Refuses to wear the shoes provided for him by the asylum. Hates the sound of the velcro. Hates socks. Likes to eat cheese sandwiches, refuses to eat almost anything else. OCD, Schizoaffective Disorder with several suspecting undiagnosed disorders. Here under court order, after violent outbreak in a previous facility.

"Violent outbreak, huh?" Lexi said, suspiciously.

"Easy, junior detective, almost every single patient in this stack had extremely violent tendencies. Listen to this guy, Anthony "Tony" Chill had a really rough past before getting to Old Dominion—and once he got there he got even worse. Says here he almost beat an orderly to death. He was then transferred to a trial program conducted by Dr. Walker, and then my mother's notes on him subside for a while, and when they started again she states that he was put back under her care—and was even less responsive to therapy than before.

"Sounds like Dr. Walker wasn't too successful," Jolene chimed in. I shook my head.

"It is *Tomorrow's Minds*. I mean it is hard to tell in the patient files but she doesn't seem too fond of it. Sounds like Walker was something of a weirdo after all," I flipped back to another file that I had looked at earlier, before Jolene had called. A file that's patient name read Marcy Winters, whose file looked similar to Tony's, save for all the violence. "Right here," I stated. "'Marcy Springs was excused from *Tomorrow's Minds*. Another failed treatment option from Dr. Walker.' She underlined 'another.'"

"'Another failed treatment option,'" Jolene repeated. "This Walker quack sounds like a person of interest," she added. And just then, like he was listening in, Kiddy called my cell phone.

"Kiddy," I said. "We are on our way to the asylum to take a look. We were just talking about Liam Walker," I said. Kiddy chuckled.

"Speak of the devil and the devil shall appear," he quoted the phrase.

"What do you have?"

"Nothing that is going to make you happy. According to residential records, Liam Walker is living in Santa Barbara, California," Kiddy stated. I balled up a fist and hit the side of Jolene's passenger door. I could feel her judgmental eyes on me.

"Are you sure?" I asked, desperately.

"Video of him at a fundraiser two weeks ago is online. It was a wine tasting for ALS. He gave a speech. Grayson, this was the same night Miranda Keats was murdered. " Kiddy replied. I glanced, in the back seat, at Lexi. She looked at me—so hopeful. "Not to mention he was in Richmond teaching a seminar the night the Kelley girl was murdered," Kiddy added to the stack

"Do you have a phone number? Email? Anything?" I asked.

"I'll email you what I have," Kiddy replied. I thanked him, half-heartedly, and disconnected from the call.

"Dr. Walker is a bust," I said.

"Why?" Jolene asked.

"His residence is listed somewhere in Santa Barbara, California now. Social media confirms it too. He's rubbing elbows at big picture fundraisers now," I said.

"Plus he has an ironclad alibi—he was seen at an event in Santa Barbara the same night your sister was murdered, Lexi," I said. "And the night Lauren Kelley was murdered he was in Richmond, Virginia, teaching a seminar."

I tapped my mother's stack of notes. "So we're back to patient files."

"We have an asylum full of suspects, don't we?" Lexi said—exhaustion in her voice. I shook my head.

"We don't have to find a patient that they failed. We just have to find the one they forgot about."

When we arrived at the asylum, which sat on a hill in Bristol, on the Virginia side, the sun had set, leaving a faint brush of plum across the sky as night slowly settled. The asylum was a mixture of history and failure. The building, what was left of it, reminded you of the old structures scattered around Abingdon. A two hundred year old building, with tall towers and gothic-like characteristics. It looked less like a hospital and more like something you'd see out of horror movie—the old, haunted asylum. Completely generic but as I looked at it, burnt in several places, mostly the southern east side, which was ultimately the last straw on a very unsteady camel, I wondered just how far off was that assumption. After all, what does it take to really be haunted?

"We don't have much light," Jolene said.

"We have flashlights, it isn't a big deal," Lexi said—an annoyed tone attached to her words. She popped open the back door, and started marching towards the asylum. "Come on, scaredy cats."

"She's certainly brave, and passionate and, well, eccentric," Jolene said, cracking the first real smile I'd seen since our encounter in the barn-shed.

"Those are nice words for: careless, misguided, and crazy," I retorted, but I smiled too. Jolene shrugged. "I don't know, we could all use a little crazy."

"She says, in front of an asylum," I mocked.

Jolene hit me, playfully. "Be nice. Most of these people really needed help—they couldn't help it any more than you could have helped your knee pain when it broke. Actually, you could've helped that because you jumped off the barn roof," Jolene stated.

"So if anyone is crazy, Grayson Grant, it is you."

"Jack dared me, what was I supposed to do?" I asked.

"I don't know, not jump?" Jolene raised an eyebrow to me.

"He already jumped. I wasn't just going to not jump, Jolene," I said, finding a smile on my face.

Lexi turned her flashlight on, and examined one of the entrances—a door that had a large hole in the center.

"She seems a little taken with you," Jolene interjected.

"Who, Lexi?"

"Some detective," she mumbled.

"She's a client," I said, jumping to my first defense. Jolene looked to me—her eyes heavy. "And besides, after the other day..." my voice trailed off, trying to make our encounter not seem like an afterthought.

"Yes?" she asked, a small smile curving on her mouth because we both knew she was forcing me to do the hard work.

"What is going on with us, Jo?"

"Is there anything?"

"I don't know."

"Well, those are the three words that make girls like me weak in the knees, Egg," she said, dryly.

"Do you know?" I said, roughly.

"I'm not falling for the Egg charm just for you to leave, again."

"If memory serves me correctly—your first love was Abingdon." And it was true, no matter what spark the younger versions of ourselves had with one another, the drive that pushed me out of Abingdon was no stronger than the anchor that was keeping her in it.

"How do you know?" she replied, trying to stand toe-to-toe with me in the debate.

"You didn't come with me," I said flatly.

"You never asked," she said, quickly. Lexi waved from the door—an anxious but hesitant amateur.

"We should get going," I said, thankful that Lexi brought us out of our day dream and into our harsh reality. Jolene didn't say anything. She didn't have to say anything. She knew, after all, what I knew—all these years haven't changed anything. Her heart and soul were still here, but not mine.

We walked towards the decaying building, which barely looked safe enough to enter. What wasn't covered in the coal colored residue of the '95 fire, were old stones that were cracked and somewhat broken.

"You really think this is worth following, Lex? This ex boyfriend's idea?" Jolene asked, skeptically.

"Naw, sugar, I just wanted an excuse to hang out with y'all," Lexi sassed as she squeezed through the broken front door. Jolene shared a look with me. I just shrugged and kept forward, following Lexi into the asylum. There were two spiraling staircases, going up either side of the main entrance, leading to an overlook. It looked as if the overlook lead to a series of broken elevators and separate staircases. Directly in front of us was a round damaged, dirty front desk. I tried to imagine what it looked like in its hay day. Golden rails leading up the staircase, maybe red carpets on the stairs themselves. Marble floor that shined like a new penny. Thoughts that were too fancy for a mental health hospital. I wouldn't know, though.

"So this is what momma walked into every day," I muttered. "Or something like it."

"You've never visited your mother at work?" Jolene asked.

"Not really the environment you want to bring your child into, Jo," I replied.

The asylum was blackened—from years of neglect and, of course, the '95 fire. I thought about Walt Rodgers, and wondered if he and his *Temporary Home* crew were actually the ones responsible for the fire. And, if that were true, why would the killer among them return here? The three of us were silent, I even paid close attention to slow my breath—doing anything I could to breathe and move as quietly as I could. Our feet betrayed us, however, as the wooden panels cracked and crunched beneath our heels.

"The ground is like charcoal," Lexi stressed, *charcoal sounded* like three syllables instead of two when she spoke.

"Be careful, Lexi," Jolene insisted. "The building is rotten and not reliable."

"Okay, where did your source say they saw something?" I asked, turning to Lexi. She looked borderline afraid, though she would never admit to it.

"I don't know—around?" Jolene turned on her flashlight, and the beam fell around black and rotten places.

"I don't see how anyone could live in this environment," Jolene's skepticism could be seen and felt through the dark.

"Well, whoever we're looking for isn't like just anyone else, are they?" I said, now turning my flashlight on and shining it down the hallway beneath the twin staircases. "Let's go this way," I said, motioning where my light beam was glowing.

"Just as good a place as any," Lexi piped up—a faux brave voice that didn't fool anyone. Her bravery outside was fleeting now.

We crept around in the dark, for what felt like an hour, shining our flashlights into unsuspecting corners and expecting to find something. There wasn't anything, though, but burned walls, decaying wood, mold and dust—a recipe for the metaphor of a clear dead end. The architecture, from what survived the fire, and could be seen in the dark, past the years of neglect and the layers of dust, was quite beautiful. Long detailed patterns of ingrained abstract designs served as a beautiful wooden trim across the top of the hallways, with dark, rich, solid wood lining the walls.

"It looks more like a house," I started—"a mansion or something."

"I think it use to be a boys' prep school—a long time ago," Jolene said, making sure she lead the way—always the police officer.

"Fitting," I murmured. Lexi was being quiet for once, she stayed close to me, only shining her light in front of her, unless she heard something, which seemed to be every ten-seconds or so.

"I think my source was wrong, y'all. I don't think there's anyone here," Lexi said, after a few minutes of silence. It was undoubtedly obvious that she was frightened, but despite that cold hard fact, there hadn't been any evidence that anyone— save for us—had set foot in the asylum for years.

"She has a point, I think," I said. We had only searched the first three floors, but the overwhelming sense of abandonment was suffocating, to say the least.

"It's your call," Jolene said, sounding positively unconcerned with whatever decision I would make. I thought about my mother's patient files—and everything Rodgers had told me at the police station.

"Rodgers mentioned he knew my mother. My mom worked on the fourth floor, so that would've been where her patients were kept. According to her notes that's where she worked the most."

"So, just because they were there once doesn't mean they're staying in their old room, how weird is that?" Lexi said, flatly.

"It is at least a place to look for any clues—evidence of any kind," I said, sharply.

"What about where Dr. Walker worked the most? He might not be the killer but maybe he has some skeletons in his closet," Lexi stated.

"Well, what floor did most of his patients reside?" Jolene asked.

"The bottom floor," I said, trying to remember the layout of the asylum in my mother's notes.

"Isn't this the bottom floor?" Jolene asked. We rounded a corner and came to a dead end at the third floor. There were only two doors left, one leading to an interior staircase, and one leading outside, to a smaller staircase.

"No, no there's a basement floor, I'm almost positive," I stated—almost excited.

"Okay, look, it is getting dark and pretty soon this is going to be too hard and frankly, too creepy for any of us to be here. You go check out the fourth floor, and I'll go check out the basement," Jolene said, matter-of-factly.

"No," I said, sharply.

"Are you kidding me, sister?" Lexi stated. "Have you seen—I don't know—any horror movie, ever? You don't separate—ever. That's how you end up *dead*." Lexi's *dead* was drawn and dramatic—Tennessean talk that was starting to grow on me.

"I have to side with Lexi on this one, Jo," I stated. The darkness seemed brighter somehow, suddenly. There was a thin layer of gray in the air that was between Jo and me. I could barely see her face but not enough to see her expression. The glow from our flashlights were enough to light up most of her body and the language there was clear—she wasn't asking.

"Don't be stupid, Egg, this is the best way to cover the most ground and get out of here," she snapped, quickly.

"What if we run into trouble? What if you do?" Lexi asked, her voice trembled for a moment.

"Yell," Jolene said, as she opened the door and began to descend the staircase. There was a dark silence that I didn't bother to oppress. I felt Lexi lean closer to me, her fingers wrapped around my wrist. I leaned forward and opened the second door, the little light that was left in the dusk sky slowly crept into the black place in which we were standing. An iron staircase sat before us and I motioned for Lexi to stay.

"What are you doing?" she said.

"There's no reason for you to go with me to the fourth floor. I'm just going to check it really quickly. "Jolene is probably right, about the splitting up thing."

"And what if there's a, oh I don't know, a Shoestring Killer, ready to kill you with his shoestrings?" Lexi snapped. "At least with two of us he'll be outnumbered."

"I don't think it is going to be that dramatic," I stated. I could hear Lexi's sigh was loud.

"There's a serial killer loose on the town, women are dropping like flies, and your dad is sitting in a jail cell right now because he's suspect number one, and I say something about providing back up and you call me dramatic?" she said. She sounded brave when she spoke back to me, but her fingernails still dug into my wrist.

"A little bit, yeah, but fine, whatever," I said, humoring her enough to let her join me. My father once told me that the best way to win an argument with a woman was to not. My father, amongst many other things, was something of a sexist. It was just something else that separated us.

We walked up the old staircase, with as much ease as possible. The floorboards cracked and cried with every step. The flashlight's beam showed the rotten floor, with holes in some steps so big one could see through them. Weaving between some of the boards were cockroaches trying to escape the light.

"Be careful, Lexi," I said, slowly, as if my own voice had the ability to snap the stairs into pieces. We walked, quietly, carefully, slowly, up two flights of stairs until we reached the landing of the fourth floor. "Just a quick look, okay?" I said. Lexi nodded—at least I think that's what she did—before I opened the door. The floor looked identical to the others, each floor a large hallway, with a nurse's station at the end, near the center of the asylum.

The corridor was wide enough that Lexi and I could each investigate each side without interfering with the other, but she refused to be more than a few inches away from me, so we took our time and zigzagged across the floor.

"See anything notable?" I asked her, as my flashlight's beam darted into one room in which the door was askew. Inside, there was nothing but a blackened mattress and the remains of a teddy bear.

"Just a pair of old shoes and a mattress," Lexi said. "Do you know which patients were in which rooms?"

"Her notes give their room numbers but I can't see any numbers in this dump. Maybe if we find something noteworthy we'll try to figure out the patient whom that room belonged," I replied.

"Look!" Lexi said, and I quickly pointed my flashlight into her direction—my heart beating fast and hard. The light hit a door that was completely open, and inside the room, what appeared to be carvings, were the words: AND I'LL BURN HER TO THE GROUND BEFORE SHE BECOMES MY COFFIN.

"Is that noteworthy?" Lexi said, her tone was dry wit but her voice was fearful dread. I slowly moved toward the room— dragging a terrified Lexi beside me.

"I'd say so, yeah." I ran the flashlight over the words once more, they were certainly carved out—a knife, one thick and sharp enough to tear through padded walls. I took a step forward, and as if I tripped some invisible line of caution, a red flagged buried among the disturbed, a violent, passionate scream erupted. It wasn't fearful, but panicked. It wasn't unintelligible, either. It was my name. *GRAYSON could* be heard from what felt like miles away. It was not loud to me, but I knew that wherever it was coming from, it must've been ear piercing. Lexi jumped and clung closer.

"That's Jolene," I said the second I realized the voice. My heart dropped all four stories before my legs could start moving. "Let's go," I yelled, and without waiting for Lexi's clinched grip, I darted down the corridor. "No, no, no, no, no," I repeated, as if my denial was anything but that—denial.

"Grayson," I could hear Lexi behind me, trying to keep up. I was already two flights of stairs downward, forgetting the fact I was standing on rotten wood. When I rounded the third landing, I heard the horrid sound of splintering wood, and a faint gasp from Lexi. I turned in time to see her collapsing through the set of stairs I'd just leapt off. I rushed to her assistance. As she fell, she managed to grab ahold of the jagged end of a step still intact. Her whimper sounded muffled, but painful.

220

"I got you," I said, as I pulled her up by her forearm, which was bleeding, and struggled to get my arm around her waist as I dragged her to the secure landing. She was bleeding from her legs, torso, arms, and hands. "Are you okay?" I asked, unsteadily—fearing my lull was risking Jolene's life. Lexi nodded her head.

"They're just scraps, I'm fine," she said, forcing herself to stand up to her feet. "Go go, I'm right behind you," she said anxiously.

We hurried down the rest of the steps, albeit with a little more caution than before, until we hit the ground floor.

"GRAYSON GET DOWN HERE!" The voice was a relief in more than one way. It didn't sound fearful anymore it sounded annoyed, or even angry. She was safe as long as she was sassy. Her voice was clearer now, and I could follow it to the end of the corridor where a door that lead to another set of stairs could be found. Lexi and I rushed down as quickly as we could until we reached the bottom, which was not made up of corridors and patient rooms. At the bottom of the staircase, the room opened into a large, oval shape, with plenty of space in the center, as if it was once used for storage or some sort of common area. Veering from the oval room, in several different directions, were individual corridors, all leading to the giant oval in the center. It was dark, the sun had finally abandoned us and in the basement, there was no outlet for outside light anyway. Jolene's flashlight, however, provided the light we needed.

"Jo!" I called out, as I pushed off the last step, Lexi dragging behind a few steps because despite what she said, she was in a lot of pain. Lexi slammed the basement door behind us, I knew it was because she dreaded what could be behind us but in that moment I was more worried about the building collapsing atop of us. Jolene didn't say anything, but instead shined her light across the walls of the oval, slow, like she was scanning something very specifically. It took a moment, and only a moment, to grasp what she was showing me. Across the oval's walls, in no particular order, pattern, design, or shape, were hundreds, maybe thousands of the same emblem. The same emblem that was carved into Walt Rodgers, the same emblem was carved into our killer's arm, according to our witness, and the same emblem that Rodgers swears was part of a cult club of patients, desperately trying to escape their walls.

There were a lot of rumors going around those days. Ugly, sharp rumors that take something away from its star. I don't like rumors, even though half my business relies on it. I prefer facts, the truth. I need the writing on the wall.

Ironically, I had the writing, right on the wall. It was spread out across a den that might belong to a villainous monster.

Extraordinary Secrets

Elizabeth's Work Journal
February 9th, 1995

*I've reached my breaking point. No, I've exceeded
my breaking point. I can no longer ignore the madness in the
dark. Dr. Walker treats these patients as if this is a criminal
insane asylum. It is not that, but even if it were, his
experimental treatments are too extreme, too dangerous, and
too violent for even the worst of people. His insanity is far
more threatening than any of the patients inside Old
Dominion. I can no longer have a hand in it. For so long I
dreamt of at least being the one beacon of light that these
pitiful faces see on a regular basis. Yet, I haven't even been
that, I'm afraid. To some extent, I've allowed myself to dabble
in the dark. Turn my eyes a different way, but worse—turn my
mind a different way. Allow my hands to be hands they never
should have been.*

*Jody, if anyone, is the light in this place. And yet he
isn't enough to bring about real change. None of us are, I
fear—certainly not me, and certainly not Dr. Walker. I'm
getting the feeling, at the end of the day, that I am just a pair
of legs around here. Tits to gawk at for the other doctors.
Only my patients seem to appreciate me, anymore. And that
isn't just here, that's everywhere.*

Alan and I have long since put our marriage in the grave. We walk around the house, like the animatronic figures you see at overpriced theme parks. We're characters that go through the motions for only one ticket buyer, Grayson, and he doesn't seem to be buying a ticket for the show much these days. I've taken to sleeping in my study, mostly. There's a small cot in there that I don't mind sleeping on, and Alan deserves the soft bed. He works hard, long, laboring hours and I do love him, I just loved my work more. At least, I use to love my work more.

Despite it all in the end, I do love my husband, but I'm afraid it's too little, and far too late. I offered to quit, several months ago, but he knew it was just a polite suggestion more than a serious consideration, so he refused. "We need the extra income anyway," he would say. "For Grayson" he would say. But Grayson has never needed the finest things of life. And neither has Alan. They aren't men who strive to put their name in a journal or be recognized by people. They just keep their heads down and walk on, like the brave men they are.

Grayson doesn't speak much to me, anymore. He's not stupid—far from it. He's the smartest boy I could've asked for, he's just lazy. Even the lazy pick up on the behaviors of others, and he has to know that his father and I aren't what we use to be. I sadly suspect we never will be, either. I've lost touch, as a psychiatrist, as a mother—as a woman. Jody's kiss was the last kiss I've had in, I can't remember when was the last time Alan has touched me. I crave another, and I know the marriage is suffering because of that. It isn't Jody, though. Poor, poor Jody, I've lost touch what it means to be a friend, too.

I've caught myself, for months now, standing in the mirror, when no one else is looking, when I'm all alone, wrapping my fingers around my throat, and pressing. I was gentle, at first, just a little bit of pressure pushed against me. It's gotten worse, though. So much so that it's hard to ignore it now. I grip my neck tightly now, and I'm not sure why. It isn't sexual, at least, I don't think so. It does something else. It takes me away from myself. It takes me away from my job, my stress, my life. It takes me away from my failing marriage and my son that doesn't seem to care. It takes me away from my failures.

It takes me away from Old Dominion Asylum.

Chapter Nine

No. Nine

When I was a kid, in the easy days before my mother died, Jolene, Jack and I would play hide-and-go-seek in the area behind our houses. Jack wasn't patient, and I would never count all the way to one hundred, so we ended up just chasing one another. Jolene, on the other hand, was good at hiding—too good. Jack and I were belittled in comparison to her skills, and would consistently lose to her. We always told her it was because she was too scared to actually run from us—that she wasn't fast enough to make it back to base before we could tag her. I think, even then, I knew the truth, though. Jolene Wire was just good at the game, not because she was afraid—she was too smart to be afraid.

The illuminated beam from Jolene's flashlight ran across the triangles all across the walls. Big ones, small ones, sloppy ones, perfect ones—triangles, with the top two lines crossing at the point to form an x, and several striped lines within the shape.

"Temporary Home," I said. "This is what Rodgers was talking about, their little club."

"Someone came back home," Jolene said.

"Or someone never left," I added.

227

"This is freaky," Lexi said, chiming in for no other reason but to chime in. The oval room, the more I looked around, was exceedingly disturbing, even if the emblems weren't decorated on every inch of the walls. There were chunks of wall missing here and there, and beneath debris left on the floor, were remains of melted and corrupted trinkets—some even resembling chains. In the center of the oval room, was a large, cement circle, that looked to be some sort of mount—which probably served as the foundation for something that crumbled in the wreckage years ago.

"We should check the corridors," I insisted, nodding to the hallways around us.

"No, Grayson, we should leave," Lexi said, firmly.

"He's right," Jolene said.

"Bet that was bitter coming up," I teased.

"Shut up," Jolene and Lexi said in unison.

"We get out of here as soon as possible, though," Jolene started. "I shouldn't be here—I'm way out of my jurisdiction." Although she said it then, in the belly of a desolate basement, I knew Jolene was less worried about her official duties and more worried that we were in over our heads, and if that was what she was thinking, as we marched down separate corridors, then she was feeling just as I had from the moment we entered the building.

We searched the corridors and they seemed more barren than the floors above. No last forgotten remnants, no personal effects left behind. There were no last minute messages of hope, prayer, or threat bleeding on the walls—just a vacant floor, nothing more, nothing less. As Lexi and I came back into the oval, defeated from the last remaining unchecked corridor, Jolene was close to the wall, studying the patterns, again.

"Jo?" I asked, I was ready to put this place behind us. I couldn't decide what thoughts haunted me the most, the idea of what could've happened here, by a serial killer, or the thoughts of my mother being connected, even innocently, to something so horrific.

"Yeah," Jolene said, turned, and caught up with us in the oval. We started toward the staircase, I was in front this time, and I guided my flashlight to the first landing—which led to the first half a dozen steps. I could faintly see, however, through the blackness, the top of the stairway, where the door stood ajar, and a sliver of moon beam from a broken window creeped past the wood and rot and onto the stairs.

The gentle twist in my stomach was enough to make me halt, completely—anchored heels and all.

"What is it?" Jolene called from the back, because even though my face was subject to the dark, her senses weren't.

Which I was grateful for, as I slowly realized the disturbing fact that none of us left the upstairs door ajar when we descended the staircase. I tried, sans flashlight, to force my eyes to pierce through the shadows and see the top of the staircase—and when I did, I only saw more shadow, darker shadows, like something was there. In a quick jerk, like ripping a Band-Aid, I shined the flashlight up the stairs just in time to see a figure dart away from the doorway and back into the upstairs corridor.

"It's *him!*" I yelled, and once again preceded to chase a mystery. I left Jolene and Lexi behind me, as I charged upward, skipping two to three steps at a time. "Hey!" I called after him, as if that had any chance of slowing down the culprit. I pushed through the door, which seemed so flimsy it nearly disintegrated off the hinges.

I sped through the corridor, rapidly approaching the front desk, when I caught a glimpse of the figure moving towards the front door.

"STOP OR I'LL SHOOT!" I threatened, despite not being armed with a gun of any kind. It worked—only for a moment—as the front door open, and the figure turned in fear of my proposed weapon, the moon betrayed Walt Rodgers'—Irusan's—features.

"Rodgers?" I said, halting before him. When he noticed I was unarmed, he leapt towards me. I fell, Irusan atop of me, before I realized what had happened. There was panic in his eyes and despite his frail body, he was surprisingly strong. His slender hands wrapped around my throat and began to squeeze. I fought, desperately, but I couldn't budge Walt from pressing his thumbs onto my windpipe. I could hear the floorboards beneath me crack and splinter and I half-wished the floor would give out beneath us.

"Grayson!" I could hear Jolene's voice echo, along with her and Lexi's footsteps. Rodgers looked in the general direction of the staircase and in a panic he left off of me. I tried to regain footing and chase after him, but by the time I reached the hospital's front doors, Rodgers was lost in the obsidian cover of the night.

Rage is a unique emotion—it is pure reaction, unwanted and unmistakable. Sadness can look like depression; happiness, like excitement, but nothing confuses itself with rage—not even anger. Anger, even at its most extreme level, pales in comparison to its mutated form—mind numbing rage. And that is exactly what I felt, in every atom of my being, as Jolene drove us out of Bristol, away from Old

Dominion, and back into Abingdon—out of the frying pan, into the fire.

"He lied to us," I said, fuming in the passenger seat. There wasn't a sound in the interior, save for my voice and the uncomfortable movement of shifting bodies on cold leather. Jolene faced forward, she didn't speak, she didn't glance, she didn't even blink. Lexi glared outside the window, occasionally looking out the back, as if Walt Rodgers was going to appear beside her at any moment.

I fiddled my hands on my cell phone—fingers shaking from either fury or lack of caffeine. I struggled to find Kiddy's contact information, attempting to send my partner a text message.

"I'm dropping you off and then I'm heading to the station," Jolene blurted out.

"He lied. I just sat there while he spoon fed me those lies," I said. "Telling me it is someone else named Jody, no wonder I couldn't find anything on Jody—there is no Jody!" I punched the side of Jolene's door.

"Easy, I'm still making payments," Jolene said, more calmly this time.

"You guys cut him loose!" I yelled, pointing at Jolene. "Cindy Parker turns up dead and you cut him loose just like that, he could've killed her right before you guys took him in."

"Don't pretend like you're the only one doing any investigating, Grayson. Don't pretend like I'm responsible for any of this," Jolene snapped.

"Let's just get home, you guys, we'll figure this out then," Lexi said.

"We have to find him, we have to find him now, Jolene," I stated, wide eyed and furious. "He will not stop unless he's forced." Sure, I was enraged. A person in my position couldn't be anything else. The Shoestring Killer, Old Dominion, Abingdon, my father, mother, Jolene, Jack, all of it—that much stress does something to a person. My mother's face was suddenly visible in my mind, clearer than it had been in years. I wasn't feeling lackluster about the case anymore, in that moment, I was just as obsessed as Alan—maybe more so. There was a fire behind my eyes and if I hadn't thought to blink, I could've burned down the world.

I asked Jolene to drop me off at my father's house, before she took Lexi to the Martha Washington, which I could tell by Lexi's not-so-subtle grunts this wasn't her favorite plan. Arriving at the Grant home, however, was a little easier said than done.

"Oh no," Jolene said, heavy breathed and regretful. I shared her feelings—the house should've never been left alone. Standing on the front porch, just beside the porch swing my mother sat on every summer evening, with her head on my father's shoulder a cup of coffee in her hand, stood Jack Hanna, screaming into a megaphone to a crowd of nearly one hundred strangers who gathered around my father's front lawn.

"What is going on?" I yelled, but the constraints of the car provided me zero answers and only discontent from Jolene and Lexi. "This is insane," I said as I popped open the passenger door, but Jolene's firm grasp on my left arm stopped me, momentarily. I looked to her, ready to growl with anger that had been building up in my gut since we saw Rodgers at the asylum, but her simple head shake and finger pressed against her lips encouraged me—if only for a moment—to not move, and not speak.

Jolene's window descended, and above the faint hum from the car I could hear the riot in front of Alan's house— once muffled, now a monstrous cheer.

"WE LIVED AMONGST A KILLER FOR YEARS," Jack said, his voice loud and pompous. "ME, MAYBE YOU, SEVERAL OF US HERE HAVE BEEN THE VICTIM OF HIS ABUSE," Jack went on—a dialogue idiot who practiced his lines too hard. "FOR TOO LONG WE LET HIM SIT UNDER OUR NOSE, TAUNTING ALL OF US!"

"Can't you stop this?" I said, looking towards Jolene. She looked at me—frowning, as if I hadn't even a small understanding of the law, or her power.

"The most I could possibly get him for right now is trespassing," Jolene explained. I nodded towards Jack, who was standing on the railing of the porch, now; his sneakers digging into the splintered, century-old wood.

"Perfect. Get him."

"What's that going to do, Grayson?" Her unblinking eyes, her straight-lined lips, tight and close, told me the only thing I needed to know: She wasn't going to get between Jack and myself. She cared too much—for both of us.

"I guess it wouldn't do anything," I stated, exhaling. She did too, out of relief. The clouds were a soft gray, a slight hesitation before a downpour. I knew it was coming—I'd be caught in the rain enough already. "Guess I'll have to," I said, opening the car door—welcoming the rain. I heard Jolene call after me, even Lexi, too, piping up from the backseat. I ignored them both as I walked toward the house. They didn't understand, how could they? This situation was too unique for them to relate—the whole thing was too unique for anyone.

I pushed by the lawn drifters, gawkers looking for a show, until I get to the star of the attraction. Jack continued to blurt out absurdities over the megaphone—harsh accusations that were filled with passion instead of content: *Alan Grant is a monster among men. The Grant household is surrounded in mystery, stacked on misery.* Buzzwords and memorable taglines. Jack could be a writer if he had the patience for a blank page, and could hold a cigarette and a pen in his hand at the same time.

"What's going on, Jack?" I finally yelled, during one of his few lulls. It was amazing how few seemed to notice my existence on the lawn until I spoke. People are too busy yelling for something to happen to ever notice if it does. It even took Jack a moment to peer down from his appointed porch-throne, and looked at me in the eyes. "Why such a party?"

"I'm sorry it had to go down like this, brother," he said to me—like he had just beaten me in a touch-football game in the backyard. He moved the megaphone from his lips, I was close enough to the stairs and the conversation was now about him and myself—not a third of the town. "Your old man, though, he's a danger, Grayson. He's unstable."

"Well, I admit he gets a little uncomfortable to be around after he's had a couple of beers but he's no killer, Jack, and you know it," I blurted out. Still, I forced myself to push out the thoughts of the bloody shoestring. I had to forget it, until I talked to Alan myself. I couldn't assume anything about my father, especially after Rodgers practically confessed to the murders by attempting to choke me to death. There were murmurs around me—hushed whispers like we were doing a staged dramatization. I only hoped those people paid up for having such great seats to the show.

"I believe the state investigators and Abingdon Police feel differently about that, Grayson. I'm afraid I feel that way about it, too. I didn't want it to be true, buddy, but it is."

"It used to take more to convince you," I said back, trying to collect my cool.

"It does," he said, quicker than I expected.

"You're not doing any justice yelling from his front porch, though," I said, growing more and more angry with every slipping moment that my best friend had constructed a riot at the very doorstep he use to knock on, every day, in order to get inside. "Get off my dad's porch, Jack. Don't make me call the cops."

Jack laughed—a subtle, nostril puff of air and a sly smirk. "Which cops? The ones that arrested your dad for killing seven people? Or the one you're having sex with?" Jack finished the sentence with a light nod to Jolene's car.

There were more whispers now—they were increasing in volume though. People snickered and nudged their neighbor.

I tried to contain my anger—not show my hand. With Jack, though, you either play your cards or you walk away from the table, and I already decided I wasn't the one walking away. "There's been a dramatic shift in the case this evening, Jack, so before you soak the town in your fountain of theories, maybe you should let the case play out."

"Play out?" he mocked me. "Play out? You think this is a thing that's going to just stop at the end of the third act? Curtain goes down and we all throw a bed of roses at your feet for catching a killer? It's not that. You're not a detective, Grayson. You're a professional stalker and you haven't the first clue about how to lead a murder investigation," Jack's words were sharp and precise. They weren't random, raw words, no, they were thought out—marinated. "You're the loser your dad pretended to be to this whole town."

"Stop it, Jack," I said. The fire was building up behind my eyes, again. Under my nails, in my joints, my teeth—everywhere inside me felt the surge of flames that were going to kill me if I didn't kill something else first.

"I think you should go, Jack," I said, hoping my voice sounded calmer than it did in my head. It didn't, my voice shook and I could only hope it wasn't audible over the tension of the crowd.

"You think he brought you here because you're some sort of master detective that was going to solve this thing? Bring home some justice for momma? He brought you home to bring the whole thing full circle, Grayson!"

"ENOUGH! My father is a lot of things but a murderer is not one of them!"

"THAT'S A LIE! I SAW HIM DO IT, GRAYSON—I SAW HIM!" He screamed—his face was red, purple, and almost blue. A thick, pompous vein could be seen traveling in a slithery fashion from the corner of his left eyebrow to his bright blond hairline. His eyes were wide, unmoving, and flared nostrils above quivering lips. I stopped—because any answer I had to say sounded childish and foolish. All I could do was pay attention to every single twitch across his face, looking for any sign that he was just trying to get under my skin. The crowd almost seemed to back away now, but not leave. They wanted the show, just as long as they weren't part of it, all the sudden. "I wanted it to not be true. I wanted to be wrong. I hoped that whatever I saw, I misunderstood it somehow. I wanted it to be the crazy cat man," Jack stressed.

"But Jack—"I started, trying to tell him that Rodgers was at the asylum, that he tried to kill me. I wanted to tell him that whatever he thought he saw was wrong because we had him—we finally had him. I didn't get that chance, though.

"Get out of here, Jack," Jolene's forceful voice called out from somewhere behind me. She bypassed me and approached the porch. "Come on, go." Jack shook his head, but did what she said, without saying a word. He stepped off the porch, and instead of walking down the stone walkway to the sidewalk, where I was standing, Jack moved left, and cut through the yard. "That goes for all of you, people," Jolene called out to the awkward people still standing around. "This isn't a mob scene. What are you people even doing here? Jerry! I see you, Jerry. If you're here who the heck is at the pharmacy?" Jolene called out.

"You okay?" Lexi asked, approaching as Jolene was shooing everyone else away.

"Peachy."

"We heard what he said, Grayson," Jolene said, very seriously as she returned. She only said Grayson when it was serious.

"Well," I started after a long breath, "I think this means, according to every movie I've seen that has an angry mob in it, that the princess must be up in the highest tower of this castle, being guarded by the evilest of monsters."

"Sugar," Lexi said, in a faux-sweet voice. "You're not as funny as you think you are, I'm sorry, sweetie."

"I mean, I don't think you should stay here tonight. It' is probably fine, but just to be on the safe side." Jolene said.

"I still have my room at the Martha Washington," I stated.

"No, I meant I think it's a good idea for legal reasons that you have an alibi. You and Lexi come stay at my place tonight. It's just all around a better idea."

I shared a glance with Lexi, to access her feelings before I agreed for both of us. "Okay," I said, catching Lexi's look of relief. She was still disturbed by the hospital. Of course she was, why shouldn't she be? When one travels that deep into the blackness, it takes one's eyes, maybe a little too long, to readjust to the light.

Jolene's apartment wasn't anything as I expected it to be—which, in my mind, was a larger version of her teenage bedroom: a *Blondie* poster, cassette tapes on the floor, and a lava lamp she thought was retro cool. Instead, she led Lexi and I into a nearly spotless apartment—no cassette tapes here.

"Nice apartment, lots of space," I said, upon entering, like I was a blind date in an awkward situation.

"There's a spare bed in the room next to mine and the couch is actually pretty comfortable, I fall asleep on it a lot of nights," she said as she gestured to a gray, lumpy mess of a couch to the left.

"Um, Jolene do you mind if I take a shower?" Lexi piped up, southern mannerisms and all. "I feel gross."

Jolene smiled and nodded, pointing upward, to the second floor. Lexi bolted up the stairs and the water was running before Jolene or I could say anything to one another. I walked into the kitchen, behind Jolene and sat down at a small round table that was off to the side.

"Coffee?" she asked, as she began pouring water into the pot.

"Do you really have to ask?" I said, burying my head in my hands. "Why, Jolene? Why is Jack fighting my dad so hard on this? Why is he fighting *me* so hard on this?" Jolene shook her head as she fed the coffee grains into the maker.

"I don't know, Egg. When Jack gets an idea in his head he sticks with it—hard. He's stubborn like that, and this case these killings have all of us a little on edge. At a certain point people just want other people to blame, you know?"

"He said he saw him do it," I said, ignoring Jolene's words whilst remembering Jack's.

"He didn't see anything, Egg. He's just trying to fuel the fire." Jolene filled up her coffee pot with warm water.

"Where was he going with it?" I asked.

"Who knows, Grayson—this is coming from the guy who beat up a man with a baseball bat on a hunch." She sat the pot in the coffee maker. "He isn't exactly in a good place. I told you. Losing his mom was a lot but his dad taking his own life really sent Jack into a dark place."

I looked up at Jolene, who had taken a seat across from me. She looked tired—drained, from the night, from every night since this started. I could smell the coffee brewing, a thick aroma that started to calm my nerves.

"Do you think Alan is in trouble?"

"Well, I won't' lie that was the most evidence we've been able to connect anyone to in twenty years, Grayson. It's not a closed case but your dad has a long road ahead of him."

"I meant—if Jack really thinks he's the killer. Do you think he'd do something stupid? Like he did with Rodgers?" Jolene focused for a minute, her lips grew tighter and her eyes bounced back and forth between mine.

"Jack is intense but he's not a murderer, Grayson." If I didn't know better, I would've thought she was offended. I didn't know better, though, so I was almost positive she was, in fact, offended. I looked down for a moment, anything to break eye contact. Jolene was something of a moral police, as well. She kept us in check, kept our best foot forward and always made sure our heart was never placed second best to our minds. The mistake she made though, was assuming everyone was like her, someone whose heart was just as pure as their mind.

"Walt Rodgers is obviously our man now," I mentioned. "What can be done?"

Jolene sighed and rubbed her eyes for a moment.

"Don't worry, I've got it, Grayson," she said, shortly. We sat in silence for the next few moments. It was quiet enough that we could hear the running water from Lexi's shower come to a stop, and even hear the violent pull-back of the shower curtain. Lexi, no doubt, still shaken up from earlier, afraid of what might even lurk behind a shower curtain.

"How do you take your coffee?"

"Lots of sugar," I started. "And cream."

"As if there were any other way to take it," She said as she added the sugar and cream and brought over a faded blue cup that had the outline of a police badge on it. I ran my thumb over the emblem, and a small piece of it flaked off onto my thumb.

"So why did you become a cop?" I asked. Jolene leaned against the frame of the kitchen's entrance—arms folded and face straight. Her eyes broke from mine, for good reason—they were softer now. She shrugged that she didn't know, a universal signal that she did. "There was a reason, right?

Because when we were kids you were dead set on being a firefighter," I smiled, and so did she.

"There was a case I heard about—rape case, fourteen year old girl. She was being raped by someone in her own home and no one really did anything about it. There weren't any adults she could trust, and the police kinda blew her off," Jolene's smile faded as she recalled the story. "I don't know, from the moment I heard that story I knew I wanted to be a cop. I wanted to be someone who helped. I wanted to be someone who people could trust."

"Pretty good reason," I said, taking a sip of the sugary coffee.

"Better than some, I guess," she concluded, unfolding her arms and taking a step closer. "And why'd Grayson Grant become Grayson Grant, *Private Eye?*" Jolene questioned, leaning in closer.

"It wasn't to be someone that people could trust," I admitted.

"So what was it?" she asked, her smile tried to return.

"I didn't know what else to do," I confirmed. Her smile faded, as I feared it would, as she retracted the step forward that she took. It was then that her cell phone rang, she blinked quickly and suddenly she was Officer Jolene Wire.

"Wire," she said. She sighed and clothes her eyes. "Okay, I'll be there in a minute," she said as she hung up the phone.

"That was a friend of mine down at the bullpen," she started. "Forensics came back on the t-shirt and shoestring," she admitted. We locked eyes and both waited for one of us to say something.

"Your mother's blood was on the shirt and the shoestring, along with someone else—they don't know whose blood, though."

"Is that good or bad for Alan?" I asked. Jolene shrugged.

"I don't know at this point, Grayson. The blood could be the killer, who struggled against your mother or—"Jolene stopped in her tracks.

"Someone else that daddy murdered?" I questioned, trying to make it satirical but both of us knew it was a legitimate question.

"It doesn't match your father's DNA or any of the victims," she nodded. "I'm choosing to look at this as a positive thing for your father right now." I nodded at her words. "They don't have anything harder on him so they can't keep him. He hasn't been charged with the murder yet but he's been told not to leave town. You can pick him up," she said. We looked at each other for a moment. It was a silent moment where our eyes didn't leave one another and neither one of us wanted to say another word about Alan Grant, Walt Rodgers, Jack Hanna or The Shoestring Killer. We just looked at each other.

"I'm heading down to the station," she said, as she turned on her heel. "It's important that we get on this Rodgers thing as soon as possible. Don't wait up." She opened the front door and eyed the staircase. I assumed she did this to make sure Lexi wasn't in ear shot, before she turned her gaze back to me. "I'm glad you're here, Grayson. I know it is for the wrong reasons, and I know you really shouldn't be here at all—but I'm glad you are here." There was a pregnant pause, as she waited for words to be returned that I didn't know how to say, at least not out loud—not in a response that didn't sound disingenuous. She waited for maybe a moment too long. A moment longer than she wanted to, and a moment not long enough for me. She shut the door behind her, and she was gone. Gone to a place where she couldn't hear my reply: "I'm glad I am too, Jo."

"It's about time you showed up," Alan said as I met him in the police station.

"You're welcome, by the way," I said with a sigh. "I know you think I had the ability to get you out of here at any moment but believe it or not a private investigator has his limits."

"I can't believe I've been arrested for this," he said as we exited the police station, and jolted down the steps. He continued to babble onward about something but I didn't listen—I couldn't. I was too worried about Jolene. The night was long, and despite her words to not wait up for her, I did anyway. I was prepared to tell her that, although I hated the nightmare had restarted, I *was,* glad to be home, to see her, to try to *move the bookmark* in this story that had, for too long been left on the same page. "Are you listening?" Alan said, as he climbed into my passenger seat.

"Yes, Alan," I said.

"I really wish you wouldn't call me that," he sighed. Jolene didn't show up, though. After she left for the station, she never returned, and I assumed she was working hard on the lead—but when I returned to the station the next morning, to bail my father from jail, she was nowhere to be found, and one of the officers had informed me that she left around ten o'clock the night before. "What's the next step, hmm?" Alan asked.

I tried to snap out of my daze, but it was hard. Alan wasn't the detective he wanted to be—but he could tell when his son's mind was somewhere else.

"I can't take you home, sooner or later another mob will show up. Jack will do something stupid, or you will. Plus, it is still a crime scene, so that's out," I said. I started down Main Street, hoping for any sign of Jolene—a desperate attempt after calling her cell phone for the fifteenth time. Her car was at the police station but I didn't see any sign of her when I picked up Alan.

"I meant about the investigation," Alan said, ignoring the fact that there were mobs gathering in front of his home. I glanced over at him.

"It's done. It's Rodgers. It was always Rodgers. All signs pointed to it and yet we just kept letting it slip through our fingers," I said, disgusted with myself.

"How do you know?" he asked.

"We saw him last night."

"Where?"

I glanced at him again—like a son who was caught out of bed after bedtime.

"Old Dominion," I admitted.   Wrinkles gathered on Alan's face.

"You went there?"

"Too much evidence was pointing there and Lexi got a lead that there were strange sightings. So last night, Jolene, Lexi and myself—we went to check it out.

"And you found Rodgers?" He asked. I nodded.

"He attacked me, too. We also found a whole lot of other weird stuff."

Alan looked out the window for a bit. Long lips that curved downward, and heavy eyes that glared at the rubber lining of the car's passenger window.

"Are you okay?"

"Satisfied and disappointed," Alan replied.

"How so?"

"If he's our man, I'm glad we got him. It's just—he's the first person, well, second person I looked into," his voice trailed off. "How is it that I didn't pin this guy twenty years ago? Wilson was all over that guy but it never clicked with me. I just never believed it was him." He looked down again. He failed, and he dwelled in it. It was a glimpse, a small glimpse into a different kind of Alan Grant than I knew—not just an absent father, but a carrying husband. Alan had always chose my mother over me, and I was okay with that—but seeing him choose her over me, and realize it was all for nothing, was even more depressing than I could've imagined.

"Alan look if it makes you feel any better, I never figured it out. The cops didn't figure it out. We just...saw him there, shocked, afraid—guilty. We wandered into it."

Alan nodded. "Better to wander than to wonder, I guess," he said.

"I mean, I thought it was this guy that used to work with mom—this guy named Jody. Rodgers put me on his trail. I didn't even have a lot to go on, really," I explained. He ticked his head toward me for a moment—he recognized the name Jody. Perhaps Rodgers didn't make him up—didn't matter now.

"Jody?" His voice was soft—but urgent.

"You know him?"

"No," he said, just as monotone as when he questioned the name. He returned his glare to the window. "Just a bunch of names on a wall, after a while."

I reached for my cell phone and dialed Jolene's number once more—nothing. There was only the immense hollowness of the thirty-second ring until I heard her voice on the other side—*You've reached Officer Jolene Wire, leave your name and number and I'll get back to you as soon as I can. Have a good day.* I'd memorized every word, every pause in the phrase and every inflection in her voice. I memorized the background noise of what sounded like dogs barking—two different dogs, barking in unison at something else.

"Eight victims," I said, laying the phone down. Alan was looking out the window, far away in a different world from my SUV. It wasn't the best timing but I had to ask anyway—there was no such thing as good timing when it came to shoestrings.

"Why was there a bloody shoestring and t-shirt hidden beneath the boards of the barn attic?" I asked, bluntly. Alan didn't turn to me immediately. He just kept looking out the window.

"Yeah, I wondered when you were going to ask me about that," he said. He looked back at me, finally. "I have a confession," he started. I gripped the steering wheel. "When we found your mother, there was the shoestring tied around her wrist, of course, but there was another shoestring there, too. Your mother being the first victim, I always assumed the killer was still trying to figure out his calling card. The killer left a shoestring behind. I kept the shoestring a secret from the police," he admitted.

"Why?" I stressed. Alan shrugged.

"I don't know, son," he started. "I panicked. I thought if I kept something that the killer had, I would be able to find out something in case the police couldn't—or wouldn't tell me. I don't know. It made sense at the time," he said.

"The t-shirt?" I asked. Alan looked to me.

"I'm surprised you don't remember. It was the shirt I was wearing when we found her, son," he went on. "You have to understand son, I just lost my wife. I was hell-bent on finding out who did it—from the moment I saw her."

"You could have botched the whole thing, Alan," I stressed as I rested my forehead against my left hand, which was propped up on the driver door. The car was silent for a moment. I couldn't believe how stupid Alan was to keep evidence away from police but I tried to imagine being in his shoes. Sometimes the hardest thing to do is give up control when you're absolutely powerless.

"So where's Rodgers now?" Alan asked, there wasn't any gusto in his voice anymore. Somewhere between the station and now he'd mellowed, dramatically. It was disturbing on a level I didn't care to think about too much.

"Where's anyone?" I answered, ambiguously. My cell rang and I jumped with my heart, in anticipation that Jolene was finally getting back to me. It wasn't, though—life rarely happens so easily. It was Kiddy, calling from the mundane of his St. Louis office.

"Talk to me, Kiddy," I said quickly and shortly. I'd apologize later, I told myself.

"You know how we've found absolutely nothing on Jody? Not anymore Grant!"

"You're a night too late, Kiddy. We found Rodgers hanging around Old Dominion. We saw a load of disturbing stuff, like a room decorated with the same markings on his arm—the same one our witness saw on the Shoestring Killer— in the asylum. He tried to choke me to death but ran away before Jolene could arrest him. He's spelling out his guilt."

Kiddy sighed on the other end of the phone. "That's all circumstantial, and you are better than that Grant," Kiddy remarked. "Is Rodgers in custody?"

"No."

"Do you know where he is?"

"No."

"Can you prove he did it?"

"No."

"Are you driving around, brooding?"

"Yes."

"Okay, then, drive to the address I just texted you and talk to the woman who lives there. Her name is Bri Cedar. She was a nurse at Old Dominion. She knew your mom, but more importantly, she knew most of the inmates by name, including your cat king—and get this, she knows who Jody is—despite us not being able to find a shred of evidence that proves Jody is even a real person.

"Great," I started. "I have Alan with me, we'll go talk to her."

"Wait, your dad?" Kiddy asked.

"How many Alans are working this case with me, Kiddy?" I answered aggressively. "Yeah, I will text you the update on it."

"I wouldn't let him tag along on this one, Grant," Kiddy had his serious tone blaring through the phone. I could almost see his nostrils flare.

"Okay," I said, as unsuspiciously as I could so I wouldn't alarm Alan.

"I didn't get to speak to Ms. Cedar for very long—she's an older lady, can't hear over the phone very well and would prefer a face to face interaction anyway, but she did make one thing clear," Kiddy's deep voice trailed off a bit, like he was looking over his shoulder despite knowing he was alone, hundreds of miles away. "For every good thing she had to say about your mother, she had a negative one for your father."

When we arrived at the residence of Bri Cedar—which was about a thirty minute drive outside Abingdon—into the country, much closer to the North Carolina State line, I asked Alan if he would mind waiting outside while I spoke with her. He looked at me, suspiciously at first but only at first. The wrinkles in his eyelids seemed to vanish and his eyebrows went back to rest. He seemed fine, more than fine—he seemed relieved.

"Yeah, I don't mind. I'll stay right here. I don't need some old lady asking me if I remember how great things were twenty years ago," Alan said, shooing away the idea of joining me on the questionnaire. I nodded my head, as if I were in full agreement. I actually had no idea what I was doing—Kiddy was too ambiguous with me.

I approached a small, baby blue house. It was cute—perfect for a starter family home. Or, as in the case with Bri Cedar, you've lived a lifetime and now it is time to return to simplicity. There were white shutters on the windows and a white trim that made the house look a little newer than it should. An old, wooden fence—that didn't really seem to go along with the house at all, stretched out to the side, blocking in a small yard area that looked more like overgrown weeds and trees than anything else.

I knocked on the white door—which seemed barely locked into the door hatch. A hard rap that could blow her door down. The door cracked open and an elderly woman, who didn't even reach my chest, with salt and pepper hair and thick black rim glasses answered. She smiled firmly, the wrinkles parting the way for her smile to appear.

"Hello," she said with a crooked smile.

"Hello, Ms. Cedar?"

"Call me Bri, sweetie," she said as she motioned for me to enter her home. "I wasn't called Ms. Cedar in my younger days, why the heck should I be called Ms. Cedar now? Come in. I don't usually have guests, so please excuse the mess, won't you?"

I stepped through her front door and landed in her living room. It was a small room, with a brownish, dark carpet that looked stained and in need of a good washing, an old television—the kind that is encased in a large wooden block of furniture, the kind that you'd use as a table today before you would an actual television. The room smelled oaky—an old smell, like closets had been opened for the first time in months, or longer. To tie the room of dark green walls, brown carpet, and a thirty year old television, were ceramic goats decorated throughout the room.

Bri Cedar sat down in a canary yellow recliner and motioned for me to sit down on a plaid blue couch that sat adjacent to her chair.

"Please, sit down. Would you like a cup of coffee?" I shook my head no—even addicts have a limit, don't they?

257

"Bri, I don't want to take up much of your time," I started. She motioned around the room, she was painfully aware of everything I'd just surveyed.

"Does it look like I have a full calendar?" she said, flatly.

"I'm afraid I have to be quick. There's a lot of things going on at the moment. Which is why I need your help."

"You're here to talk about Old Dominion right? A fellow called earlier asking about it. Told me his associate would be dropping by later to ask more questions. Can't say I'm surprised. Although, I am surprised it took twenty years for someone to call me."

"Why is that?" I asked, shifting on the couch. The couch wasn't soft—but instead was stringy and course. The fabric poked out from its pattern and would cause itches across my body.

"Well, the last days of Old Dominion Asylum were sort of suspicious to say the least. After all, several people were looking strangely towards Dr. Walker and his practice, many of the patients who actually had caring families started to complain about their loved ones conditions worsening under his care. Not to mention the mass breakout that happened just before the horrid place nearly burned to the ground. It might have all been happenstance but it wasn't easy to ignore the coincidences surrounding it."

"Dr. Walker was a strange guy, huh?" I inquired. I was fairly sure Rodgers was my man, but it helped to know if he descended into darkness, who blew out the light.

"The man was a freak," Bri said, and her tone sent a shiver down my spine. "He did things none of us are sure about."

"What does that mean?" I asked, focusing more intensely on Bri now than before. I had my suspicions of his practices. Bri's cold and black tone suggested something else—something worse.

"Dr. Walker was a kid playing with dolls. He liked to poke and pull and twist and find out what made a human being a human being without being one himself. He didn't let anyone on his private floor, save for his patients and his own special team of nurses and doctors. I worked on the main floor, and I wasn't even allowed to take the elevator down. I was a nurse for fifteen years before I started working at the asylum. Walker rated like I didn't know my way around a hospital bed."

"Did you know any of those patients?" I questioned. Bri thought for a second, leaning her salt and pepper hair gently against the yellow spread of her recliner, and tilted her eyes upward.

"I was there a long time—too long. There are several patients that are just blurs to me now. Mixed names and faces,

259

and sometimes not even that much. I remember a few, not as many as I should but more than I probably want to."

"Where does Walt Rodgers fall on that list?" I asked. Bri lifted her head up, as if Walt had just walked through the door. She stared blankly, somewhere around her television, thinking—pondering the name.

"Walt Rodgers," she repeated, dazed, drifting. "Rodgers, yes, I know that name. He came to us pretty early after I started working there. 1989, I believe. I remember because Bush became president that year. Yes, he was one of Dr. Walker's patients. Well, eventually. It wasn't for another four years before he started the *Tomorrow's Minds* project."

"I can't seem to find out too much about that program," I said, nonchalantly.

"Never found out, either. We all thought he was doing something crazy. Using some kind of aggressive force to try to force the patients to break their vices or their mental illnesses through some type of savage behavioral learning, but that's as much as we could speculate. No one was allowed on that floor and anyone who was down on that floor, patient or employee, wouldn't talk about it. He ran a very, very, tight ship.

"There's a guy that I heard used to be part of it, maybe a patient or something. His name is Jody, but I don't have a last name," I said, knowing the farfetched stretch it would be that

Bri knew someone from over twenty years ago by their first name alone.

"Oh yeah, of course I remember Jody," she said and a smile popped up on her face. What did I know?

"You remember him?"

"Everyone remembers Jody, I promise you that." Her words were swift, and upbeat. She was pleasured by the remembrance of him. "Jody was everything Dr. Walker wasn't—charming, sweet, funny, and respectful. Jody was the best of us. The good that man would've been able to do if he had some sort of medical degree." I frowned, thinking back to the names, and hoping I hadn't gotten mixed up along the way.

"So, Jody wasn't a patient?" I asked. Bri laughed.

"Not hardly, Jody probably had better mental health than any of us."

"I just couldn't find much on him," I explained.

"Well, that was probably for a reason," she said. "See, like I said, Jody didn't have any medical credentials, he was a song and dance man."

"I'm sorry—a song and dance man?" I repeated, doubting the words I'd heard. Bri let out a quick chuckle.

"Yeah, he was an entertainer. His job was to keep the patients' spirits up—give them something to laugh and clap to in between the pill swallowing and the group therapy sessions. He would bring his guitar and teach them songs, I believe he taught a handful of women how to waltz. He was just a fellow that made you want to be a better person. Always greeted you with a smile, always wanting to help. But, there wasn't the money in the official budget to hire someone like him so he was paid under the table and on paper it looked like the extra money was going to arts and crafts which was pretty close enough to the truth."

I looked away for a moment. Jody didn't sound like someone capable of doing the things The Shoestring Killer would do. If Rodgers wasn't my guy, Jody was my next lead. The further this case developed, the further away I felt from the end. It was a sinking feeling—a terrible, murky, suffocating, sinking feeling.

"Something on your mind, son?" Bri asked bringing me back into reality.

"Well," I started. "Just not what I was expecting."

"This is about what has been going on in Abingdon, isn't it?" she asked, suddenly. My eyes glanced upward to meet her gaze. She was sitting closer to the edge of her seat now. The mustard recliner squeaked and groaned as Bri shifted her weight in the seat.

"That obvious?" I asked. She shrugged—with a proud smile, self-diagnosed detective.

"I'm not a dummy, kid. And besides, it is all anyone is talking about right now, and like I said, I'm surprised someone didn't come to me twenty years ago. I tried to speak up but everyone was bugging the investigators with a thousand theories. No one took anything seriously, it seemed."

"You think someone from the asylum is involved? Dr. Walker?" I asked.

"Well, I don't know about all that—although it wouldn't surprise me. We did, after all, lose two of our own," Bri said.

"Two?" I asked, raising an eyebrow to her. She nodded her head, slowly, as if I—the detective—should know the answer.

"A doctor in the hospital, and then, of course, Jody." It felt like my brain smeared into my heart.

"Jody was a victim?" I asked, suspiciously.

"See that's another reason you couldn't find anything about Jody. That's a name he started going by as a nickname to a few of us at the hospital—Me, Elizabeth, a hand full of patients. That's not his birth name, though. His real name is Joseph Farmer, but we called him Jody," she explained.

There was that sinking feeling again. It was getting harder and harder to see, now, and the mud I was sloshing around in was now up to my chest.

"Jody is Joseph Farmer?" I asked. She nodded. I stared at the stained brown carpet in Bri Cedar's living room. Grayson Grant, motherless private investigator who is chasing ghosts in a ghost town.

"Are you okay, sir?" She asked.

"Ma'am," I started. My mouth was dry. "I am Grayson Grant. I'm Elizabeth Grant's son.

"Wait a moment," Bri blurted out. She smiled and it seemed a tear gathered in her eye. "I should have known the second I saw your face. You look just like her," she stated. Her smile disappeared though, when she finished connecting the dots. "And that means your father is Alan Grant," she stated.

"Yes," I nodded. She looked away from me, almost as if she didn't want to cause a scene.

"I don't want to speak ill of a man when his flesh and blood is standing in the room," she stated.

"It is okay," I said. "Most people don't seem to mind."

"Alan Grant had a lot of buzz around him at the time of her death," she stated. "I know it was serial killings but that father of yours was a jealous man. Elizabeth came to work all the time talking about how upset he was about her working long hours, or talking about Dr. Walker, Jody, or any of the other men. You know he was actually jealous of her male patients? What kind of a man acts that way?" She stated.

"Sounds like Alan," I nodded. My phone began to ring, whilst staring into space. It was a number I didn't recognize, but it caused panic in my gut all the same. I stood from the prickly blue plaid couch and moved toward the door.

"Thanks for your time, Bri. You've been a big help." I nodded and stepped outside the door. I could see my father, his head leaned back on the passenger seat headrest, through the dirty windshield of my car. My phone continued to buzz and I finally answered it.

"Hello?" I said, uncertainly.

"Gray," I heard Jack's voice on the other end. I immediately tensed, as if he were suddenly going to appear in front of me, ready to fight over my father's guilt or innocence. "Gray?" he said again, after I paused too long before answering.

"Yeah, I'm here, what's up?" I said, coldly and shortly. It was everything I could do not to verbally attack him once again for forming a mutiny outside of the Grant house. There was a vibration in his voice that sounded worrisome. An uneasy tremble was in the word that he repeated. "What's going on? Are you okay?" I asked, the compassion I had for my friend fought through in a time I didn't want it fighting.

"It's Jolene," he said, softy and quickly. My heart paused. His voice became heavy breathed and agonizing. "She's missing."

Elizabeth's Work Journal
April 2nd, 1995

If anything happens to me, if I'm not there to see my little boy grow up, tell him I'm sorry.

I'm sorry, Grayson.

Chapter Ten

Broken Strings

I drove back to Abingdon twice as fast as I did heading to Bri Cedar's house. I barely spoke a word to Alan on the return drive, just enough to let him know what was going on and that everything else had to hit the back burner until Jolene was found and safe. We were both quiet, both wrestling with our own imaginations about where Jolene was and what might be going on. In any other situation, one might just assume that she was an adult who was perfectly capable of taking care of herself—she was a cop, after all. There wasn't anyone who felt safe enough with that line of thinking, though—not anymore.

I argued with Alan that I was going to take him somewhere safe but there wasn't a chance he was going to miss out on the search for her.

"How dare you, Grayson? She grew up with you. I watched her grow up from a toddler to the police officer, and beautiful young lady she is today. You think you're the only one who cares about her?" he spat at me while we pulled up to the police station. Jack was pacing back and forth in front of the building—he looked pale with sickness.

"No, Alan," I said gently. "I know I'm not the only person who cares about her." Jack met me at the car door—eager.

268

"Where is she?" he asked me, desperately.

"What makes you think I know?" His eyes darted over to Alan as he stepped out of the car. I could feel the tension and although I couldn't see Alan's face, as I didn't feel comfortable taking my gaze off of Jack, I knew he was giving my old best friend a glare that was insulting enough in itself one would want to punch him in the face, whether he killed someone you loved, or not.

"What's he doing here?"

"Helping me solve a case," I said, quickly.

"So he gets out of jail and boom, Jolene goes missing," Jack blurted out.

"Easy, Jack—he's been with me since I bailed him out. He doesn't have anything to do with this. Besides, don't assume the worst has happened to Jolene. She's a smart woman—a tough woman."

"We can't chat all day, we need to get out there," Alan said. There were police officers shuffling in and out of the station rapidly, and civilians could be seen in the streets packing their cars down with supplies of all kinds. There was going to be a massive manhunt for Jolene Wire—this town was going to save her like she always tried to save them. It would be beautiful, it would be poetic. I looked to Jack, he was too angry to admit it but he agreed with Alan. This was no way to find Jolene.

"We either put on pause whatever crap is going on between us or we work separately. If all we can do is hold discontent for each other, we aren't going to help Jolene," I said.

Jack took a second to cool down and nodded his head. "We should work together. We know Jolene best."

"Then get in the car," I demanded, as I returned to the driver's seat and slammed the door.

"Mr. Grant?" My dad and I looked to my window, where we heard a commanding voice. Agent Killian was approaching the car rapidly.

"Agent Killian," I said with gritted teeth. "Man, this really isn't the time."

"Save it, Grant. Officer Wire informed us what the two of you discovered at an abandoned hospital for the mentally ill? Are you kidding me? I thought I told you to keep out of this?"

"You did say that," I replied.

"So why are you and an officer of this city deliberately breaking the law?"

"Because I want this killer found, sir," I said, matter-of-factly.

"You've endangered an officer's life, Grant. If Ms. Wire has been targeted now because of your antics, that is on *your* head. And don't think I haven't noticed the trouble that surrounds you and your father. I don't know if he has an alibi for the past forty-eight hours but I'm betting that you don't. So trust me, we'll be talking to you really soon.

"Sure, we can talk as long as you want, as soon as we find Jolene," I said.

"I'm not playing with you, Grant. This is the end of the line for you," Killian blurted out. And, without contemplation, I fired back. Swiftly, unapologetically, I approached the out of town agent, quick stepped—enough to make him draw back a bit on his back heel. I was close to his face, too close, but it was the only way he could see the growing fire behind my eyes.

"Listen, I get I've screwed this up and I get that I, nor Jolene, or my dad or anyone else should have been involved in this but at the end of the day we're all trying to do the same thing. You're snapping at my heels like I'm the bad guy but deep down you and I both know I'm not, and Alan isn't it, either. He's crazy, I'll give you that, and he is pointlessly obsessed, I'll give you that one, too. We are talking about Jolene now, though, sir. We're talking about an outstanding citizen of this community, a brilliant police officer and a good

271

friend to not just me but most of the people in this town. So I don't care if I leave here in cuffs or a body bag, just as long as we find Jolene before you have yet another victim from the Shoestring Killer on *your watch.*" My words subsided but I could still feel my lips twitching and vibrating. Killian didn't break eye contact with me, and I didn't blink. He nodded slowly, and I breathed quietly.

"Let's get out there," he said, and the hunt for Jolene Wire began.

I called Lexi from the car and told her what had happened, she panicked, but tried to hide it. After we explained the situation to her, that Jolene didn't return home after she let us into her apartment, isn't answering her phone, and her car is still parked at the station. We told her where we were starting our search, the same woods that we found Walt Rodgers in, and she, without questioning, decided to join. The four of us, Jack, Lexi, Alan, and myself, waded out into the thick brush and broken trees until we found the clearing where a small stand of trees stood, organically fencing in Irusan's kingdom of felines.

"Who could live out here?" Lexi asked.

"This is a giant waste of time," Alan mumbled, ignoring Lexi.

"Have a better idea, Alan? Know something we don't?" Jack snapped.

Alan shook his head and rubbed the back of his neck. He looked tired, out-of-breath. There was a reason he didn't insist on doing a lot of on-foot investigating with me—old men and old parts.

"It's unlikely either one of them are here, but it is a good place to look for any signs," I said. I was still convinced that Walt Rodgers was our killer, but now that I'd calmed slightly from seeing him at the asylum, I started to wonder. If it were him, would he really have been so surprised to find me looking there, after he gave me the idea about the asylum in the first place?

As I walked through the brush, I really began to hate that my lead suspect, Jody, turned out to be another body in the investigation.

"What the heck is that, crickets?" Lexi asked, remarking upon a loud cracking coming from the woods.

"Cicada," Alan answered, flatly.

"What?" She questioned, looking at me.

"Bugs, Lexi," I said, a little annoyed.

"Gross," she sighed.

"Grosser than crickets?" I asked.

"I just remembered what they are," she said, her eyes squinted, lips perched, and her head retracted, like she just tasted something disgusting. A shiver must've danced across her, as she jiggled her arms like she was doing the wave. Lexi wasn't as brave as she wanted you to believe her to be but that, however, in itself, was brave to me.

We made it through the clearing and into the stand of trees, the smaller clearing—where Walt Rodger's house sat— was coming into view and a daunting feeling brushed over me as all of us reflected upon what we saw before us. The house was torn to pieces. Large chunks of wood were missing, the windows were broken, and the front door not only was off the hinges, but several feet away from the door frame, lying flat on the murky ground surface.

"What happened here?" Jack asked, his voice proved him to be as taken aback by the sight as the rest of us.

Lexi let out a quick scream, and covered her mouth.

"That's sick!" Alan said, retracting back almost as loudly and as quickly as Lexi. I turned to the two of them, as they peered upward, into the high branches of a few of the smaller trees. Hanging off the edges of branches, scattered all the way through the stand, were the caucuses of dead cats. Ten, twelve, maybe more, cats hanged by their necks, draped across a line of trees at around the same height, to where they all stretched down to around the same length. It was a horrid sight—the kind you could barely peel your eyes away from, which is the worst.

"This is ridiculous," Alan sighed. I moved my eyes over to Jack, who didn't budge.

"That's disgusting, let's get out of here," Lexi said.

"Not until we search the place," I demanded, as I stormed to the house. I kept hearing Jolene's voice rattle around in the cages of my head. I could hear what she would say, sense what she would do. I was so far off the mark of what I should be, and she was the embodiment of that—all of it would be for nothing if Jolene had gotten harmed in the process.

The house was empty, and there were nothing but damaged belongings and forgotten memories left inside. Walt Rodgers, Irusan or Shoestring Killer, whoever he was, whatever the name, was gone. I upturned every bit of furniture I could, looking for some sign that Jolene had been there, some clue that I could detect. I sighed and flung the table chair I was holding against the wall.

"What's your problem, Grayson?" Jack yelled out to me. I could feel my left eye twitch uncontrollably, ill-rationally. I turned to him. I knew there was a look in my eye that was unexplainable, because for the first time since I arrived, Jack looked uneasy—he looked scared.

"JOLENE IS MISSING!" I screamed, as loudly as possible. Suddenly the rotten cabin was smaller, more confined—constricting. I was bursting at the seams and beyond the seams were panels of wood, casing me in a heinous entrapment. "JOLENE IS MISSING AND I'M NOT A DETECTIVE!"

There was silence, instantly. My voice subsided and there was nothing but a low, inaudible hum that resonated in my throat that even I could not even hear—only feel. Jack looked down, and around, as if he'd dropped something on the floor.

"Let's just sweep the place and get out, okay?" he said in the most distant, uncomfortable tone he could attain.

"Are you hearing me, Jack?" I spat out, and though my best friend didn't look at me, I knew my words landed harshly on his ears. "Do you hear me, Jack? I should never have come here—none of us should.

Jack nodded his head slowly, as he pushed a sleeve up his shirt in order to rub his arm. I could see, on the surface of his pale-white skin, a tattoo of a murder of crows spiraling up his arm.

"Yeah, that's your problem, Grayson," he said in a humble voice. "It shouldn't have been you...that's been your motto for a lot of years, inspector. The truth is though...if not you, who?" There was a break in his speech where I think he wanted a legitimate answer, though I was far from prepared to give him one. "Let's be real with ourselves for a moment. Whoever the Shoestring Killer is, he's probably the reason Jolene is missing right now. I know you don't want to admit that but there's no getting around what we're staring at, okay? So we just have to swallow that fact, and break this down. We have to find her."

Jack's words were blunt, cold, crisp, but pure. He was right and it pained me to admit it. Not because of some childhood minded jealousy game that even boys like us managed to play—but because he was right about Jolene. She was in trouble, and if we didn't find her soon it would be too late.

We stormed out of the cabin, desperate to canvas more grounds. I decided I would return to the asylum, and hope to find a better clue in the daytime, even allowing myself to think that somehow Jolene returned to the asylum herself for the same reason—despite the fact that her car was left unattended to just a block from the police station. Jack was going to check some of the other trails, with a group of guys he knew that might be able to help out, with the idea in mind that Lexi and Alan would help out back in town.

We regrouped in the clearing outside the cabin, unable to ignore the limp bodies of the Irusan felines that dangled in the trees.

"What kind of sick freak would harbor all these cats and then hang them?" Lexi asked, as we began to push through the woods.

"He wouldn't. He loved them too much," I said, taking a glance at the closest one to me, just before it was out of view. It was a tabby cat, large, fluffy.

"Maybe it wasn't him. Maybe it's a little payback for torturing a community. It would serve him right. It's just not enough—not nearly enough," Alan said. It was just as Alan's fatigued sentences wore on, that I noticed the noose around the tabby cat's neck. My stomach turned and I could feel breakfast regurgitating in my throat.

"Maybe," I said softly, feeling the sickness settle in my chest. "Except Walt Rodgers isn't the Shoestring Killer, either," I said as I paused long enough to point up at the tabby cat. Jack hesitated for a moment, Alan did too. Lexi actually stopped, turned around, and retraced her steps to get to me. I pointed to the cat's noose and although it took her a few moments, she finally saw what I was pointing at and let out a small, subtle gasp.

"What is it?" Jack asked, impatiently.

"Well, Alan was partly right. Someone did this out of spite. But it wasn't because Rodgers is the Shoestring killer."

"How do you know?" Alan asked, who was now looking up at the tabby.

"Because all of these cats," I said as I gestured around the clearing within the stand. "Are hanged by shoestrings."

After a few moments, we collected ourselves, and moved forward. We walked away with very little that afternoon. Walt Rodgers probably wasn't the Shoestring Killer but he was on the killer's bad side—but why?

As Alan and Lexi began marching through the woods again, Jack held back until I was close enough to him that he could speak to my privately. His hand grasped around my forearm and pulled me back, locking me into my stance in the Earth.

"We don't have time for this, Jack," I said, annoyed. Jolene's face flashed through my mind.

"I haven't even begun to let your old man off," Jack whispered. "As far as I'm concerned he's still guilty."

"Then why don't you march up there, kick him to the ground like you like to do so well, and beat him until he tells you where he hid Jolene while he was with me? Since that's exactly where he's been ever since I bailed him out."

Jack shook his head and smiled at me, as if there was a punchline being told and I was the only one who didn't get the joke. Maybe it's because I'd heard that one before.

"You don't even know, man. I'm here to keep my eye on him and maybe on you, too," Jack said, as he let go of his grip and walk forward. I wanted to tackle him. I wanted to punch and kick and beat him senseless. I wanted to shove the idea down his throat that I loved Jolene just as much, maybe more than him or anyone else in that stupid town. I wanted him to know, through blood and tears, that he was wrong. I did nothing, though, but move forward, pushing through silently in the woods. In the woods, there's only nature and the mind. The unending questions and the resurgent scream of the cicada.

I have seen too much unsuspected death for any one person. Too many final faces burned into my cerebellum, which flicker on in the darkness—like a nightlight in the calm of my childhood slumbers. I saw my mother's face, cold, hardened, lifeless, when I was just a boy. And now, standing somewhere on the Abingdon side of the Creeper Trail that runs through the state, I saw another lifeless face. My eyes flood, my soul shatters, and I crumble as I watch two police officers, who were doubling as avid members of our search party, pull Jolene's limp body up from the murky nature, right off the path, somewhat buried in the ground.

Jolene Wire was dead.

"Clear out," I heard Agent Killian say to me, as he pushed through the group and singled me out. "Now, Grant, I don't want to see your face until I'm ready to see it, do you hear me, Grant?" I connected eyes with him for a brief moment but I didn't reply. "I mean it, Grayson. You are trouble. This entire thing reeks off your stench. Take a good look, Grayson, because you're the reason she's here." Killian stomped off, sputtering some non-descriptive words I couldn't and didn't want to hear.

Alan tried to reach out to me, pressing his hard, cold hand on my shoulder. I shoved it off. There was no comfort now, nor should there be. As soon as we made it back to town from searching Rodger's cabin, we caught a squad car fleeing in the opposite direction. We followed it to the Creeper Trail. Jack stood off to the side, by himself—occasionally shooting dirty looks towards Alan. Lexi stood off to the side from me, as if she were waiting around for me to fall, so she could catch me, but not too close, in case I might crush her on my descend.

I watched Jolene for as long as I could before the coroners zipped her into a body bag. There were tight markings all over her neck, just like every other victim, and on her left wrist, the shoestring responsible for the markings, tied in a bow.

"This shouldn't have happened," I finally said aloud, to no one in particular, save for me.

"This wasn't your fault, son," Alan started. "I don't care what that jerk-off said."

"I don't care what he said," I lied, shrugging the idea, and a cold chill, off my spine. "But he's right. It is my fault. This was a case for the state, not for Grayson and friends," I murmured. I walked away, passed my father, passed Lexi, and passed Jack, whom I glanced at for only a moment as I continued. His eyes were repelling away from my own, as he watched blankly at the body bag. His jaw flexed and he breathed heavy.

Jolene, Jack and I use to play hide-and-go seek behind my parents' house. Jack and I would always lose, because Jolene was too good at hiding. And now, more than ever, did I wish I were better at seeking.

I did nothing for the next couple of days. I officially checked out of the Martha Washington, and moved my things to my father's home—to my old bedroom upstairs. I stayed, secluded and sedated until the day of the funeral. I'd replaced my hourly coffee with a bottle of whiskey I found in Alan's cabinet, and sleeping pills that I swiped from his nightstand. The Grant men certainly had their vices.

At least three times each day that I stayed cocooned in the Grant house, there would be a knock on my door. Alan was desperate for me to pull myself from the pit I had found myself in, but I refused to answer him. Lexi couldn't even get me to crack the door open. I had become numb throughout the two day period. Somewhere grief and sadness morphed into a depression that was unforgiving.

On the day of the funeral, I forced three cups of coffee down my throat—black, no sugar or cream now. I needed the surge to force myself into a tie and drag my bag-of-bones to the cemetery where a small service would be taking place. It was hard, even considering Abingdon. Jolene was the best part of home for me. Without her in it, it just wasn't home anymore. It was just another place.

The service was beautiful, at least, what I could attain. My mind drifted into dark places, into wonderfully light places, too. Moments that seemed like snapshots, now. A brief negative locked in a darkroom, somewhere. Jolene and I on our first date. Jolene's surprise sixteenth birthday party. Jolene and I, sixth graders and sneaking out of gym class. Jolene and I, our last fight before I moved out of Abingdon. I told her I wouldn't let her go. It was one of the several lies I told her whilst living here. I needed to float on—away from this place. And you can't float when you're weighed down. I watched as each member of the Wire family paid their last bit of respect at the face of the casket. Her father's tears covered the mahogany. Her mother gently kissed her fingertips and pressed it atop her husband's tears. I wish I were weighed down, now.

Alan stood near the back of the crowd. The Wire family had personally invited him to attend, claiming they trusted him beyond measure, that he wasn't responsible in any way for Jolene's death, or any of the others. He was still cautious, of course, considering that not many other shared in the Wire's sentiment—like Jack, who stood near the Wire family. I found myself somewhere away from all of them, even Lexi, who was also standing alone in the sea of mourning faces.

The cemetery where the Wires decided to bury Jolene was an old, small, almost private cemetery. It was located atop a hill surrounded by several trees. Six or seven men had arrived early and dug out a six-foot grave with shovels. As the service ended, and members began to scatter, I remained—standing beneath a large pine tree that looked over what was in process of becoming Jolene's grave.

Jolene's casket sank into the ground, a ship surrendering to the sea. As the crowd broke away, whispering tears and prayers, I noticed the ground. It was murky. It had rained too much, too soon—for a funeral, anyway. All of us would leave with mud on our shoes. That's why I stayed. I deserved the mud. I watched as the diggers picked up their shovels and began to repack the earth with the dirt in which they stole. There was a spare shovel, that didn't look as big or a sturdy as the rest. It was obviously a spare.

I approached them slowly, hoping in some way to go unnoticed, and retrieved the shovel. As the rest of the men started to toss dirt, I scooped up a bowl of it, with the shovel, and dumped it onto the smooth casket. One of the diggers stopped in his steps, glared up at me in confusion and almost laughed—a sly smirk.

"We have it covered. You don't have to do this, pal," he explained. I sighed and nodded, but continued to pour ounces of dirt into the ground.

"I helped put her in this bed," I started. "I might as well tuck her in."

Long after the diggers finished, and I was drenched in sweat, I leaned against the pine tree overseeing Jolene. My cellphone continued to ring but I didn't bother to even read the caller I.D, let alone answer. Lexi, annoyingly enough, had returned to the cemetery and remained in Alan's parked car at the bottom of the hill. It was clear she was worried about me. I should have apologized to her—but I couldn't pull myself away. I just stared at the fresh mound of dirt on top of the grave, hoping that I would wake up from a bad dream, or be the recipient of a terrible prank.

Footsteps approached my left, and I refused to look at Lexi, who was no doubt there to lecture me in the ways of grief.

"Not now, Lexi," I said, sighing.

"Not your southern belle, Gray," Jack said approaching, and leaning on the other side of the tree. I looked to him. He looked calmer, more collected than he had before. I hesitated at first, but I decided to let down my defenses. This—whatever it had become—was bigger than the both of us.

"Are you okay?" I asked. Jack shrugged and looked toward the grass his shoes were kicking, haphazardly.

"No more okay than you," he replied. It told me everything I needed to know.

"I was just thinking about the good times," I said, peering back over at the mound of dirt. "Not any of these times, investigating times. Not even really the days we dated either, because I already had one foot out of this town by then. I'm thinking of the old days. That roller rink where we use to skate. Do you remember that place? It had an arcade," I explained. Jack chuckled.

"I still have the high score on one of those Pac-man machines," he said, actually smiling.

"Man, only because I left town," I teased.

"Why did you leave?" Jack asked, after a few silent moments. "I mean, I said I understood. I do understand. I guess what I mean is, why did you leave when you did?"

I gestured to the graveyard in front of us. "This is why. This is all I saw when I was here. In actuality or just in my head. There was just death. No matter the good stuff in my life, you, Jolene," I paused at her name. "Hindsight is a pair of glasses I could've used in those days," I said.

Jack nodded. I knew the subject was raw, it was raw for anyone who was close to me back then. It was raw for him, too. Jack and I never recovered from that move—not like I thought. I suppose long distance does damage to more than just a romance.

"Do you remember your first date with her? With Jolene?" I asked him, changing the subject quickly. Jack grimaced and eyed me.

"This is weird, Gray. Let's not go there, man," he said. I smiled, albeit, it was only for show.

"Come on, man. It's okay. We're celebrating her life, now. We're not having a pissing contest," I said. Jack sighed and dragged his elbow against the pine for a moment.

"She made us go on a picnic on the Creeper Trail—not far from where she was, you know, found."

"She made me hike, too," I said, reminiscing. "Our first date was a movie, though. Simple, fun—just like us."

Jack shifted uncomfortable for a moment, and then leaned off the tree. Our gazes left the burial plot and moved towards one another. There was a heavy weight on his chest, that much was obvious, and he was looking for someone to help him carry it. So, I reached out my arms, sport of speak.

"What's going on, Jack?" I asked.

"I owe you an apology," he admitted. His eyes bounced from my stare, to the ground. "I've been treating you like all of this is your fault. I know that, even if your dad did have something to do with it, you haven't, or wouldn't. And as for Jolene, well if anyone cared for her as much as I do, it was you. You'd never want this—not in a lifetime. So, for being cold, distant, straight up rude. I'm sorry," Jack finished. I nodded my head, in full acceptance of his apology.

"It's a stressful time, Jack." I said, as it were a reasonable explanation for action.

"I don't want you to mistake me," Jack said, nearly cutting off my response. "I still think your dad is involved, but I've been taking that out on you. And, well, I shouldn't."

I sighed, and gritted my teeth. I could hear my teeth scraping against one another, it fueled my stress.

"Jack, you are kidding, right? How hard are you going to hang onto this theory that Alan is the Shoestring Killer?" I spat out. Jack's mood turned on me in an instant. His calm demeanor shifted dramatically to aggression.

"No, man, you don't know what I've seen. I know things. I've been gracious enough to keep it to myself because I don't have any hard evidence on him and I didn't want to hurt you all these years, Grayson, but I know. Because I've *seen* it."

"Then why don't you tell me, Jack?" I dared.

"Are you going to listen?" Jack stalled. "Or are you just going to try to give your pop a faux-alibi?"

My body tensed. I was furious but terrified. Jack was a lot of things, but a liar didn't seem to be one of them. At least, not when it counted. We were both victims, though, to be honest. We were introduced to true violence at an early age, and I *saw* just as much as he's claiming. At the end of the day, though, the ghosts in your closet are just your own dirty laundry.

I hadn't the energy, or the desire to fight him. There was only tension and grief left inside—not energy. He held up a hand, as if were him that stopped the debate.

"I'm not here to fight with you, Gray," he said as he pulled his cellphone from his back pocket. "I wanted you to hear this." He handed his cell phone over to me, and gestured for me to take it from his hand. "Listen to the voicemail." I took the phone from him but stopped just short of checking the messages.

"Why?"

"Just do it."

I pressed the voicemail button on Jack's phone, and moments later a soft inviting voice echoed through my ear.

"Hey, Jack—it's me."

"Jolene," I said, breathless. My chest felt heavy all the sudden—this was the weight Jack needed help carrying.

"I just wanted to talk to you about a couple of things for a minute. Grayson, Lexi and I went up to Old Dominion Asylum, in Bristol, we got a lead there and since Grayson's mom use to work there we thought maybe there was a connection. Anyway, we saw a bunch of stuff I won't get into

over voicemail but we did see Walt Rodgers out there. Don't go beating him with a ball bat again until we know more. I'm leaving the station now, but I wanted to talk to you about something else besides the case. Jack, I know you have a theory that involves Alan and I'm not dismissing you or the theory or anything like that but you have to realize the damage you're doing to Grayson right now. Even if Alan is guilty, which, for the record, I think you're wrong about that, but even if he is look at what it is doing to Grayson. He's your best friend. I don't know. You two mean something to each other and you both mean something to me. I know it's kinda weird, and none of this, us, our friendships, the case, none of this is normal. I just—I care about the two of you and I just..."

Jolene's message wasn't over but she'd stopped talking...she sighed into the phone and I closed my eyes and pretended she was beside me, talking to me, with me. I came to once Jack spoke.

"She opened my eyes a little and left me a gift of one last message, and I wanted to share that with you," Jack said. I opened my mouth to reply but Jolene's voicemail continued.

"I just don't know what to do now. I confessed my involvement in Grayson's investigation because I think it is

getting to the point where it is too big for us—for Grayson, for me, for you, for even the department. The state detectives are asserting that very strongly and they're getting to the point to where they're phasing out the department— Hey, are you okay? Do you have shelter, a place to stay? Do you need help?"

I frowned, trying to make heads or tails of the message's detour. Jack noticed my expression.

"Yeah, she runs into a homeless man at the end and starts talking to him—trying to help. Jolene was always the girl scout. I stopped listening after that." Jack explained, but I was listening to her voice too closely.

Why don't you walk with me back to the station and let me see if I can't find a place for you to stay tonight, okay? Maybe get a hot meal. That sounds good, doesn't it? Let's go. Oh, need help with your shoes? They're falling off your feet. Here, let me help you with that velcro. Oh, goodness, sir, are you hurt? That looks bad—have you seen a doctor? Hold on, Jack, I'm sorry, you're probably cussing me for leaving a voicemail in the first place. Just, call me later, okay? Please think about what I said.

I closed the phone, shocked and dismayed by what I had just heard. My throat felt full, so does my chest.

"She said she'd just left the station," I started. Jack nodded.

"No one saw her after that," Jack completed my thought. He didn't find anything suspicious about the message's conclusion. He started talking, about Jolene and what she said, but my mind was racing with visuals. Lexi telling me she saw nothing in the cells but a pair of shoes. Patient files my mother brought up, that distinctly said that one of her patients had an obsession with hating his velcro shoes—a patient that desire normality. A patient that desired to wear shoes, normal shoes—shoes with shoestrings.

I tried to keep up with the trail, to deduce what was happening, to make sure I hadn't hit yet another dead end but I hadn't. It wasn't Jody, he was the victim known as Joseph Farmer. It wasn't Walt Rodgers—Irusan was telling the truth when he said the Native American marking on his wrist was shared with several. And most importantly, it proved that the Shoestring Killer was not Alan Grant, no. It was Franklin Butler, one of my mother's favorite patients.

I cut off my conversation with Jack quickly and raced down the hill. I didn't need him to be involved—not yet. Lexi, excitedly, got out of the car and approached me.

"Is everything okay?" she asked.

"As good as it could be in this situation. Lexi, I know who it is," I said with near glee.

"What?" she asked

"The Shoestring Killer, I know who it is. Finally, we can nail this guy."

And as I stood at the bottom of the hill, my hands clamped around Lexi's wrists, I thought for a moment, about Jolene's message, how the case had become too big for all of us, and wondered if my continuation would in any way dishonor her memory but there was a thirsty vengeance that returned to my veins and I don't think any voice of reason would've stopped me in that moment—not even Jolene's.

Why?

Three Months Later

Chapter Eleven

Dr. Feel Bad

I was no longer a private investigator. I was a shell of my former self. After Jolene's funeral, I went home—my parents' home, the place I grew up. In my eyes, it had stopped being my home the moment I moved away but for the first time in years there was a strange comfort in seeing it. It wasn't Alan, it wasn't the memories—it wasn't any of those things. There was just something about the familiarity of it all, though, and that was enough for me. Pain you understand is more comfortable than pain that surprises you. It's why we cry for the elderly when they pass, but cry a little harder for the young when it's their turn.

I called Kiddy a few days later, after ignoring most of his phone calls and tendered my resignation over the phone. He argued with me, fought with me for days after—even threatening to come to Abingdon to get me. The calls stopped, eventually, though.

Lexi was disappointed with me, I didn't charge her for any of the work that I did on the case, but when I told her I had quit and I wasn't going back to St. Louis anytime soon, she angrily threw the money in my face, anyway.

297

Alan doesn't mind my being here. In truth, I think he kind of likes it. There hasn't been anyone in the house for a while, other than him, and he likes the company. He doesn't, however, like everyone else, seem to like that I've dropped the ball completely on the investigation.

Well, almost everyone else. I went to the police one final time, spoke with Agents Strout and Killian. I told him that I'd deduced the killer's identity, that he was a mental patient named Franklin Butler, from Old Dominion Asylum, that use to be under the care of my mother. I got another lecture and they threatened to arrest me but they didn't. Despite knowing the identity, Franklin couldn't be found. His trail seemed to go cold after the fire. There was another sweep of the asylum, all the way down to the bottom floor—but nothing was found. They don't come out and say it—but they still believed Alan had something to do with it. Despite police officers finding the shoestring in the barn, which Alan finally admitted to swiping from the crime scene, no one could compile a case against him. After all, Alan was in jail when Jolene went missing and he was with me from the moment he left the police station until after Jolene's body was found. Atop of that, he even had an alibi for Lauren Kelley's murder. He'd taken me to stay with my grandmother—his mother's house, in Boone, North Carolina.

It was odd, though, that the shoestring my father swiped seemed to be the only evidence of blood not pertaining to the victims. Franklin left no trace behind of DNA, so forensics teams could never connect him, biologically. It was another reminder that these murders were more calculated than passionate. He had time to plot.

Footage from the police station showed Jolene leaving but by the time she stopped to Franklin, she was already out of shot. There was footage of a man, mere minutes earlier, lurking around the station that matched Franklin's description but no positive match could be identified.

I woke up early, somewhere three months into my stay at Alan's house. Three months since we all gathered together, and put Jolene in the ground. I couldn't go back to sleep. An orange beam cracked through the window blinds and turned my gray room into a sunrise painting. Only my eyes were open, I couldn't possibly think about standing up or even moving, yet. I glared at a wood paneling—following the different grains along the wall.

I couldn't force myself to go back to sleep. The sunbeams spread throughout my room, warming it in a golden lens. I could hear Alan rummaging around in the kitchen just below me—most importantly, putting on a pot of coffee. By the time I got downstairs, there was already a cup of coffee ready in an old Butterfield Bluejays mug he got once when we went to a game in '93.

I found Alan on the porch. He was sitting on the swing, enjoying his own cup of coffee. I raised my cup, in a nod of thanks. He nodded back.

"You drink yours black, right?" he asked. I nodded my head, again.

"I do now, with a little sauce mixed in." I sat beside him on the swing, and watched a quiet Abingdon in front of me. It was early in the morning, there was a crispness in the air—like the world hadn't woken up yet, somehow we'd beat it to the punch. Birds chirped back and forth, a subtle reminder of the things we don't hear once the wheels start turning.

Alan and I hadn't had too many moments like this in the past three months but when we had them, they were nice. We'd found a way, somehow, to stop arguing with each other. A couple weeks after Jolene's death, he just dropped the entire thing all together. Now and again he'll mention my mother, but never the case—never the killer. Perhaps he had some closure for at least knowing who did it. It had to bother him, though, on some level, that police hadn't found him yet.

"Nice weather we're having this morning," he said, taking a slurp of his coffee. I nodded, again, in agreement. I nodded a lot, in those months, I think. "Maybe I can get you

300

to pick up a few things for me at the hardware store?" He asked. I turned to him slightly, eyeing him.

"Why can't you do it?" I asked, bluntly.

"I guess I could," he shrugged. "Just thought you might like a chance to get out of the house, I guess."

"If I wanted a chance to get out of the house I'd pack my bags and go back to St. Louis, do you want me to do that, Alan?" I snapped. Alan watched me for a moment, as if he expected me to smile and laugh and tell him I was kidding. He dropped his grin when it was clear I wasn't doing a bit.

"I want you to do whatever makes you happy, son," he said, sipping his coffee again.

"What does that mean?" I said, defensively, laughing into my cup. "All you've wanted me to do for months—for years— was to come out here and help you solve mom's case."

He looked bothered when I mentioned the case, like I was pressing a sore wound on an ill-stricken body. Maybe that is what I was doing after all.

"And now you just want me to what? Get arrested by trying to do more? Strout, Killian, the police department made it very clear that one more interruption from me in this case is going to land myself into some serious trouble. What do you want from me?"

301

Alan's face turned on me. It was full of wrinkles now, he was frowning, almost fuming. He didn't say anything, but he tensed up, as if he were ready to lecture me—father and son, the facts of life, the hard lessons.

"Don't be an idiot," he finally said, but in a soothing voice.

"What?" I asked.

"You heard me, kid," Alan started. "Maybe it was wrong for me to nag you until you came out here. Maybe I wanted you to be this unreasonable superhero in all of this, or maybe I was just looking for a way to connect with my son again. I don't know, pick which answer pisses you off the least. The thing is though, I never wanted you to come back here to stay," his words subsided and he cut his eyes over to me. "And I don't mean that you're not welcome here. Of course you are...this is your home. I never chased you when you went off to St. Louis. You know why?"

"I assumed because you were in knee deep into a conspiracy theory about the case and didn't really notice," I said, harshly. He waved his hand at me like I told a bad joke.

"I knew when you left. I knew what you were doing, and I didn't say boo. I missed you. Of course I missed you. You didn't need to be here, though. You were the kid whose mom got killed in his own house. You were pitied or taunted and you never felt right about this place, not since then. And who

302

could blame you? Living here after that was just a recurring nightmare. I'm sorry I didn't get you out, sooner, myself," Alan finished.

"If being here was so bad and you knew it, why didn't you leave way back when? Why are you still here?" I asked, my voice had eased. We were civil with each other now—progress. Alan tapped one of his cracked, worn knuckles against the wood of the swing.

"My best friend, Bill Tate made this swing for your mother and I for our wedding present. Elizabeth and I would sit on this swing every evening and have a cup of coffee, or tea, or wine, or whatever we had a taste for that week, and we would watch main street, or the stars, or you and Jack playing cops and robbers out in the yard. It took a long time for me to be able to sit in the swing, again," he sipped his coffee and stared out into the distance—I followed his eyes, and looked in the same direction. I knew, however, that we were seeing two different things.

"I couldn't leave, Grayson. My wife was here. For better or worse, I loved her and didn't want her to die. And leaving without any justice being done just—I felt too guilty, Grayson. I couldn't leave," Alan explained.

"But you're wanting me to?" I asked.

"I want you to take your life back, son," he pleaded. I scoffed.

"Jolene and I might not have exactly been marriage-bound but I loved her. I truly, truly did, Alan. So if I can't leave, then who better to understand that than you?" I questioned. Alan threw his heavy, hard arm around my shoulders and pulled me close for an ever so awkward side-hug.

"Because look at what it did to my life, son. Twenty years practically wasted. I never got very far on the case. I got arrested. My relationship with you has been a joke. I basically stopped being a father. I stopped being a man. I retired and became an introvert. I haven't dated, I haven't gone to a poker night, I haven't gone fishing, I haven't done anything like I use to do. I completely changed myself because I couldn't let your mother's death go. I'm not telling you that you have to forget Jolene. I'm not even telling you that you have to fall in love with someone else or get a hobby or go back to St. Louis. But I am telling you, Grayson, you need to move on."

Alan let go of me and stood up from the swing. He took one last gulp of coffee and sat the cup on the porch railing.

"I think I'll go to the hardware store myself," he said, pulling a ring of keys from his jeans pocket.

"Alan," I called out. He stopped and sighed.

"I really wish you'd get over calling me by my name," he murmured.

"You and mom," I blurted out. "Were you good? In the end? Or were you going to divorce?" I asked. Alan turned around and locked eyes with me, like I read his private journal.

"She died before we could really answer that question," he replied. "And for twenty years I've wondered what the answer would've been."

That afternoon, I ignored another phone call from Kiddy, which to be honest, had me taken aback due to the fact he hadn't bothered me in weeks. I almost answered, but in my last couple of seconds, I turned into a coward once again. Instead, I found myself spending the afternoon organizing and dismantling Alan's lunatic board within his room. It had been three months since we deduced the identity of the killer, but yet he'd refused to dismantle the string of evidence and theories he had webbed up in his room. I guess he was used to it.

As I made a pile of photographs and maps, and stacked papers with witness accounts and drawings, I ran across my mother's file on Franklin Butler once again. I shook my head, as I combed over Franklin's file, wondering why it took us so long to realize he was the killer. His file was practically screaming it. Although we all missed it, it made me wonder how Alan, who had the information in his possession for twenty years, somehow failed to at least follow through with one half correct theory. Perhaps he was a worse detective than myself.

About that time, there was a knock on the front door. It was a little unsettling. Alan had a key, of course, he didn't need to knock on his own front door, and no one else bothered to come by the Grant house, not anymore. The masses still suspected Alan, heavily, of being involved in the murders, somehow. The ones that didn't suspect him usually believed him to be a crazy man who *never quite got over what happened.* It was like a slogan that was carved in a sign that hung from the porch. I wondered if people would say the same thing about Jolene and me. Twenty years of trying to escape what my father had turned into and I was on quick path to becoming it myself.

The knocking wouldn't subside, in fact, it only got louder, more violent. Enough to bother me from what I was doing. I jotted down the steps and the knocking continued to rumble the front door so much I could feel it beneath my bare feet in the vibrations of the wood flooring.

"Keep your pants on, I'm coming!" I yelled at the door just moments before I twisted the knob, and flung it open. To my surprise, before me, with her left hand deep in her back jean pocket, her strawberry blonde hair dangling in curvy strands down to her shoulders.

"Lexi," I said, seeing her before me. She wasn't smiling at me in an *It's so wonderful to see you after all this time* kind of smile. It was a smirk. An, *I took you by surprise* kind of smirk. "What are you doing here?"

"What are *you* doing here?" She asked as she pushed by me, entering the house while I still stayed at the door—open mouthed and confused.

"Seriously, what are you doing here, Lexi?" I asked, following her into the living room. She surveyed the area, like she was house hunting.

"I wanted to see what was happening here," she explained. I gestured openly to the living room, where an empty popcorn bag, random articles of clothing, several empty or half empty soda cans lay scattered across the coffee table, and several bottles of beer and liquor laced everywhere from the television stand, to the coffee table, to the mantel above the fireplace.

"Obviously nothing," I said, sharply. She looked at me—taken aback. Lexi lifted her hand, flat palm facing me and gestured forward, like an awkward high five.

"Can you pump the breaks here, Grant? I don't know what your attitude is about but it isn't anything I've done," she said, just as sharply in her reply as I had been with her.

"I remember you throwing a bunch of bills in my face," I tested.

"I remember you acting like a jerk," she protested. I sighed, but I couldn't contain real contempt.

"That's fair," I said, nodding. "So serious talk," A calmer, more inviting voice now, "What are you doing here? What brings you back to Abingdon?"

"You do, of course," she said with a frown, like I was the last person in the room to get the joke. Suppose that was true.

"Why?"

Lexi slowly shook her head as she walked across the living room, eyeing every empty soda can, empty bottle and dirty plate that she saw, like she'd stumbled upon a crime scene and had to investigate.

"Is this how you've been living for three months?" she inquired.

"More or less, I guess, why? What are you *doing* here, Lexi?" I repeated.

"For you!" She said aloud, angrily—dramatically. Her hands waved in the air like she were trying to signal me. "I mean you can't be serious about livin' like this, sugar. You gotta go home at some point. You either accept that you've gone as far as you can on this case, and go home, or you pick yourself up and you do something else about it. You can't just stay like this, stuck in a weird limbo."

"What do you know about it, Lexi?" I flopped down on the couch.

"I know Jolene meant a lot to you, that much was obvious. You can't lay in your grave too, though, Grayson," she pleaded with me. "You cracked the case—that's what I hired you to do. I didn't hire you to bring him in, or instill some kinda vigilante justice. I just wanted a name and a face. You gave me both," she said, earnestly. I looked up at her as she crossed the floor and sat on the edge of the coffee table in front of me. She smelled wonderful—a fragrance for swooning. Her eyes locked with mine and I remembered what Jolene said, just before we went into the asylum. *She's taken with you.* I pulled back from Lexi and looked down.

"He won," I said, flatly.

"What?"

"He won. Franklin *the Shoestring Killer* Butler won. Just when we find out who he is...he's gone. We haven't heard a peep out of him in three months." I stood up from the couch and walked away from Lexi. I didn't like to be still when anxiety clouded me, and being that close to Lexi wasn't helping. "He stopped. He just left town, or retired, or something. He stopped. I get close to him. I get really close to him, Lexi—and then," my voice trailed off. I didn't want to push out the words that had been rattling around in my head for weeks, now. Words that have never fallen on anyone's ears. "He took Jolene. He won."

Lexi stood from the coffee table. I couldn't see her face, my back was turned to the living room—I glared at the French doors because there was nothing else in which to glare.

"I don't know where to start on how *wrong* you are about, well, everything," Lexi stated. "How about we start with the fact that you're not the center element here, Grant. This man, this twisted, disturbed man, isn't putting on a show for a one person audience, sugar. It's deeper than that, it has to be," she concluded.

"Does it?" I asked. "Because that's what it feels like, Lexi. I mean why? I've gone over that file a thousand times these past three months. He was semi-violent but he was never a threat. He had to start for a reason and he started with the woman that was trying to help him. It doesn't make sense. It's just—he's a monster! He took my mother and he took Jolene because he could."

There's a reason you see police investigators take a back seat on the cases that hit close to home. There's a fog that drifts over the sky of their intelligence. It hides the sun, and allows you to hide. Even then I knew I was hiding.

"So that's what this is, huh?" Lexi stated. "You think he's killed your mother and Jolene because he has some kind of problem with you?" Her questions didn't seem believable. I shook my head.

"I just think—I think he was making a point with Jolene. I mean it couldn't be coincidence, could it?"

"Either way, let's say, out loud, what this is really about," Lexi said, firmly. Her arms crossed over one another. "You're turning into him, your dad."

"Well, that's what you want to hear," I said, sarcastically.

"No, I'm sorry but it's the truth, Grayson. You're letting yourself fall in a rut. Blame yourself for Jolene's death all you want but she was a police officer, Grayson, and she would have faced Franklin with or without you because he was a threat to her home and she wasn't going to allow that to happen. Jolene was too strong for that, wasn't she?" Lexi stressed. I nodded my head slowly, but broke her gaze.

"I guess you want me to go home, then? Go back to Kiddy's agency, beg for my job back, apologize for vanishing for three months until he forgives me and we kiss and make-up?"

"I'm all for the making-up part, but I'm not too wild about all that other," a third voice came from the front door. I jumped—startled. Standing in the hall just in front of the French doors, was Flynn Kiddy, holding a folder underneath his left armpit. He wore a tan Members Only jacket, and he had more facial hair than usual, which was disturbing to me for some reason. He flicked a chubby finger over his mustache, combing it out of the way of his lips. "That drive is stupid, by the way," he said.

"Kiddy?"

"Has it been that long? You don't recognize me? I swear I've only gained three pounds."

"Kiddy," I said, in awe of him standing in my living room. Flynn Kiddy was the type of guy that didn't leave the comfort of his own couch unless he had to, during his off time. He only ever did anything if it were important: work, or his family. Guess I fall under one of those categories.

"Okay, I've gained five pounds. To be fair, though, a lot of it is stress eating because of you."

"What are you doing here?"

"Well, mainly because you're a douchebag that doesn't answer his phone calls," he explained.

"Did you do this?" I gestured toward Kiddy but looked to Lexi.

"Well, yeah, you think we just showed up here at the same time? You really are a bad detective."

"He's not adequate, no," Kiddy said.

"Excuse me?" I retorted.

"I'm not even sure we should tell him," Lexi said, looking to Kiddy.

"I'm having second thoughts as well," Kiddy stated. "In fact, we should've stopped on our way in, and checked it out for ourselves."

"Tell me what?"

"Maybe we should just tell the cops what we know?" Lexi questioned.

"*Tell me what?*" I asked, annoyed.

"I doubt they'll look into it. They haven't been very helpful thus far."

"*Okay!*" I yelled. "I get it. You have something and you want to involve me—so much so that you came all the way from St. Louis to do so. I get it, but if I'm going to even think about it you have to talk to me first."

Kiddy just stared at me for a moment, not contemplating his words, not filled with emotional charge—just blankly staring, as if he were waiting for me to finish with an intelligent thought. I turned to Lexi, who was more acceptable, despite her own quirky ways.

"I thought you wanted me to go home and move on," I said.

"I just want you to get out of your rut. I don't want you to become Alan Grant. I'm not stupid, Grayson, I know the truth—you don't have a home—not anymore, not yet."

I paused, it felt like the breath was knocked out of me. Lexi looked around the room. "You can't keep doing this. You can't keep sitting here. Jolene isn't coming back."
I looked down for a moment. Lexi's words made sense but she got something wrong. I wasn't looking for Jolene—I wasn't trying to dig her body back up. I learned at an early age that death was a full-time commitment. That was the problem, actually, I wasn't convinced I was still alive.

"What do you have, Kiddy?" I asked, looking towards my boss. Kiddy dropped the file on the coffee table that he'd been holding.

"What is this?" I asked, picking it up and thumbing through the pages. They were admission papers to a hospital in Bristol General Hospital, the patient's name was Maxwell

Bryant, and he was being admitted for burn wounds and psychiatric care. There were other admission papers behind Maxwell's, all of them needing the same care.

"Admissions papers to Bristol General Hospital—look at their reason for admission," Kiddy said, digging his sweaty fists into his pockets.

"Burns and psychiatric care, sounds like Old Dominion. Is that where they were taken?"

"We think so," Kiddy nodded.

"I don't recognize any of these names, though, Kiddy," I started. "Maxwell Bryant, Wallace Turner, Deela Snow, who are these people?"

"Aliases. Fake names so they couldn't be traced back to Old Dominion," Kiddy explained.

"That's a cool trick, who pulled that off?" I questioned, looking over the papers once more.

"Well, his name isn't on the papers, but enough phone calls got me the information that Dr. Walker had a few friends in the hospital at the time, and were able to get the patients in the hospital before any major investigation was done during the asylum fire," Kiddy said.

"We should talk to some of them, shouldn't we?" I asked—feeling a pulse within me that hadn't been awake for three months.

"I can do you one better. We found him, Dr. Walker. Wasn't easy, but I found him. His whole California living was a hoax. He retired and lives in Bristol now. I think it is time the good doctor gets a little chatty, don't you?" Kiddy said.

"You don't have to though, Grayson," Lexi interjected. It was strange, Lexi's voice being the one of caution and reason. Three months ago she was ready to fight for justice, even if that justice was dirty. Three months is enough time to change perspective.

"Franklin had been somewhere in Bristol this entire time and it was because of Dr. Walker. He was never any help. He created monsters and then he let them off the leash. He deserves to at least be confronted. He may know where Franklin might be," I stated.

"Told you he'd say something like that," Kiddy interjected.

"Let's go see the doc," I said, eagerly.

As we walked out of my father's house, Lexi grabbed my hand. Her cold, slender fingers folded in the spaces between mine and latched on like hooks, anchoring me down. I stopped and looked back at her. She wasn't crying, but her eyes were wide and her lips were small. There was something in her mind, somewhere, dying to leap out.

"What is it?"

"Lexi, what is it?"

"This is real, you know," she said.

"I know."

"This can't be some dark pit you fall into and can't get out of, okay?" Lexi stressed.

"Okay."

"I mean it, Grayson. You can't become Alan about this— no matter what we find, no matter what we do."

"I can't become Alan, Lexi. It's impossible."

"How do you know?" Lexi asked.

"You wouldn't let me," I retorted. The fog that was congesting my vision, making the past three months almost unbearable, was clearing. I didn't have to hide behind those clouds anymore, and with the warm friendship and familiarity of Lexi and Kiddy—it was like the sun, through the fog, was a solar flare.

"So what do we do? Walk up, knock on his door, tell him we think he's a crime-doctor and we want to know what he did with a serial killer twenty years ago?" Lexi asked as the three of us arrived outside of Dr. Walker's house. It was a nice home, three stories, brown brick stone with a large, wrap around porch. The architectural work was beautiful and, it reminded me of some of the buildings in St. Louis. There were large, beautifully framed windows but all the blinds and curtains were pulled closed—not surprising. Closed blinds are the only windows anyone ever want to peep through, anyway.

"How about you pretend you're selling girl scout cookies?" Kiddy teased.

"I don't think I should pretend that I'm selling anything," she muttered under her breath.

"We'll just tell him we are journalists doing a piece on Old Dominion and would like to talk to him a little bit about his days there," I suggested.

"Three reporters about a failed, half burned, abandoned asylum from twenty years ago?" Kiddy raised an eyebrow.

"Do you have a better idea, Kiddy?" I asked, frustrated.

"How about the truth? Tell him we're private investigators, we know Franklin Butler has killed several people, we know he used to be his doctor, and maybe he can shed some light on where he is? We don't mention the asylum, we don't mention Bristol General, or how several patients arrived burned and left without so much as a notice, we don't mention that he was a weirdo who did experiments on patients. We're just straight forward. Dr. Walker might be crazy but he isn't an idiot. He's going to see through half-baked attempts to outwit him."

"It seems like a risky move, Flynn," Lexi said.

It was Kiddy's call. Kiddy had a dozen cases like these.

"Okay fine, we'll try that," I replied. Without leaving Lexi any room to rebuttal, I opened the passenger door of Kiddy's Volvo, and marched up to the dark green door that separated the rich brown brick. Kiddy and Lexi were one step behind me, and when I knocked hard on the door, I felt the breaths of all three of us freeze, as the latch on the other side of the door flicked over the moment I knocked.

The creaking sound the door made as it barely popped open sang loudly—old houses have loud voices. On the other side of the large, green door, stood a man no taller than 5'8. He had black, thick rimmed glasses that looked like he'd owned years before they came back in a retro hipster fashion. He wore a plum-colored sweater and gray pants, and behind his glasses, large, darting green eyes surveyed the three of us.

"Yes, can I help you, strangers?" his words were off putting but his voice was very soft, warm, inviting. It was the kind of voice you wanted to love and that's exactly why you hated it so much.

"Um," Kiddy hesitated—it wasn't like him.

"We're reporters for *Bristol Daily,* and we're doing a throw-back issue, talking about historical events and things of that nature that have happened in the past thirty years. We're doing a piece on Old Dominion Asylum, and since you were one of the head doctors who ran the facility we were hoping you could talk to us a little bit about your time there and how it affected your practice once the asylum was unfortunately burned?" I said, smoothly as possible—you learn to lie when you're hustling a customer out of a good deal. It reminded me of my more domestic cases. It was hard for me to believe that over three months ago I didn't seem to care about anything but getting the highest dollar out of a desperate soul.

Dr. Walker smiled, his lips tight and never parting, his eyes sparkled, I could see it, even through the glasses. He surveyed each of us again, and without losing a hint of the smile, he shook his head.

"Nope, you're lying. Try again," but instead of pausing for one of us to speak, he slammed the door.

"Um," escaped Lexi's mouth—appropriate. The three of us shared a look of uncertainty but Kiddy's quickly changed to anger as he balled his fist, leaned forward and banged on the door once more.

"I didn't come all the way from home for this little man to slam a door in my face." The door flung open once more, but the look on Dr. Walker's face remained calm, almost pleasant and inviting.

"Yes?" he asked, politely.

"Listen, we're not from some newspaper like my very absent minded partner here says we are," Kiddy said. Walker shot uncomfortable eyes to me, and then back to Kiddy. "The truth is, Dr. Walker, we are private investigators. Well, two of us are, this one here is a client and she keeps following us because apparently she doesn't have a job or anything more important to do," Kiddy said.

"I told you earlier I am a travel agent slash musician," Lexi hissed, bitterly.

"Anyway, we're investigating a string of deaths we believe to be committed by Franklin Butler, an old patient of yours at Old Dominion," Kiddy started again. "If it is okay with you, we'd like to talk to you about your time with, or around him. It may not seem like much but trust us, it will really help us figure out where he went. We're just trying to get him in prison or in a hospital—where ever he belongs, it is not the streets," Kiddy finished.

I was surprised, like Lexi, who literally took a small step backwards whilst listening to my partner speak. Flynn Kiddy wasn't a charmer, and at times he could be very annoying to be around, but he was good at what he did—and it is a shame there were moments in our time together that I let that slip my mind.

Dr. Walker paused, squinted his eyes despite the fact he was wearing those ridiculous glasses, and nodded his head. "Yes, I remember Franklin." His eyes darted over to me. "You—I know you, don't I?"

"No," I said, quickly, keeping a strong gaze with him. "I don't frequent asylums."

"No, I know you. You're taller now, stronger, and you clearly have some sort of five o'clock shadow-don't-own-a-razor-type thing going on," he said, as he rubbed his smooth face, while gesturing to my scruffy one. "I don't forget faces, though, never have. I've seen you before."

Kiddy looked at me, smiled and smirked, then gestured back towards Dr. Walker.

"What?" I asked, defensively.

"Just tell him," Kiddy said, nonchalantly.

"What do you mean just tell him?" I questioned.

"Just tell him who you are," Kiddy said. It was starting to sound like he was bored with the whole thing, already.

"I don't see what that has to do with anything," I stated.

"Oh my gosh you are so difficult," Lexi started, louder than Kiddy and myself. "His name is Grayson Grant. Grant probably rings a bell because there was another doctor that worked under you at the asylum. Her name was Elizabeth Grant. This is her son, Grayson. Well, apparently it is Edmond Grayson, but he doesn't go by Edmond. It's just Grayson. Grayson Grant, meet Dr. Walker. There. Now everyone is up to speed." Lexi was a wildcard. Dr. Walker cut his eyes over to me. He sized me up, eyes bobbing up and down like basketballs—as if they were organic lie detectors.

"You are Elizabeth's son?" his smile grew wider.

"I am," I said, in a muffled voice.

"I was sorry to hear about her passing," Dr. Walker said, his voice soft and warm. "Do you believe Franklin was also responsible for your mother's death?"

"I know he is," I said, firmly.

"Then please, come inside and have tea with me and we'll talk about it," Dr. Walker said as soon as I answered him. He opened the door wider, and gestured me inside. Kiddy and Lexi started to follow but Dr. Walker halted them at the threshold. "Excuse me, I'm sorry, I am only inviting Mr. Grant inside the house at this time," he said, in such a voice you would think he was offering all of them the wonderful opportunity to *not* enter his home.

"Excuse me? Where he goes I go, buddy," Kiddy said, angrily.

323

"You'll have to understand, mister—I'm sorry, I don't believe I caught your name?" Dr. Walker implied, his serpent smile made me cringe—the worst kind of grin is one that takes yours away.

"Flynn Kiddy," he said, with pride.

"Hi, Mr. Flynn Kiddy, as I'm sure you can understand I did not expect visitors today and also as you can see I'm a bit startled by the prospect. I do not often entertain and inviting Mr. Grant in my home here is more than I would normally do but since his mother's death happened because of a patient of ours, I feel extremely responsible and would like to attempt an apology I should've delivered twenty years ago," Dr. Walker spoke with quickness and charm. It was easy to like him if you didn't already know how horrible he was inside.

"It is fine, Kiddy," I said, turning to my boss and Lexi—both of whom looked disturbed by it all. "You guys can wait in the car or something. I just want to interview Dr. Walker real quickly and we'll be out of his hair. Go get a bite to eat. Or tell Lexi one of those so-called jokes you tell," I patted Kiddy on the shoulder, to reassure him that I was okay with this plan, even if he wasn't, and entered into Dr. Walker's house. Kiddy and Lexi were dumb struck, and I could hear the blunt words of Kiddy and Lexi, most of them did not need repeating

"Come, come, sit down, please. I'll just step into the kitchen and put some water on to boil," Dr. Walker said, as he gestured to a golden armchair that sat beside a glass end-table. The chair squeaked as I sat down. There was a smell I couldn't ignore—cigars and air freshener, a cocktail of contradiction. I could hear him rummaging around in the kitchen, and it gave me a moment to observe the sitting room in which the doctor had left me. The walls were green—a pea green, actually, with a gold and white trim. There were several antiques, cabinets and hutches. A brown ottoman sat in front of me, and that's when I noticed the golden shag carpet beneath my feet. I chuckled to myself, wondering when the last time the house had been decorated.

"I hope you like tea!" He called from the kitchen.

"I'm more of a coffee man," I said.

Liam Walker entered the room, slowly and patiently, made his way to a brown armchair that sat adjacent to me.

."It should be ready shortly. I stopped drinking coffee about ten years ago," Walker stated. "It's terrible for you, you know, medically speaking."

I shrugged. "Helps calm my nerves, I guess," I said for small talk.

"Oh," he started, and he paused as if he were contemplating the words. I couldn't really follow his train of thought, but then he held up a finger, as if he were asking me to wait for a moment and then he reached into his sweater pocket and, to my surprise, withdrew a small handgun. Before I could panic at the thought of my life ending, he pointed the pistol at his own temple. "I hope you're not a nervous person."

Chapter Twelve

Malpractice

Dr. Walker sat, not six feet from me, holding a gold plated handgun at his temple, as calmly and elegantly as if he were holding his teacup.

"Dr. Walker!" I said, in shock. "What are you doing?"

"It's a beautiful piece, isn't it, Mr. Grant? Gold plated. It's a replica of a piece I saw in a museum once. I called up a gunsmith friend of mine and had one made for my own enjoyment. The one I saw was a pre-World War II model PP presentation pistol for King Carol II of Romania," Walker explained, as if everything happening in the room was completed natural.

"Yeah, yeah, it's beautiful—why is it against your head?" I asked, quickly.

"Oh well you see," Walker laughed. "See, I plan to kill myself."

"Why?"

"Well, you see, Mr. Grant, my life has come to a point where I no longer believe I can continue on under any charade that I can avoid past sins—and now must either face prison or face a bullet. If your investigation has lead you to Franklin then it has certainly lead you to me. You've seen me,

327

how I live, I think it is safe to assume I would not do well in prison."

"Okay, fair enough, I'm just here to ask questions, though."

"You are here because you know I have secrets, too, don't you? Don't lie, I have a gun to my head and it can't get much worse than this," Walker said.

"Okay, yes, I know a little bit about what went on at the asylum. I know you did experiments or something, had an entire floor devoted to it. And I know you had a lot of patients, including Franklin Butler, who were eager to get out."

"Yes," Walker said, nodding his head. "Yes, they had those symbols they carved into their arms. The Native American emblem, resembling their teepees. A temporary home. It was very clever, I give them that—they were disturbed people but very bright. Now if you'll excuse me, I have no idea how loud this gun will be as I've never fired this weapon before."

"Wait!" I yelled, hoping he would hesitate on the trigger. He did, and sighed as he did so.

"Suicide isn't as easy as I'm making it look and I would very much like to get on with this while I still have the courage to do so—do you mind?"

"Yes, yes I mind. Look, you can blow your brains out all over this carpet—which is ugly as sin by the way—but answer me a few questions first, okay? Go out on a high note," I challenged him. He stared at me for too long. His eyes were small, his lips were thin, tightly stretched. Finally, he lowered the gold-cased gun onto the arm of his chair and nodded slowly.

"That is a fair request I cannot deny that, Mr. Grant. Please, continue with your line of questioning." At that moment, the hissing of the hot water from the kitchen sounded and I nearly jumped out of my seat. "Well, that's just poor timing, isn't it?" he said with a chuckle, and stood from his chair and exited back into the kitchen.

He wasn't gone long, soon Dr. Walker was back with two burgundy mugs, one in which he handed to me as quickly as possible. "Be careful, it's hot."

"You're not what I expected," I admitted as I sipped the tea out of politeness. I wasn't a tea drinker, at all, actually.

"Did you expect a mad scientist?" he said, almost giddy.

"I did, yeah," I said, not entirely sure I was wrong. "From everything I read and heard," I admitted.

"I won't try to deny it," he said, interrupting me. "I was a little mad, back in those days. I had a series of complicated experimentations going on at the time that I knew I wouldn't get a unanimous vote of approval from the board, so I decided to keep it hush, hush under the guise of a pre-approved program."

"*Tomorrow's Minds*," I answered, filling in the mad-lib gaps he was leaving open for me.

"Yes, excellent that you know your stuff, Mr. Grant," he said, like it was a game show and I was contestant number one. "*Tomorrow's Minds* was supposed to be a way of conditioning the patients to enhance their functions and make them stable creatures that could walk and talk in the real world without our help. Therefore, the only patients I could use were patients that, on paper, gave us plausible reason to believe they had conditions that could be tamed. Unfortunately, those patients had promising futures and couldn't be disturbed. The board would never have it. So I thought I would try my luck with some of the more, wayward patients," Walker said, leaning back in his chair after sipping his tea. "So I threw out the board approved therapies and conducted my own—privately. It worked—or it seemed to for a time. It wasn't as bad as all that, there weren't any ice pick lobotomies, or anything of that nature," he said, nonchalantly.

"What did you do?" I asked.

"Conditioning is very strange, Mr. Grant, and my methods were strange too, I'll admit. There were, let us call them, techniques I used. Pain, starvation, fear, manipulation, used most of these together too, to find new ways of controlling the mental handicaps from within," Walker started. "There was one patient in particular I will never forget. He checked himself into Old Dominion Asylum. Said he had these sexual urges that wouldn't go away. Bad ones, the kind for people he shouldn't have them for—children, Mr. Grant," there was a proud smile on his face now. There wasn't much regret—not really.

"Now, he agreed to all these treatments. I forced a negative conditioning into his brain. When he thought of children, he was to be punished. He would be hit, or denied food, or strung up in chains for the rest of the patients to yell at him, scream at him, and scold him for his urges."

"That's sick," I said quickly and bitterly. Walker shrugged.

"Be that as it may, when he was discharged from the hospital, he left confidently that he would not do anything of the sort ever again. I heard from him a couple of years later, he was still cured—no setbacks, no temptations. Whenever he saw someone that was to his fancy, he would suddenly feel the stomach pains of hunger or the humiliation of pain."

"And you did this with a hospital full of mentally unstable people?" I asked.

"Well, you act as if all of them are like Franklin Butler, your serial killer. Most of the patients, even Mr. Butler, wasn't all that violent when they first came to Old Dominion. Your little-to-no-knowledge of the mentally handicapped is very alarming, Mr. Grant. I hope you don't shudder when you find yourself around these people. They're all around us, with various forms of disease it would be a shame to know you look at them all as criminals," he said, matter-of-factly, as if I were the one to be ashamed.

"My only problem with the mentally impaired is that they're dropped off at places like Old Dominion, and allowed to be tampered with by people like you," I said, losing my cool. Kiddy was always better at this—too bad it wasn't his mother.

"My work? And your mother's work?" Walker said, a little too pleased with himself. "Because, it should be of some note that although Franklin was only in my program for a brief while, he was under the care of Dr. Elizabeth Grant for much longer. In fact, I discharged him from my program within the month—he just wasn't fit for the therapy, his cognitive capabilities were too wavering. However... Mr. Butler, along with several other patients, spent a large amount of three years under your mother's care."

"What are you implying, Dr. Walker?" I asked—teeth pushed in friction, anger filled.

"Mr. Grant I'm not implying anything. You simply made an assumption about me and I just want you to know the facts: Your mother spent a lot more time with Mr. Butler than myself. Now, does that excuse me for my wrongdoings? Of course not. It's caught up with me. I know it. I knew it in the moments before my hospital went up in flames."

"Moments before?" I asked.

"Yes," Walker said, with a sly grin—like he'd just told me the answer to a secret riddle. Maybe he did.

"You did it. You set the asylum on fire," I stated. The doctor nodded and stroked the handgun that lay on the armchair beside him.

"I knew it had all gone to hell, so I thought I would send it there in flames. I wasn't counting on the impressive response time by the local fire department. I was lucky to have gotten away with it."

"All the evidence, everything about what you were working on down there," I went on. "You let it burn up in the asylum. I've been back there, you were on the basement floor."

"I made sure my work went up in flames. Now, are we trying to analyze my own wrongs or are we trying to catch a serial killer, here?" Walker asked.

"Do you know where to find him?" I asked, bluntly. Dr. Walker tipped the last drop of his tea, from the looks of how he titled the cup nearly atop his nose. He savored it, I guess he planned for it to be his last cup. It was intriguing, to watch a man interrupt with life when he planned for death to be a swift and soon step. It was eerie how peaceful it seemed.

"If I knew where to find him, Mr. Grant, I would have already ended his life," Walker said as nonchalantly as every other alarmingly calm sentence he'd spoken in my presence.

"He's a monster," I stated.

"He's worse than a monster, Mr. Grant."

"So if you knew how dangerous he was, why didn't you say something sooner? If you knew he was the Shoestring Killer, why didn't you come forward?"

"We already went over how much I didn't want to go to prison, correct?"

"You just let this go on, knowing who he was?"

"You can point your finger at me all you want to, Mr. Grant. I am not the monster. Nor did I create him."

"When did you know?" I asked.

"I knew his obsession with being able to tie his own shoes. I knew his anger over meticulous things, like being forced to wear the asylum's velcro variety. Who gets that violent over shoes? I knew that there was a potential danger within him, that's why he didn't survive my program. That's why I gave him to your mother for care in the first place. I knew what was lying within Franklin Butler. Although, I will admit—at the time the murders started, I wasn't sure he was capable of being that violent. Not at first," he trailed off for a moment. "I don't know where to find him. I don't know how he gets away with it. If you came here looking for those answers, I'm sorry," the smile was gone now. There were only intense eyes that didn't blink, only watched me.

I stood from my chair, sat the cup of tea down that I'd barely touched, and moved for the door. "Thanks for the tea. I think we're done here. Thanks for nothing, Dr. Walker. Do me a favor, if you blow your brains out, at least write down a note. I don't want to be a suspect in your murder case, if there would even be one." I reached the doorknob, disappointed my visit turned out to be a dead-end that got me no closer to finding Butler. I placed my hand on the golden knob and was about to pull the door open, ready to admit my defeat to Kiddy and Lexi, when Liam Walker called out with the most intriguing statement he had uttered since I entered his home.

"I can give you the why."

"What?" I said, turning towards him. "You can?" I let go of the knob and entering back into the sitting room.

335

"I can explain why he went for your mother, and why he went for the poor women he chose after that."

"You're serious?"

"Mr. Grant this would be a very poor time to lie, wouldn't it?"

"Then what is it?"

"Come on, I'll show you," he said. He stood from the chair, tucking his gun into his sweater pocket.

"Yeah, I'm not sure I'm too keen on going anywhere with you, pal," I stated, flatly. He waved his hand. I could smell cigars again.

"No, no, please come on. I just would like to show you my basement. I have stacks of information I've saved from the hospital, or accumulated over the years. I think I even have something of your mother's, if I'm not mistaken," he said, matter-of-factly. "It explains everything."

I was hesitant, but needed what information I could get. I could feel the phone in my pocket buzzing. No doubt Kiddy or Lexi asking for an update. I nodded my head slowly, unsure of if I were making the right choice. Giddily, Dr. Walker escorted me through his house. It was similar to the sitting room, filled with furniture one would likely find in an antique shop, the hallway was lined with wood paneling and the floor changed from a shag carpet to a vinyl flooring.

At the edge of the hallway, just near the kitchen, was a yellowed door. Eagerly, Dr. Walker opened the door and offered me to walk down the steps first. I refused, and Walker must've seen the sense in it because he didn't insist any further. He walked down the steps and I followed, slowly and hesitantly. The basement looked like a doctor's office, mementos, no doubt, from his former practice. Walker's numerous degrees were decorated on one wall, with several stacks of white boxes underneath. The basement was fairly open, once we got past the staircase. There were a few surgical utensils and equipment which disturbed me, considering he wasn't a surgeon. On a mantel place, oddly placed on the far wall, were numerous awards and photographs—presumably of the doctor's career.

"I believe the item of which I was speaking is in one of these boxes. Please give me just a moment to locate it, okay?" Dr. Walker said, cheerfully.

I reached into my pocket to retrieve my phone which had started buzzing again. I had multiple text messages from Lexi: *"Grayson, where are you?" "Get your butt out here." "Seriously, if you don't answer me back, Kiddy and I are going to bust the door down."* I almost laughed, picturing the two of them becoming some kind of duo. I sent a text back telling her to hold off on her breaking and entering urges, because I was close to uncovering something that might help. I don't know how truthful I was being with her. I don't know how truthful I was being with myself. The *why* factor rarely matters in cases like these. *He was beaten by his father, repeatedly* or *he was bullied at school* or *he watched his parents die in front of him.* The *why* someone does something is never usually a good way to find someone. It does, however, give something to the people they hurt. I don't know if it is closure—but it is something.

"Here it is! That was quick!" Walker laughed subtly. "Now, Mr. Grant," he said. I turned to see him returning back to me with a box under one arm. "I have some good news and some great news."

"Okay," I said, suspiciously.

"The good news is, I've located your mothers things, and not only do I give them to you as a parting gift, I believe they will shed some light in otherwise dark places," Walker said.

"That sounds pretty good, actually, Dr. Walker," I said. "What's the great news?"

"The great news is, I've decided before I depart from this green Earth, that I might have one last go at a small hobby I use to have in that asylum basement of mine," he said as he turned his back to me for a moment. I couldn't quite see what he was doing, but before I had time to question it, he turned around and faced me. His smile was wide—the *all your teeth* kind of wide. He reached into his sweater pocket, and withdrew the gold plated pistol—this time with a silencer attached at the end of the barrel. "Don't worry, Mr. Grant. It will only hurt for a moment." His reassurance sent a chill up my spine and before I could react in any other way, the gun had sounded, the bullet had left the barrel, and I collapsed on the doctor's floor.

Chapter Thirteen

Nice

There was only blackness when sound returned to me, though I didn't understand what sounds I was hearing. It was repetitive, though. The same sound, at the same volume, the same frequency.

"Julius," I finally understood. That's when I was able to realize I could also feel things. I felt something soft, but with weight, move across my torso. It wasn't until then that I suddenly felt the pain from my right shoulder. "Julius, get down from there!" I heard his voice, again. It was complicated what I heard and what I could understand. I was awake, I knew I was awake, now—but my eyes were closed, and I wasn't sure how that was possible. I was starting to remember but I was also forgetting. *What was that name?* I moved my body and suddenly felt cold hands against my stomach. I was no longer wearing my shirt.

"There, there, Mr. Grant please be patient with me, alright? You have a minor flesh wound. I told you it would only hurt for a moment, didn't I? Trust me, you'd be in a lot more pain now if I hadn't administered a healthy dose of painkillers and sedatives." I opened my mouth to speak, but something inaudible came out. "Oh, I'm very very sorry Mr.

Grant, I'm afraid you haven't gained control of your patterns of speech yet. The sedatives are wearing off, just give it a few moments. I must say, I am surprised you passed out. After all, it is only a flesh wound."

I recognized the voice. I knew it was Dr. Walker, I was just having trouble remembering how I got into this position.

"I told you that you'd be okay. I am an expert marksman. Remember when I told you I had this pistol commissioned? The commission was to an old army buddy of mine. I was briefly in the service. I didn't do much good, I'm not the kind of man that needs to be protecting our country but it paid for my medical schooling so—why not? Turns out the only thing I was ever any good at in the army was shooting. I won a competition we had on base. You know, just fun stuff. I suppose it was misleading when I said I hadn't fired this gun before—if it makes you feel any better, I wasn't lying," Dr. Walker's voice clashed with the sounds of metal and vibrations under my body.

"Lexi," I was finally able to mutter

"Lexi? Is that the young woman you arrived here with?" Walker asked. I couldn't answer, only repeat her name again.

"Well, you sent your friends outside a text message just before I shot you, saying that you were getting much needed information and to not bother us—thank you for that. That made all of this a lot easier. Gives us more time. I went ahead and sent one more though, just to be sure we would have our privacy," Dr. Walker said. "Julius, get down!" I heard again. I was finally able to pull my eyelids open. I could feel a crust break when they parted, like the result of a long sleep after a bitter cry. The world was watery—fuzzy, didn't make sense. I blinked, and blinked again. There was that soft feeling again, a soft heavy feeling landed on my chest this time. I saw a black blob in front of me. I couldn't see, but I could tell it was alive.

"This is the stupidest cat I've ever seen," Dr. Walker said, picking up the cat and tossing it back to the ground. "And I've seen a lot of stupid cats."

"Irusan," I muttered, because at the time, somehow it all connected.

"Irusan," Dr. Walker muttered. "That sounds familiar. Is that some sort of folklore? British or Irish folklore, correct?"

"Rodgers," I stressed, though it was hard to speak, still.

"I'm afraid I have no idea what you're speaking about, Mr. Grant. Don't worry, I'm sure you'll make sense to us both in no time."

342

I felt some pressure on my shoulder, a surge of pain and I let out a yell. "Now, now, Mr. Grant...I must ask you to keep it down. You're on too many painkillers to feel where I shot you, and the pressure I'm placing on you, you know, to ensure that I bandage you correctly, is just that—pressure.

"Lexi," I said again. "Kiddy," I added.

"Your friends will have to wait, Mr. Grant. I am not going to kill you, don't worry. This is, however, a sound proof basement. The silencer was just for good measure and, if I am being honest, because I've wanted to use it ever since I bought it. There is little chance they heard the gunfire or any attempts to contact them vocally. Although I wouldn't need soundproofing for the latter, now would I?" He laughed at his own, sick joke. "I wasn't lying to you, though, Mr. Grant, I do have something that belongs to your mother."

I could hear the clamoring of Dr. Walker as he shuffled through the box, my eyes had adjusted now and I could see. I was lying, strapped down, to a stretcher in the middle of his basement. By my left, was a tray of surgical tools, in which I'm sure he used to pull the bullet from my shoulder that he put there in the first place. I started to hope the painkillers wore off so I could tell the good doctor where to go.

"Ah, here we are," Dr. Walker said, as he turned around and held up a small, 5' by 3' notebook. "Your mother's journal," he said as he flopped the leathery, worn black book onto my stomach, as if it were a coffee table. He reached into his sweater pocket to retrieve his glasses once more. "This is quite exciting, seeing this book again. It's been a while since I've read it. I don't usually like to read books more than two or three times but, it sure is hard to resist the classics," he said, and his smile seemed mocking, now.

"Let me read to you some of my favorite passages, okay?" he said, eagerly. "Now this one is the first one, it seems as though this journal was to be some sort of account of her process at Old Dominion. She wasn't consistent with her writing but, when she decides to write in it, it sure is juicy. Now, where was I?" Walker adjusted his glasses and glared at the journal. "Ah, yes," a smile erupted. "*My dream job has arrived. Oh, how I never thought I would see this day! All those years of hard work. Tears on satin sheets, midnight phone calls from my dorm room to my mother's house, waking her up from her chronic pain long enough to tell me: It's okay, you're going to make it! Oh how I wish she could see me now. I wish she could see that I've made it, and a charming place called Old Dominion Asylum is exactly who to thank. Dr. Liam Walker and the wonderful medical board*

344

of Old Dominion Asylum has welcomed me to be part of their psychiatric team," *he* snapped the journal shut. "Well, you're welcome, poor Dr. Grant. Now this was the 28th of June, 1993 so you were just a child when she joined the staff," Walker explained.

"There's a lot of hope there, in that first paragraph," Walker went on. "Let us choose another passage, shall we?" he flipped through the pages, his fingers dancing on the edge of the paper. "Ah yes, here we go," he started. "This is from early '95: 'Franklin experiences several different mental illnesses, including Schizoaffective Disorder, and a serious Impulse Control problem. I often wonder if there is some kind of trauma induced disorder, but much of his history before coming to us is unknown. He, through proper medication and care, has become a very excellent patient. I'm very proud of the progress he's made. He's actually quite adorable," Dr. Walker said, finishing the quotation.

He looked over at me, like he just caught my hand in the cookie-jar. The doctor smiles more than anyone should.

"Did you hear that, Mr. Grant? She finds your killer adorable."

"Franklin," I muttered.

"Yes, yes, Franklin," Walker said, pandering me. "But you want to know more about him, yes? The why factor? The doctor stepped away from the makeshift operating table, long enough to retrieve a stool on which he sat down upon, while he adjusted his glasses.

"Well, let's work backwards, shall we?" He held the journal close in hand. "There's a simple reason why he chose the victims he chose."

"Nothing in common," I said. I could feel myself start to make sense of my reality. Either the pain medication was giving out, or I was adjusting to it.

"Very good, Mr. Grant, these women seemingly have nothing in common—not age, race, height, weight, profession, social circles, politics, nothing. However," he paused, dramatically as he tapped the cover of the journal. "We *can* connect Franklin to your mother and considering she was the first victim and he traveled all the way to her home from Bristol, I would say that at the very least the assassination of your mother was at least partially purposeful," the doctor said as he moved towards his surgical utensils.

"What are you d-doing?" my words slurred.

"Oh, I'm preparing my tools for *my* fun, after we solve your case." As the sedatives began to wear down, my anxiety rose. Dr. Walker was going to help me, alright, but only moments before he kills me—or worse.

"You-u c-can't."

"Don't worry. Like I told you, I won't kill you, Mr. Grant. I never killed Franklin, and I kept him down here for an unprecedented amount time. I'm simply altering some functions within your brain. I can prepare you for the world of *tomorrow*." Dr. Walker was more mentally unstable than any of his patients, and there I was—in his lion's den.

"Now, as we said, we have blondes, social workers, African Americans, Koreans, and twenty year olds and forty year olds and there's just not a lot of consistency with poor Mr. Butler," Dr. Walker said. It didn't matter to me anymore, though, I couldn't focus on the why behind the reason when I was staring at my own death in his very smile-clad face.

"Shall we look at another page in your mother's journal?" the doctor asked rhetorically, flipping through the leather-bound book. "'Franklin is even letting me put on his shoes for him, although he refuses to attach the velcro straps. His personality is so vibrant, so energetic. He's come a long way from the quiet loner he once was when I met him almost a year ago," Dr. Walker quoted from my mother's personal words. "Well, it sounds like Franklin worked very well for your mother. He never worked so well for me, even when I wasn't well," he gestured to my being strapped to a stretcher, "you know, doing stuff like this."

"She was a g-good doctor," I said, I tried to wiggle out of the restraints Walker had me in but they were harnessed too tightly, and I was too weak from the drugs and pain from the bullet.

"That she was," Walker agreed. "So let us get down to the brass tax. What is left, Mr. Grant? Hmm? Use those *detective skills* of yours, and tell me what is left here. These victims have seemingly nothing to do with one another, yet Franklin clearly chose them for a reason, didn't he?"

The room seemed to vibrate to me. The wooden walls inhaled and exhaled like they were not walls at all but ocean waves, and soon Walker and I would be swept up by the tide.

"My mother," I said slowly, forcing my brain to stay in reality as much as possible. "She was so kind," I pushed out. "Kind to him," I added.

"Yes," Walker said, eagerly.

"Carol Hanna," I said, thinking about Jack's mother. There was nothing in common between our mothers. They were just nice women who took care of Jack and I the best way they knew how to do, and as I thought about these things, I assumed the answer and projected it out loudly as my groggy voice would allow. "They're nice."

"Bingo, Mr. Grant! These women were nice to Franklin Butler. They were nice. Starting with your mother—just trying to put on his velcro shoes. At least, that's how it started. The rest of the victims—just women who tried to help out a burn victim, or a man who can't keep his own stupid shoes on his stupid feet," Walker went on. The phrase *burn victim* vibrated through my head.

"Why?" I said.

"Why would he harm the nice ones? Well, it started with your mother," he said as he flopped the journal down once more, onto my chest. "The why is terribly important, isn't it, Grayson Grant? We know why he picked the ones he did but why did he target nice women? Let us discover it," he said, gleefully as he flipped through my mother's journal.

The basement door broke open, and had I not known better, I would've sworn it screamed as the hinges clanged down the wooden steps. Dr. Walker's face went pale, and then nearly green as he realized my company wasn't as patient as he'd hoped they would be. Kiddy and Lexi raced down the stairs, Kiddy already leaping off the landing by the time Lexi reached the bottom. Walker hesitated, but when he decided to reach for the closest sharp object—a scalpel—Kiddy had already arrived at the doctor and flung a fat, balled up fist into his nose.

"Kiddy," I said—the experience was somewhat sobering. Lexi arrived on the scene and assisted Kiddy in getting me off of the stretcher.

"What happened?" Lexi stressed, stepping over Doctor Walker as she helped me stand. I shook my head.

"Walker is a nut, that's what happened," I said—my knees feeling like Jell-O.

"How did you know to break in?" I asked—my legs felt like mush.

"That last text you sent," Kiddy said. "You ended it with 'thanks,' and that just didn't settle right with me," Kiddy scoffed. "Let's get out of here, now," he said, putting one of my arms around his shoulders

"Wait," I said, as I paused to bend down and pick up the journal that had fallen to the floor.

"What's that?" Lexi asked, deciding that now she would be my support, as she put an arm around my torso.

"Answers," I replied.

Julius brushed up against my leg and purred. I looked down at him and suddenly felt a great swell of pity. I thought about the cats I saw, hanging like ornaments, in the stand that Rodgers lived in.

"Grab him," I said, gesturing down at Julius. Lexi bent down and picked him up. He clung to her, instantly. She smiled, resting her cheek gently against his ear.

"Mr. Grant," Walker said, rising slowly from his punch from Kiddy.

"Be careful," I whispered to Kiddy, who started to move forward. "He has a gun in his sweater pocket."

"No, no," Walker said, waving his hands. "I'm not going to try to kill anyone, I told you that, Mr. Grant. I know I have to pay for my sins. Just remember something," he said. "I'm not the only one with sin," he said, smiling. None of us said a word to him. We marched up the stairs and what once felt like walking in three feet of water started to feel like land, again. As we got to the sitting room, I felt an eerie shiver up my spine, like Walker was going to come out of the catacombs, grab Lexi, or Kiddy, and this was going to start all over, again.

It didn't happen, though. We made it to the front door, and as Kiddy reached for the knob, we heard the faint sound of a gunshot. I felt bad, because I chuckled, but it was only because I wished I had one more moment with Dr. Walker, so I could tell him that his basement wasn't all together soundproof.

Chapter Fourteen

Home

The ride home was quiet. I filled them in on what happened, and while they were trying to piece it all together, I was busy thumbing through my mother's journal to find the answer as to why Franklin might target friendly women—and men, considering we still had no idea if Joseph "Jody" Farmer was also Franklin's victim. And if he was—why change the way he tied the knots? Why be so sloppy about it?

"So wait," Lexi said, running her fingers through her hair.

"He was going to do what to you?"

"Beats me," I shrugged. "Give me a lobotomy, I guess." I couldn't get Walker's words out of my head. I didn't want to believe he had my mother's journal. How did he have something so personal? But every word of it sounded like her. The way she would talk, the things she knew about Alan or myself, her handwriting. The passages about Franklin or her patients were few and far between."

"What about the cat?" Kiddy asked from the driver's seat, seemingly unmoved by the fact I was just in grave danger moments before.

"And he did it because they were nice to him?" Lexi asked, still confused by that part.

352

"It doesn't make sense to me, either," I said.

"But what are we going to do about the cat?" Kiddy asked, annoyed as Julius tried to sit on his shoulder whilst he drove.

"Did he not give you any idea about how to find him though?" Lexi continued to quiz me.

"He burned the asylum," I started. "He wanted the evidence of everything he'd done gone. But he still had a box full of my mother's things and he still had a lot of his equipment from the hospital. No way he just waltzed out the front door with all of that stuff," I said as I thought out loud.

"Someone please do something with this cat," Kiddy sighed.

"I don't think we looked deep enough," I said. I flipped through my mother's journal. I caught a scene that disturbed me: A kiss shared between her and Jody. My stomach turned. Another page, the second to last, as a matter of fact, in my mother's journal caught my eye. It made me stop. It has somehow become deeply folded in the binding of the book, as if it were a page that was to be remain hidden. I read the lines over, and then read them again. I braced the book in my hand tightly. I felt a swirl in my stomach again, the same time I felt my head spin again. A mixture of vertigo and vomit. "We didn't look deeply enough at all."

"I need your help," I said, hours later, standing in the tree stand clearing where Walt Rodger's hut sat. Rodgers was sitting on a boulder outside the home, and as I bent down and placed Julius the cat on the ground, the feline went directly for him. "I am choosing to ignore how you almost killed me at the asylum if you're willing to forget how scared I have made you," I stated. Rodgers smiled a bright, dopey smile and scooped the animal up in his lanky, pale arms.

"Hello kitty," Rodgers said, seemingly ignoring my statement. Lexi and Kiddy stood several feet back. Lexi, because she was disgusted by the sight, and Kiddy because he was well, Kiddy. "What's his name?" Rodgers asked.

"Julius, I guess," I said, nonchalantly.

"Julius," he said with glee.

"He belonged to Dr. Walker," I said. Rodger's smile vanished instantly. He almost looked repulsed by the cat at that point.

"Cat needs a good home now. Walker is dead," I explained. Rodger's neck nearly snapped as he looked up to me so quickly.

"Did you kill him?" he asked, softly. I shook my head.

"He did that, himself."

"What do you want from me?" Rodgers asked, as he stroked Julius' fur continuously.

354

"You were in Walker's program. I know you know that asylum all too well."

"And?" Rodgers rocked back and forth.

"I think the Shoestring Killer is hiding in the asylum somewhere—somewhere Walker use to hide his experiments and everything he wanted to keep when the place burned."

"The basement," Rodgers said.

"No, it has to be somewhere else. We've seen the basement. Police have seen the basement. No sign of anyone living there," I said impatiently. Rodgers smiled an unwarranted smile.

"I know where to look."

"Will you show us? Will you show me?" I asked.

"It's Jody? Jody the music man killed these people?"

"No, Jody is dead," I answered. "The Shoestring Killer is Franklin Butler." Rodgers' smile faded. He looked down at the cat.

"Franklin was my friend. But, he took my cats. Franklin always hated my cats."

"Will you please help us?" I was getting desperate. He took a moment to respond—maybe too long, long enough that I wondered if his eventual agreement was to be trusted. He agreed, though, and I was too desperate for someone who could help speed things up.

"Okay then," I said to Walt Rodgers as he arose from the boulder where he sat. "Be prepared, Irusan. You're going home."

"Why do we always have to come here at night," Lexi complained, as Kiddy pulled the car up to Old Dominion Asylum. Lexi made it sound like our visits to the asylum were a regular occurrence. Still, it was easy to understand her position. It had been a long day and the sky was falling on us—appropriate. If Rodgers could find him now, though, I couldn't live with giving Franklin another free night where he had the potential to hurt people.

"Is everyone ready?" I said, turning back from Kiddy's passenger seat to look at my team: Kiddy, myself, Lexi, Walt "Irusan" Rodgers, and his newest cat, Julius. It wasn't the team I started out with, at all. I thought momentarily about letting Alan in on our newly found piece of information but I decided against it. I wanted him safe. It was bad enough Lexi and Kiddy were with me. I wouldn't have anyone else die on my watch—not like Jolene.

"As ready as we're gonna get, Grayson," Kiddy said, nodding toward me. I gave him something of a smile, back. It was an oddly warm feeling, coming from Kiddy. Perhaps killer hunting can bring out the human in people like Flynn Kiddy and myself. There was still a chance for hope.

"This could be nothing," I informed. "Just because we think we have all the answers doesn't mean that, and even if we do, it doesn't mean we'll catch him here. We just have to take it for what it is a chance."

"What if the police find out?" Lexi asked.

"They might be petty enough to arrest you anyway," Kiddy suggested.

"If Franklin's in the cell next door it will be worth it," I replied, as we all exited the car. Kiddy naturally walked a little bit ahead of us, and as we closed in on the door, Rodgers instinctively took the lead. Lexi held back and instead of running face first into the darkness, I held back, too.

"Are you okay?" I asked her, as we entered Old Dominion.

"Don't worry about me, Grayson. We have bigger things going on, here," she said, flatly.

"I'm not worried about you—you're too stubborn to let something bad happen to you," I teased. I could hear her scoff in the darkness. The sun hadn't vanished completely, but just as before, if we stayed too long, we would be dancing in the dark.

"I know it's creepy, but the thing we were afraid of last time, is with us now," I said, gesturing up into the figure that I assumed—and hoped—was Rodgers. "It just goes to show you that you can never be sure what you should really fear, and what you shouldn't," I said, feeling a little too heartfelt. "Just a detective tip for you," I said, in order to mask it.

"It isn't that, sugar," she said—her twang ever-so-present. "It is just—I'm not worried about if there's something here to be afraid of," she explained. "I'm worried there won't be something here to be afraid of," she explained. "I mean, how long can we keep doing this? And how long can Franklin hold off before there is another victim? Tomorrow? Or another twenty years?" I didn't answer her. The questions, whether they appeared so, or not, whether she meant them to be so, or not, were rhetorical. No one could answer how long we would be able to last before the exhaustion of the case wore us too thin to be able to exist in it, any longer. Or how long Franklin could wait before he insured more death.

"Stay close," Rodgers yelled in his highest whisper, as we began to descend down the staircase.

The basement floor was just as we saw it months ago—the triangle *temporary home* emblem was everywhere—maybe even more places than I remember it being, across the rounded room that served as a central hub for the various hallways that sprouted from the middle.

"This is where we ran into each other," Rodgers said, in a pitiful voice, as if were by complete happenstance that we were both here. "I thought you'd found the secret place."

"Where is the secret place?" I asked.

"It's right here," Rodgers replied.

"That's just a floor, nitwit," Kiddy muttered.

"Shine your light, Grayson," Lexi said, turning on her flashlight and shinning it where Rodgers pointed, the center of the circle. I turned my flashlight on and did the same. There I saw the large round metal circle that served as some sort of architectural talking-piece. It never occurred to me that the circle could be something more. I was battling a million.

"It's a door?" I asked. Instead of answering me, Rodgers gestured for us to help him move it, as he bent down and grasped one side of the rim. Kiddy, Lexi, and I sat down our flashlights and joined him at the circle. I regretted never thinking this was more than just a marking for the center of the room. The large circle looked like metal in the dark, but was actually pure stone—and heavier than anything I'd ever attempted to lift. It took us several tries but we were finally able to flip the stone over and reveal a large gaping hole in the floor, which seemed to stretch downward for too long—long enough that there was no ground, just blackness.

"Wait, this can't be it," I said, turning to Rodgers.

"Franklin is just one man, there's no way he's strong enough to lift that stone by himself. This is ANOTHER DEAD END!" I yelled in Rodgers face, although it was my fault. It was my fault that I thought I could take Dr. Walker's word at anything. The man was deranged, possibly worse than Franklin ever could be.

"There's another way," Rodgers said. I reached around the ground for my flashlight.

"What do you mean there's another way?"

"I don't know. There's another way—none of us know where it is because none of us who ever went down there came back."

"Try to give us some English we understand, sweetheart," Lexi said.

"Dr. Walker," Rodgers started. "He would make us lift the stone and then he would throw us down here—in the pit. Then he said he'd go take care of them and he would leave. Sometimes he would go back up the stairs, sometimes he wouldn't. He would vanish though, and we could hear him down there. Hear his laughs—hear his demands and we heard the screams of the others. They weren't coming back. They knew it. We knew it, too," Rodgers continued, his voice shaking and cracking. "He would throw them down there. Just to scare them. Just to scare us—or worse."

A shiver went up my spine. It meant something worse to me now—after all, I had a firsthand experience as to how Dr. Walker would treat a person after having a few minutes alone with one. Deranged and disgusting.

"There has to be another entrance then," I stated, firmly. "You said he would go upstairs, though?" I asked. Rodgers nodded.

"Probably to throw off anyone clever enough to take notes," Kiddy said.

"Either way we should check out all the areas, entrances, all that," I explained. Kiddy, Lexi, and Rodgers didn't exactly seem to agree but they went along with it, anyway. After all, it wasn't as if we were going to jump into a gaping hole that, none of us knew how far it went or what was on the other side—save for Rodgers, and he wasn't any more eager to enter Walker's secret passage from there, either.

We moved back up the stairs, this time my own flashlight guiding the way. I could hear Kiddy heaving behind me. Too many stairs for a man who has spent an entire adult lifetime avoiding one. Lexi was braver than I expected, although she was between Kiddy and Rodgers. I suppose part of it was because she already lived through it, once.

"What was it like, Walt?" she asked him.

"Scary," he aptly replied.

When we were back in the corridor, I let Rodgers lead the way, expecting him to have some idea of how else to get to Walker's floor.

"Do you have any idea where this other entrance might be, Walt?" Kiddy asked.

"The doctor walked up the steps when he would send someone to hell," Rodgers said, too calmly for my comfort. He walked down the corridor, out to the main nurse's station.

"If there is another entrance, maybe it's in his office?" I asked.

"Like an actual secret door, Grayson?" Lexi said, the draw on her southern accent indicated her level of disbelief in my statement. "I am definitely in a Scooby-Doo cartoon," she finished. Kiddy actually chuckled at that, but before he was able to open his mouth and reply with some of the dry-wit Kiddy is accustom to spewing, Rodgers' stopped walking.

"Rodgers?" I asked. It was only on our flashlights that we once again had to rely. Therefore, it took a moment for all of us to see what it was Rodgers had already seen. Our eyes attempted to adjust in the dark, but it wasn't happening quickly enough. Narrowing my eyes and approaching Rodger's left shoulder, there, not running, not wavering, but standing perfectly still on the other end of Walt Rodger's beam, was Franklin Butler.

He stood taller than I expected, but hunched over, not as if he were disfigured—something much more psychological than that—he looked exhausted. It reminded me of the security camera footage outside the Abingdon police station. It was Franklin that we saw. His eyes were big, but the skin around them was like a shadow—fossil colored. He wore dark clothing—charcoal gray from head to toe. His hair was thin—black, but very thin. He was like a walking corpse. His face—it wasn't a mask he wore. It was *his* face. A burned face. A face that looked like it came from hell itself. *Burn Wounds.* Walker's words were realized to me.

It was strange—surreal, some might say, to see the man who murdered your mother stand before you. He was a man, but he didn't look like one. Instead, he looked like a child the size of a man. The man-child, as his appearance was burned into my cerebellum that moment forward, was holding something large in his hands that looked to be something like a cinder block, and had his arms stretched up above his head, as high as they could be.

"Okay, okay," Kiddy said, trying to calm down a silent crowd when it was he who needed to be calm.

"Frank," Rodgers said, like they were meeting up at a high school reunion. Franklin didn't reply. The black-blue sky coupled with the moon and stars shined in through the window. We were all standing a few feet behind the nurse's desk. Kiddy moves up a couple of inches and it made Franklin uncomfortable. He started shifting and moaning something of a growl. It sent a chill across my body—like a wave.

"Franklin," I said, as I stepped closer, Kiddy did as well, and this made the Shoestring Killer even more upset. He stomped his foot on the floor and I could literally hear the boards cracking. I glanced at Lexi but I couldn't tell if she saw it. "We're not here to hurt you, Franklin. And we're not here to," I paused, debating on how to word it. "We're not going to lie to you and trick you, Franklin. You're going away, for a long time. But not like here, or like Dr. Walker's house, either. You'll go to a better place. One where they're not so *nice* to you," I said.

Rodgers looked over at me, a little perplexed but didn't say anything. Franklin hadn't moved—his eyes were perfectly still looking-glasses, and all of us were waiting for the rabbit hole. All of us except for Lexi, who'd somehow shed her inability to function within the confines of Bristol's Old Dominion Asylum.

"Franklin," she said, with a heavy accent on the *a*. She moved forward, and although I wanted to reach out and stop her more than anything, Franklin didn't jolt, he didn't scream, he stayed perfectly still. Somehow, that bothered me worse. "Listen honey, I know you're scared—none of us are going to hurt you. It's really important you come with us, though. You know what has been going on and it has to stop, okay? If it doesn't you could get hurt too," she said, calmly, as she took another step forward.

"Lexi please," I called out.

"Don't step any further!" Rodgers pleaded. Lexi didn't move forward, but she did stay where she was, right in the center of the creaky floor, between Franklin and ourselves.

"Don't listen to these guys yelling, okay? I won't yell at you...why don't you put that thing down and take my hand?" she asked, and she extended out a friendly hand. Silence erupted in the asylum. I could hear a very faint heave of Kiddy's breath, and the small crackles of boards splintering as our weights shifted. It was several moments later I realized I was holding my breath, waiting for something to happen. Lexi inched closer and closer, and Franklin hadn't made a sound. He watched her—unprovoked, with kinder eyes than previously. Kiddy's flashlight didn't leave Franklin, but Rodgers' was wavering—too antsy for the cat king, I suppose.

"Stop," I said to Lexi, as she approached closer to Franklin, but she waved her hand at me, as if to say she had it.

"Franklin, do you want to take my hand? Do you want us to help you get out of here?" she asked, softly—her accent not so intrusive this time. It was obvious what she was doing—playing nice—I just didn't know if it would distract him long enough for us to do something before the anger took over. Franklin almost nodded, and began to slowly lower the cinder block. Kiddy and I exchanged a look, surprised, eager, even. Rodgers glared, unable to take his eyes off of him—skeptical. Rodgers was decent—if it weren't for the cat thing.

Franklin slowly lowered the cinder block, as he watched Lexi's hand. I'm unsure what happened in the next moment. Maybe Lexi's hand shook from nerves, or maybe he was ready to make Lexi his next victim, or maybe the conditions of Franklin's mind began to squeeze once again, because he screamed, louder than all the times prior. His screams were so loud that it placed an unnatural fear within me. The Shoestring Killer lifted up the cinder block and with a fast, hurling motion, summoned it to the weakened floor between us, while simultaneously moving toward Lexi.

The following events that transpired, occurred rapidly—so blurry I felt blind. Rodgers and I leapt towards Lexi and The Shoestring Killer. As the cinder block collided with the splintered boards, the flooring gave away, and just as Rodgers had pushed Lexi out of the way of the collapsing floor, and just as I had thrown myself between Franklin and Lexi, with full purpose to attack the Shoestring Killer, Rodgers and I fell through splinters of a burnt yesteryear.

I landed roughly, in the basement floor on the edge of a corridor entrance right next to center room. I was certain my leg was broken, at least my knee was damaged. An unmistakable pain jolted through my right leg. My heart was pulsating and vibrating through my rib cage and a piercing sound echoed in my head. The corridor I was in smelt terrible, and as that was the least of my concerns, I pushed out all the thoughts of *why* it smelled the way it did. The basement was the color of crow, now—a thicker black that prevented me from being able to see anything.

"RODGERS?!" I called out. There wasn't a reply. I saw his body fall with mine. I crawled into the hub, or at least what felt like the hub, the darkness of a starless space was surrounding me now. I crawled until I could get a better look at what happened above. The floor had given out, but I could no longer hear any rumbling upstairs. "HELLO?"

I blinked several times, trying to push my eyes into a state of vision—to overcome the shadows that had snuck inward. I couldn't—I was in a coal furnace. A hot and black pit in which I couldn't crawl out. I tried to stand, and although I accomplished doing so, walking was a much slower task. I heard a faint scream—it wasn't Franklin's tantrum cry, though, this was Lexi. My lip quivered and my hands shook. I stepped firmer, and limped across the room. "No," I whispered to myself for a little motivation. "Not again."

I began to get in the swing of my limp but just as I picked up any kind of momentum, I tripped over something obscure. I fell flat onto the cold floor surface. It felt like I was there for an hour as I tried to get myself loose from the random bits of fallen debris.

"Kiddy?" I called out, pointing my voice in the general direction of where I believed the stairs were located. I didn't hear anything. "FRANKLIN!" I followed up with anger flowing through my veins and voice.

There were moments, many moments, throughout my investigation in Abingdon where I felt the cool hand of defeat slipping up around me. An idle hand of ultra-unrealism that would ultimately equal to being a jester of longevity that would hang over my career as a private detective, a former citizen of Abingdon and a human being who lost his mother. It wasn't until I saw Franklin, wide eyed and terrified with a cinder block over his head that I ever thought that idle hand could reach out and grasp the man responsible. And as I leaped for him, to stop him from hurting another person I've come to care about—my fingertips scarcely touch him.

The basement entrance opened suddenly—what was left of it. I still couldn't see through the ebony filter of the night but I heard everything. A creaking down the stairs—carefully, purposefully. I wondered then if it were Franklin, or was it somehow Rodgers? I stayed as still as I could. I saw the stable shades shift, I knew there was a person somewhere in the room with me but he or she didn't speak—then again, I hadn't either.

"Lexi? Kiddy?" I finally called out, fearing the eyes of a monster had finally found me. Somehow the silence had gotten even more silent. An uncomfortable nothing was suddenly something and I knew I wasn't alone with an ally.

"Franklin," I addressed the figurative elephant in the room. "You know why I'm here," I stated to the black air. "You're not stupid. I know people treat you like you're stupid but you're not stupid." There was no answer, but I knew he was listening. My knee was throbbing— I could feel the swelling with each step of pressure I forced. I didn't know where I was walking—but I tried to make it a circle. I knew I was near the center, and I attempted to not get near the gaping hole in the middle of the room that lead to the "skeletons" of Dr. Walker's closet.

"But I know what you did, Franklin," I started— taunting a man I knew I shouldn't taunt. I couldn't help it. For whatever disturbance that had ignited the fire within him, there was an anger in me that burned just as hot. "And I know what was done to you," My voice was silenced with a jolt from behind. My chest pushed forward and my neck whipped backwards as I felt large, firm hands jab against my shoulder blades. I stumbled forward, top heavy—any balance I should've had was betrayed by my weakened knee. I fell forward, and to my dismay found myself spiraling downward—into the gaping hole of the basement floor. I had found the rabbit hole we had feared earlier. I fell for what felt like forever until suddenly there was ground. Wherever I was, it was small. The darkness was still ripe, not so much that I couldn't see the small confines I was stuck in—it was quite literally a pit. I looked up, as if I were stuck at the bottom of a wishing well that was hopeless. I saw a figure blocking the entrance from above. It was Franklin, I was sure of it. I could feel his eyes locked on me. I looked back, refusing to blink. What followed was a screech like before, followed by what I think was meant as a chuckle.

"Go home," a raspy, broken, whisper-voice said, and with that the voice and the man disappeared.

I screamed for Franklin to come back. I tried to climb the smooth walls of the pit—it was impossible. I couldn't climb, I couldn't see—I could barely stand. There was no way back up from where I came. I had no choice but to admit I had fallen, and pray that someone would pick me up.

Chapter Fifteen

Velcro Shoes

In the days following my mother's death, I would segregate myself away from friends, and even family. Alan would drag me out of my room and force me to be sociable. It was around that time that I started turning the barn's top floor into my own private nest. A place where I could hide away from Abingdon and everyone in it. In fact, that's exactly what I use to call it: *My nest away from everything.* Alan heard me call it that one time, and he laughed at me. It was not the kind of laugh you would expect from a father to his son—one of silly malarkey and intrigue. It was the kind of laugh that ridicules and mocks. Alan replied to me: "You're not in a nest. You're in a pit, and the more you dig deeper into it, the harder it will be for you to climb out." I knew, deep down, he was trying to keep me from turning into something I shouldn't—ironically, the very thing he turned into himself. It never sat right with me, that laugh and that response. As I scratched the walls of the hole I found myself in at Old Dominion Asylum, I could just hear my father, with his hands behind his head, leaned back in his seat and uttering the words: *I told you so.*

The pit was bigger than the size of a well, but I had no idea by how much. As soon as I stopped pacing in my small space—I concentrated on feeling the walls around the bottom of the pit as opposed what was at chest level and above. Finally, I found what seemed to be a door. It took several minutes to pry it open, and could feel my fingers start to bleed as my flesh worked hard against the cold structure.

I tried to steady my breath and my anxiety about what was happening above me. Franklin was able to get away from Lexi and Kiddy, and neither of them had come to my rescue. My fears were slithering out from my brain. Had he already robbed me of two more people that meant something to me?

The room I found myself in was most unsettling, but it was better than being stuck in the small pit. It was half the size of the basement floor, and along the edges of the walls were springs of lightbulbs that gave off the tangerine light. The orange bulbs shined light not only on myself, but on a myriad of madness that sank whatever good feeling I had left about this case.

Dr. Walker's entire life was stuck down here—there were files, video tapes, stained surgical equipment—even clothing that let me know bodies might not be too far away. In fact, I was sure if I did digging I would find actual skeletons—so I didn't dig. I could tell it was the work of Dr.

Walker—everything he confessed was here, and it made me wonder how a man as sick as him could've eluded any measure of suspicion for so long. It occurred to me that Rodgers must had told the truth. Walker would throw patients into the makeshift well and then bring them into the torture room in which I found myself. It was also how he was able to keep his equipment from burning in the fire. We were completely under the facility, in a hidden level no one seemed to know about but Walker himself. Any evidence he needed to hide was locked away here, at some point or another.

Among the evidence of Walker's madman-mania, were personal belongings of Franklin Butler. I knew they belonged to Franklin, too. It was just too obvious. Scattered by my feet, along with almost every other area of the room, were pairs, or individual shoes. Most of them, the shoestrings had been tied or removed completely—nothing in-between. I studied the area, trying to determine what I was looking at but could only make assumptions.

A few of the tattered shoes hadn't shoestrings at all, but velcro. It reminded me of what my mother's journal said, about Franklin and his shoe habits. It was obvious to me, in that moment, that Walker swiped the journal after the murders started. If anyone else got their hands on my mother's journal—they would know exactly what was happening.

There was a bundle of gathered blankets—old, stained, nasty sheets. The kind that belong to the homeless, the kind that belong in dumpsters. They were wrapped in a makeshift bed. I needed to move on. Now that the room had opened up, there was a desperate need to find a way out.

I was tempted to stay, however, upon looking at the violent scene where Franklin was living. It is rare when one has the opportunity to look at something so troublesome in its nakedness, and once one does—one has a difficult time relearning how to blink. I was pressed to find Franklin, and more importantly, to find Lexi and Kiddy. I moved across the room, traveling to some of the darker corners, hoping the light bulbs would light enough of the path that I could find a way through. I pressed my hands against the walls, searching for a door or passageway—so I could escape the dungeon in which I'd been trapped.

I searched for what felt like a half an hour, and I began to panic. My sweat was cascading down my forehead, nose, and lips. I could scarcely breathe. The basement air strangled me, and just when I felt like there was no exit from these asylum catacombs, just when I felt the hospital would claim another life, with its bare hands around my throat, I felt something else, something real—a shoestring around my neck.

The pressure of the shoestring tightened along my throat—I tried to fall backwards away from the lace, but I could feel his body—Franklin's body, behind me, keeping me locked in, pulling on either side as the string cut off my ability to breathe. I tried to fight him off, pushing and squirming. Franklin was a large man, though, and stronger than even he knew. His arms acted like bookends on either side of my torso. I grabbed at the string with my hands, trying to move it but Franklin's large hands pressing in the back of my neck reminded me I was no match to budge him.

"Did you see the velcro shoes?" I heard the same raspy-whisper voice from earlier, slither in my ear. "I don't like velcro shoes. I like shoestrings. I—" Franklin stuttered for a moment. "I like shoestrings. I can choke you with shoestrings."

Moving around as much as I could, I found a way to fling my arm up in the air, and bring it down quickly, jabbing my elbow into his stomach. He grunted in a short excerpt of pain and loosened his grip enough that I was able to rip the shoelace out of his grip. I ran forward, but the darkness was crippling—even with the lightbulbs. I tripped and was united with the cold, hard ground quickly. I could feel my knee pain surge through me, again.

I was able to get to my feet and without hesitation, I turned around and threw a balled fist into the abyss—it landed. A sucker punch in the purest of forms. I struggled around the room, feeling along the sides for a door, again. I kept my ears on Franklin, as he stood up. I panicked as I waited for the sounds of his footsteps to grow louder, but in that moment I felt a small iron door handle. I pushed down on the lever as quickly as I could and passed through the doorway. Before me were a series of stairs that I discovered as I tripped over them in the darkness. My knee throbbed with pain. As I climbed up the stairs, I could see the shimmering stars of the night sky and realized I had made it out of the asylum. At the top of the stairs, I was able to gather my surroundings better. The staircase had led me to the south-side of the hospital, thanks to a side door history seemed to have forgotten.

I was able to enjoy a precious moment of fresh air in the midnight dark before Franklin reapplied the shoelace around my neck.

I fought, struggled, twitched as I felt the air leaving my body. I fidgeted, like a fish that had been caught, but hadn't been put out of its misery.

"I don't need help. I don't. I don't need help with my shoestrings. I have. I can tie my shoe strings," Franklin's voice grew a little louder—but not enough to make a difference. "I don't need help. I don't need any of them," he went on, violently.

There was a moment, where Franklin's shoestring around my neck pulled my neck and head back far enough that I could see the sky. My eyes watered, unfocused pools hovered over my irises. The clear, bright shine of the stars were fuzzy instead—damp bulbs, if anything. When facing death, the ideas and memories that passed over me are not the things I would have imagined I would have thought about in the end. I thought about the victims. I wondered what they saw at the end. What they thought about, what they felt, whether they saw shining stars, or damp bulbs like me. It was that realization, whilst being choked, there were those only, those two ways to look at it.

And as the stars began to fade, and I knew my life with it, I thought of Lexi—and that despite it all, I was glad she walked into my office all those months ago. I thought of Kiddy, and how fortunate I was that he gave me a shot that I clearly didn't deserve. And Jack, too, and how my big regret is that I never made peace with him. As the life faded from me, I knew that would be his regret now, too. I even thought about Alan and the sorrow I felt for him as now *he* would lose a second life to the Shoestring Killer. Lastly, and perhaps most earnestly, I thought of Jolene. I somehow knew that in her last moments, she didn't see bulbs. She didn't see stars, either. She was too busy fighting back.

There was a sudden jolt and I fell to the grass below—but I could breathe. The pressure around my neck had disappeared. I gasped for several seconds as my ears tried to focus on the commotion behind me—there was an altercation for sure. Shaking, I pressed my hands against the Earth and lifted upward, desperately trying to stabilize my breath and body. I turned to find Franklin struggling for dominance over Lexi. It was obvious what happened—Lexi sideswiped Franklin with as much speed and strength as she could. It was enough to knock us over—it was enough to save my life. Franklin was furious, I could see his eyes widen in the moonlight. They glowed and it terrified me.

As shock was wearing off of my body, I moved forward to be the interrupter that Lexi was for me. Franklin had her forced to the ground. He was behind her, also rolling around on the grass, and his hands around her neck. There was more than anger pulsating in my veins—there was something else, hate, fear, vengeance—something. It was that feeling, and only that feeling, that pumped enough adrenaline in my body to pull Franklin off of my client, and back onto the grass away from her. I straddled him. I didn't want him off the grass. I didn't want him off his back. I wanted him vulnerable, afraid—like all of them were afraid.

I reached to a flat, smooth part of the grass behind us, where the man had just attempted to kill me, and picked up the shoelace that he intended to be the murder weapon.

"Grayson," I heard Lexi call as she stood up. I wrapped my hands in the ends of the shoelace—confirming a nice tight grip.

"Tell me, Franklin," I said, as I wrapped the string against his throat and pressed down as hard as I could. "What does it feel like? On the other end of it? How does it feel now that it's finally caught up to you?" Franklin moved, shifted, and fought. I could barely keep the upper hand. In fact, I knew at any moment I could lose my advantage. He was choking, now, though, and Franklin was not stable enough to realize, it seemed, that he was a stronger killer than I was a man.

His eyes screamed when he couldn't. There were tears, there was panic. His fists didn't beat me but beat the ground beside him—pulling grass from the ground.

"Did you watch their eyes, Franklin?" I asked. Franklin's face was beginning to lose what little color it had left. I could hear Lexi call out to me again—southern accent and a worrisome fear cocktail. "Did you watch their eyes like I am watching yours? Did their fear not slow you down? Or did it fuel you?"

I felt like the madness was exchanging to me. As if somehow it was connected to the string laced through my fingers. It was obvious enough that I noticed it—just subtle enough that the situation didn't bother me.

"I've fantasized about this, Franklin—for too long. For way too long," the string looked like it was about to break—the durability of a shoelace is frail, and my anger was breaking it further. It occurred to me that Franklin didn't kill in anger. It didn't make me any less angry, but it made me all the more compromised.

"Grayson!" Lexi yelled. And I yelled. I let go of the string and hit Franklin's chest as I leaned in, screaming into his face.

"But I can't, Franklin! You sick, sick man! I know. I know what happened," I panted from fear, anger, exhaustion. Franklin didn't move, he didn't fight me off of him. In fact, he lay their patiently. My knees—even the hurt one—were digging into his forearms, my fist still balled on his chest. "I know the why," I whispered. "It doesn't—it doesn't excuse the what....but I know the why," I said, breathless. A tear traveled down my face, and just as I wanted to spit in the burnt face of the man that killed my mother, and get off of his defeated body, I saw, in his eye, one trickle down his face as well. "Don't even think that's okay," I said, bitterly as I climbed off of him and stood up. Lexi joined my side, and fortunately we only had to hover over him for a few more minutes before police arrived on the scene.

The police arrived and began to assess the scene as First Responders took care to bandage us. Lexi began to inform them that two more persons who were with us were inside, but Kiddy emerged from the asylum's entrance, bruised and bloody like Lexi and myself. It was a relief to see my partner, but when the realization of his safety wore on, the realization that Rodgers wasn't with him, occurred.

"There's a body in the basement," Kiddy said. "It is the body of Walt Rodgers. You can check with Abingdon PD, he was a suspect in a string of murders but turned out to be a person of interest who had key information to leading us to him," Kiddy finished, gesturing to Franklin, who was now in handcuffs and being escorted to the backseat of a squad car. I grimaced as a first responder cleaned a wound on my rib cage. "I tried to save his life, but," Kiddy's voice trailed off. A moment of pity found its way to Kiddy's face. The officers finished taking our statements, and asked us to come down to the police station to give a more detailed account of everything—after the first responders escort me to the hospital. I refused any emergency room visits and eagerly wanted to get down to the police station.

Their acceptance of our accounts seemed skeptical at best, and continued to question why we're acting outside of the law—private investigators or not—I decided it was best to name drop the state investigators who had threatened me. I could get in serious trouble, but I decided I should be the one to face charges—not Kiddy or Lexi. Kiddy also explained what happened at Liam Walker's house. He described we showed up for a simple interview but the former doctor pulled a pistol on us and even shot me in the shoulder before he turned the gun on himself.

As we waited at the precinct for the officers to run our story, I caught a glimpse of a beat cop locking a loud, clanging door to a holding cell that held Franklin Butler. He looked sad—like a caged pet that couldn't understand why it was being confined. He knew, though. I knew he knew. When I nearly killed him—he knew. And I wish I could say there was a better reason why I stopped, but there isn't.

I fantasized again, like I did when I nearly killed him. I fantasized about walking up to those bars, and baring my soul to a man who had taken so much from me but didn't realize it. I wanted to tell him that he stole my mother from me, from everyone. I wanted to tell him that despite whatever happened to him, he stole something that didn't belong to him and that didn't make the bad of his life go away. I wanted to tell him how taking Jolene was beyond dirty, whether it was intentional or not. I wanted to tell him that for twenty years he's made me sick to my stomach, that he made me a worse version of myself, that he stole what were supposed to be some of my father's highlighted years and tossed him into a whirlwind he couldn't escape. Lastly, I wanted to tell him that he would suffer—and that no matter what kind of place he ended up in, he would never be the victim anymore. He would always be the criminal. And how glad I was that he was still alive—so he'd have to live with it.

I couldn't do those things, though—life doesn't work like the silver screen. This wasn't that forties noir that I wanted it to be, with the fedora hats and the glass door that read *Grayson Grant, Private Eye.* It wasn't something you could tie up nicely in a bow, where the villain got to get handed a swift supply of justice, where the hero got to gawk. There wasn't a hero here, as far as I could tell. The real heroes were people like Jolene, and Walt Rodgers. Like the little girl who was brave enough to tell us about the scar carved into Franklin's arm. I wasn't a hero. I was too emotionally compromised to be a hero. I was too broken to be one, too.

And after I realized why Franklin became a killer, I started to contemplate the number of villains in this story.

We got back on the road when it was nearly daybreak. State investigators Strout and Killian, though furious we acted against them, were just glad it was all behind us. They vouched for us, on some level, and Bristol police let us go. As we drove home, the sky looked like it was losing all of its darkness—like ink, draining. It was slowly becoming a midnight blue, with a hint of something lighter underneath. The drive was quiet although it shouldn't have been. We were survivors—not just of the night but of an entire existence. A twenty year nightmare had ended and we were lucky enough to wake up and feel the fresh air of life—true life.

We stayed in silence, though, the only sounds were the sounds of the car as Kiddy drove us back to Abingdon.

"What's next?" Kiddy asked, finally breaking the silence, and his voice—it sounded like it was being ripped open from a deep sleep.

"Yeah, that's a good question," Lexi stated. I sighed and kept my eyes glued to the window. I could tell by the pavement on the road when we crossed back into Abingdon. There was a familiarity about it that I didn't get elsewhere.

"Coffee," I stated. "I need coffee."

Kiddy was fast asleep back at the Martha Washington. The sun was rising, and although I should be exhausted, I couldn't sleep. Lexi couldn't either, as she talked all the way from the Martha Washington back to my father's house.

"Thanks for the lift," I said, interrupting her as we arrived. "Even if you stole Kiddy's car to do it," I stated.

"Borrowed," she corrected. The house looked calm, unprovoked. It was any other day at the Grant house but it was all about to change. "I can't wait to hear what your dad says," Lexi said.

"Yeah, he's going to hate I didn't take him with me," I confessed.

"Your dad sent me to you because he knew you could get it done, even if you refused to talk to him about it," she said. I nodded as I sipped a cup of coffee that Lexi had bought for me while I checked Kiddy into the hotel. I grimaced as I retracted my tongue.

"I forgot to tell you it is really hot," Lexi said half-serious. I clinched the paper cup and despite the singes on my tongue, I laughed.

"Coffee looks better on you than alcohol," she said, her smile balancing out.

"Thank you," I said, as I looked to her, "for coming back for me. I owe you one."

386

"Sugar, you owe me two," she smiled. "I dragged your lazy butt out of St. Louis in the first place." We actually shared a laugh, a good laugh, a real laugh, and while we did she gently clasped my hand. I paused for a moment, before clasping back.

"Do you know why I made the switch to coffee?" I asked, rhetorically. "Alcohol made me sleepy. I'm tired of sleeping. People sleep as much as they do so they can get away from their today, their tomorrow, their yesterday. I'm okay with all that—sleeping doesn't take away yesterday, and days like today make me want to keep one eye open for tomorrow." Her eyes glimmered—perhaps I said something meaningful.

"Coming in?" I asked, as I opened the door. Lexi shook her head.

"I should let the Grant boys feel a pride of justice for a few moments before I ruin all the fun. Besides...I think I need to find some of Walt's friends in town, tell them what he did for me. He deserves to have a better name than he does," Lexi said.

"Irsuan isn't a good enough name?" I asked with a smirk.

"Later, Detective," she teased, and I shut the passenger door. Lexi rolled down the window, though, and called out to me one more time.

"Hey Edmund," she teased. I turned back to her. She leaned over, peering out the passenger window. "Why did you stop? You said you know the why? What is it? Why did he go after the nice ones? I mean, if it made you stop?" she asked. I felt my heart sink, again. I hated that feeling. I shook my head.

"For another time," I said as I gently blew on my coffee and turned around towards the house.

I paused for a moment, before I entered the house, wishing my coffee had cooled down enough so I could sip, but I knew it hadn't. I took a deep breath of procrastination before entering the house. I was pleased, relieved, unburdened after twenty years and I couldn't wait to give that satisfaction to Alan, but I was serious when I told Lexi I was afraid of how he'd respond to not being more involved. Alan had devoted himself to something he didn't get to see through. I wondered if I should have felt more guilty for leaving him out, then I remember Rodgers, and how closely the rest of us came to dying in that asylum, too. It was a safe bet, I thought, as I opened the door and stepped inside, that had my father been with us at Old Dominion Asylum, he might not make it out alive. I felt better, knowing that he was here, in the comfort of his own home, safe.

I smelt the faint scent of smoke from the kitchen and walked down the narrow hallway. As I rounded the corner, calling out for Alan—and asking him if he was burning something on the oven—I found him sitting at the kitchen table, scared, unmoved. Across from him was Jack, who puffed a cigarette in one hand, and tantalized a handgun—my handgun—which lay on the table between them.

"Well, hey there, Grayson," Jack said, exhaling. "I heard you were out catching a killer. Looks like we both have something in common these days, after all."

Chapter Sixteen

Who Kills a Killer?

When we were kids, after our mothers died, but before we grew up and were able to realize how mad we were about it, Jack and I were put into a grievance program. The kind that tell you exactly what to feel, exactly when to feel it, and exactly how to handle yourself once it is being felt. It was the kind of program I chuckled off—fancy degrees and flash cards weren't necessary to tell me that my mother was dead and that she was never coming back.

During those sessions, which were Mr. Hanna's idea, as apparently Jack was having horrible night terrors, we would spend our time divided into two sections. In the first section, we would talk about who we lost, what they meant to us, and what they would probably most likely say if they were with us in the meeting. I always found that last one to be redundant— if my mother was with me, I would have needed a group of strangers telling me it was okay that I cried about her at night.

The second section of the sessions were different. We talked about how we lost them, what it means for our future, our family's future, and why we lost them; If we even know the answer to that question. I was never good at the second portion. I could never talk about how I lost her, why I lost

390

her. It was something, though, that I could always do the first half—Jack couldn't even do the first half of the sessions. He would always get too angry, uncomfortable, and storm out. So that's what the perception became in Abingdon for Jack and myself. I couldn't bear to admit how I lost my mother. Jack couldn't bear to admit that he ever had one.

"Jack," I said nervously, as I entered the kitchen. Alan didn't budge. He looked onward, through me, beyond me. He was playing it as peacefully as he could, because he knew there wasn't any peace—not here.

"Have a seat, Grayson," Jack said, gesturing to the seat beside my father. I walked around the table and sat down on the bench beside Alan. Jack wasn't holding the gun up in any serious threat, but he continued to adjust the gun on the table, as if it ticked back and forth, the barrel facing me, then Alan, then me again and so on while he glared at the two of us.

"So, hombre, I hear that you found the monster in all of our closest," he took a long drag on his cigarette, with ease. "Any truth to that or is Abingdon just starting another little ghost story?" News traveled fast from Bristol. How could it not though? Jack was wearing a plaid flannel with the sleeves rolled up. His blonde hair in a ponytail and a red-orange under the eyes that made him look like he'd either been up too long, or seen too much—knowing Jack, it was some sort of mixture. The cigarette danced around his lips, flicking over a tooth as he waited for my reply.

"Heard the news and thought I would come over here and see your old man in cuffs. Guess you didn't find who I thought you would," he said.

"Jack, there was a lot that happened and I would like to talk to you about it if that's okay," I said, rationally.

"Well, the way I see it," a ring of smoke drifted to Alan and myself. "The only thing any of us have here," Jack was gesturing to the three of us, "is time." His eyes moved between Alan and myself.

"We got him, Jack. Franklin, he was hiding in the asylum after all," I stated.

"And what did you do once you found him?" Jack asked. I hesitated for a moment because there was a tone in Jack's speech, a look behind his eye that told me he wasn't hoping for the answer he was expecting.

"He's in custody, Jack," I admitted. Jack nodded and breathed so hard through his nostrils I could see them pulsate.

"And you are content with that?" he asked, as cigarette smoke wafted from his nose.

"He can't hurt anyone now," I stated, hoping that it convinced myself, along with him.

"That's a lie!" Jack yelled, slamming his hand on the table. Alan jumped in his seat. I'd never seen my father terrified, not like that, not that badly. My best friend took a moment to collect himself, parting a fallen blonde lock that had begun swinging across his face like a pendulum. He positioned his hair and then took another puff of his cigarette. "If he's alive, and in the system, there's always a chance he could hurt someone else," Jack said, firmly.

I nodded and slowly rotated my coffee cup in my hand, allowing it to make a ring on the table. It reminded me of Jolene.

"Unfortunately, that's the only option I had, Jack," I explained.

"You can't seem to find the preverbal big stick, brother," Jack retorted. My teeth were grinding against each other—the tips sawing at each other like I were filing them into fangs.

"What are you doing, Jack? What are you even doing here?" I asked.

"I have a secret I never told you, Grayson, and I've come to apologize." Jack's eyes now moved to Alan and didn't budge. I glanced at my father, who didn't seem to break his concentration, either. "You see, I've let this go for too long. I

393

was hoping there was another answer here but there just isn't one, buddy. I didn't want to be this person. It wasn't my place," Jack kept tapping the gun. It made me nervous—triggers on guns tended to pull before anyone ever intended.

"Go ahead—*big stick,*"I taunted. Jack took out his cigarette and pushed the ashy end onto the yellow wood of the table. As he smothered it into the splinter, I felt Alan move uncomfortably on the bench.

"Your father is a murderer, Grayson,"Jack said, flatly. He reached into his back pocket and pulled out another pack of cigarettes—soft pack this time. He fingered a stick out of the packaging and reached for a lighter that lay on the table—a black one, with a big white diamond on it. "Aren't you going to ask me how I know?" he pressed his thumb on the igniter and a small, perky flame stood erect. He leaned the smoke's ash-end to the flame and as soon as it caught, like a humble camp fire, Jack inhaled and leaned back.

"How do you know?" I played along. Jack nodded, like it was a game he knew I was participating in at this point, and he wanted to play by his rules.

"Because like I've said before, brother, I saw him do it," Jack said strongly, and quickly. Teasing this story like he had, for this long, made me doubt he had anything believable. I admit, that even in my assured moment, I was almost caught amiss by Jack's performance. A weak smile sprouted on his face, as if he knew he'd found a door in which would take him under my skin. I had a tell, a small tell: one that I didn't even know about—my eyebrows, maybe, or a twitch under my left eye. There was something that he recognized was off, within me, if even for a moment. He was my best friend, after all, and best friends have a way of seeing the dirt within each other, even if we think we're clean.

"Aren't you going to ask me who I saw him kill?" Jack teased, he was pushing his next piece forward in his twisted game.

"No," I muttered. "You're going to tell me, anyway," I added.

"Joseph Farmer," a ring of smoke danced around our heads as the words left Jack's lips—like gray confetti, revealing a bleak truth that entered my nostrils. Without meaning, my eyes cut over to Alan. He was still, but now he had an expression on his face—one almost of glee.

"You're so full of it, Jack," my father blurted out. "You've been seeing stuff in your head for twenty years, now. You just make stuff up, boy. You always have. You couldn't handle it—and that's okay, but it doesn't mean you can make me a bad guy just because you were scared of a bad guy you didn't know, then," Alan said. They were wise words—rehearsed words. I found myself wondering how many times had Alan wanted to tell Jack this, just the past few months, or all these years?

"I saw him, Grayson," Jack ignored every word of my father—he didn't even blink. "I came looking around one day, for you. I heard him getting in a fight with someone. They were here, in the kitchen. I tried listening in by the kitchen door, but I wanted to see what was going on so I peaked," Jack stated, laughing a little. Not the kind of laugh you want, though, the kind that tells you there's no more room for tears. The kind that leaves you laughing because your emotions don't know which direction they're going anymore. In those moments that I was fearing for my life, I feared for Jack's as well.

"The two of them were yelling—and I mean yelling. It was mostly Alan, saying that he—Joseph Farmer, who I didn't know was Joseph Farmer until later—made a big mistake coming around here. Your pop said he wasn't welcome. I thought maybe, maybe in my dumb kid brain, that Joseph was the bad guy. It was getting dark, but I could still see what was happening, even though Alan thought he was alone. Joseph said something, I'm not sure what—something about your mother, Grayson, and that's when Alan lost it. He pushed him and punched him until Joseph was on the floor. And once he was on the floor, Alan started choking him," Jack's account of the story made me uncomfortable—it was detailed, it was intense. And after reading my mother's journal about the kiss they shared—made me all the more hesitant. I thought about what the nurse, Bri, said about Alan. Jealous, Bri called Alan Grant. It was untrue, though. We had our killer. It was not a stretch to imagine Franklin killing Jody, the nice song and dance man from the asylum. Besides, I was still sitting on valuable information I could promise Jack didn't know.

"Next thing I know, your dad, he stops choking," Jack added.

"This is so stupid," Alan said.

"Joseph doesn't move, though. He doesn't budge. I freaked and ducked from the window, I ran back home and I didn't talk to you for a day or two. Then—Joseph's body was found—his body dumped, a shoestring tied around his wrist.

"It was then I knew that your dad was the Shoestring Killer. I couldn't say anything, he lived beside me. I would've risked everyone's lives if I had said anything," a tear ran down Jack's face, and now his fingers were wrapping around the handle of the gun. As his fingers collected around the handle, my heart beat a little harder.

"Listen, Jack," I stated.

"Think of what he did to us, Grayson! Forget that he's your dad. Forget that he's responsible for who gave you your life. He's taken more than he's ever given," Jack pressed.

"If you were so sure it was him all this time, why didn't you ever tell me? When we grew up? Why help me track Rodgers? You beat that man for no reason!" I stressed.

I studied my friend for a moment, and realized, possibly for the first time ever, a side of Jack that wasn't collected, that wasn't thought out, analyzed by a cool exterior.

"I either hoped that you'd figure it out, or that there were more people involved and we could focus on finding those people—like Rodgers—together. I hoped I was wrong. I hoped it was something else, a bad dream, one of those night terrors I had when I was a kid. But, when I saw that evidence the police found in the barn—that's when I knew I was right all of these years," Jack said as he removed his cigarette from his mouth and subtly gestured it toward Alan.

I sat—at a crossroads— desperate to keep what I knew to myself, but knew it was also the only way to reach Jack. Decisions pressed into stressful situations are not decisions at all—they're just inconvenient happenings.

"Jack," I stated, softly. "I have something in my back pocket. I'm going to reach for it, okay?" I said, hoping that his trigger finger didn't feel like dancing. "I'm reaching for it,

I just want to show it to you okay?" He watched me intently, as I pulled my mother's journal out of my pocket and dropped it on the table. The three of us looked at it for a moment, Alan opened his mouth to speak—there was even a little noise of realization before he halted himself.

"What is that?" Jack asked. The notebook was laying beside the gun, and I thought of how appropriate that was for the situation.

"That's the last answer," I started. "That's my mother's journal and the page I have tagged, that had been folded in some kind of secret—that's a passage she wrote days before she died. It was the second to last thing she ever wrote," I explained.

"Grayson?" Alan said, he was anxious—for good reason. Jack picked up the journal with one hand...careful not to move his other hand away from the pistol.

"Read it," I said. I could see skepticism embody my friend, but curiosity always wins against skepticism. Jack started scanning the words but I stopped him. "Out loud." Jack stopped, eyed me for a moment, then to Alan, and nodded his head.

"Boy, do I have something to tell you," Jack started, reading my mother's words. "I am full of extraordinary secrets, but this one takes the cake. The kind that bubbles up in your chest, lingers like an unspoken idea. The juicy kind you'd tell girlfriends if you were still young enough to have sleepovers. For thirty years I was at peace with being a good, clean girl. An unhappy one—but one that had a loving husband, a bright son, a cute house on a good street. If I wanted to, I could be Dr. Grant for the rest of my life. And in all honesty, I probably will. This job, for its weaknesses, for its depression, it has given me something. A realization I never had before—a surging shot of clarity. One I use to see in Alan, one I use to see in Jody, but one that Franklin has now provided. He sees me with eyes no one else does. I'm just a doctor to a lot of these people—or a quack, a fraud. I am mistake, a mother, or something in between. To Franklin, though—I was just Elizabeth. Simple, lovely, warm, Elizabeth. Last night, I slipped into his room. He was practicing tying shoelaces. He is so cute. He was so surprised. My hands around his neck, my legs around his waist. I gave him what he saw: Simple. Lovely. Warm. Elizabeth."

Jack dropped the journal onto the table and its hard thud-bang was the only sound that could be heard in the Grant's humble kitchen. The wheels were turning in Jack's head, and though I felt like speaking would be too violent—

like stomping while standing on thin ice, my only choice was to talk Jack down from wherever he was trying to go.

"Franklin is going to go away for the rest of his life because of what he did, Jack," I started. "I know you want this to be Alan, I know it makes more sense to you if it is but it isn't. Dr. Walker took advantage of Franklin's mind..." I tried to force the rest out. "And my mother, she took advantage of the rest."

"Wait just a minute, son," Alan started but his words stopped there. He didn't have an argument and he knew it.

"Franklin killed women that were nice to him because the lines between sex and violence became distorted to him. My mother blurred those lines, purposefully, Jack. He needed someone and she took that and used him—in a way in which he could not consent. And we have to live with that very real fact," I said, flatly. "And the trauma—the only nice person around hurt him, in an extremely personal and private way. He was conditioned then, Jack. The trauma made him revolt against anyone else that was nice to him. Decent people, like your mother."

Jack shook his head a few times, his eyes were pierced to the table, but he didn't look at us. He didn't look at me— or Alan; I don't even think he was looking at the table.

My father looked downward. I couldn't imagine what he was feeling: anger, depression, denial. Honestly, all of it would be valid.

"This is some pretty heavy stuff, Grayson," Jack finally said. "You realize you're dragging your mother's name through the mud, don't you?"

"I'm not dragging it through the mud, Jack, I'm just pointing out where she left it," I replied. His eyes shot up at Alan.

"You going to sit there and let him deface the woman you loved oh so much?" Jack said.

"I have nothing to prove to you. If you were going to shoot me you would've done it, already. You haven't, though. You sit there and cry. You cried waiting for Grayson to get here, and you're still crying. You've had twenty years to cry. You've had twenty years to cope with it, or better yet, you've had twenty years to kill me. Why have you waited so long? If you really thought it was me, if you really wanted to take out your own brand of justice then why have you waited for so long?"

"Alan," I stated, getting nervous about the tension that was clearly rising in the room.

"No no, it's okay, son. I want to know. I want to know what kind of a man it takes to be sitting on top of this gold mine of information and hasn't done anything about it all these years.

You live beside a killer and you, what? Sit in your room and smoke pot all day?"

"Alan," my voice was becoming a background of reason. Jack's face was expressionless, except for his eyes—his eyes were screaming.

"You know what I did? I had no idea who the killer was and I sat up in that room upstairs and I put every piece of information together that I could. I researched and hunted and tried so hard to put together something that would lead me or someone else to the person responsible and I did it because I loved my wife and I loved my son. You? I don't know what you love or what you care about because I don't know how many times I've seen you—albeit at a distance—over the last twenty years and you haven't so much as given me the finger, let alone try to avenge your momma or anyone else that psycho took from this town."

"Alan, easy," I said, trying to interject. He wouldn't have any of it, though. My old man was stubborn, like me—a Grant family trait. There was enough tension among the three of us that even if I did interject, I wouldn't know how to stop it. Jack had a gun, and with each passing moment he seemed more intent on using it. And Alan, with every passing moment, seemed all the more *content* with him using it.

"So go ahead, Jack. If you are going to be a man and stick to your true convictions for once, instead of just talking about it like you potheads always seem to do—then do it! Pick it up, kill me!"

"Alan!"

"Do it!"

"Dad!"

It's true what they say—sometimes, in moments you know might be preceded by death or destruction, time can slow. It's an anomaly—it deviates from time how we know it. I felt it when I fell through the first floor of the asylum. I felt it when I landed in the pit. I felt it in that moment in the kitchen, when Jack reached for the gun, instead of his fingers dancing over the handle—flirting with the trigger, they grasped onto the handle. And, as Jack, on pure emotional rage and temptation, aimed the gun at my father, I instinctively reacted. With a quick jolt, I aimed my coffee cup toward Jack and tossed the scalding coffee onto his face.

His reaction was appropriate—he screamed and grasped his face, closed eyes and misdirected his gun when he fired, which resulted with a bullet in a kitchen cabinet. I stood up from the moment that I threw the coffee in his face, pushing the yellow table up and against him, knocking him onto his back. Alan jumped to his feet, bent down and reached for the gun that Jack had dropped in the process.

"Pathetic," Alan scoffed.

"Call the cops, dad," I said, breathless from panic and adrenaline. He nodded and handed me the pistol as he left the room. I didn't point the gun excessively at Jack, like Alan had begun to—instead I held it peacefully by my side, and offered a hand in which to pull Jack up off the floor. He glared at me in refusal, and pushed the table off of his body. "Don't test me, Jack," I said.

"No, you win. You finally brought the big stick," he said.

"I wasn't trying to trick you, Jack—that journal, Dr. Walker, all of it is real," I insisted. Jack nodded.

"And that all very well may be true, brother, but what I said is too, so where does that leave us?" Jack said as he collapsed his face into his hands. I didn't answer. I just watched him, as he lay on the kitchen floor, able to get up but refusing to do so. "So is that it, then? I try to put this to bed, once and for all, expose your daddy and all you have to say is your mom was to blame?" I balled a fist—white knuckles digging into the side of my leg.

"All you did tonight Jack, all you proved was that you could ruin a twenty-five year friendship," I stated. The police sirens were loud and obnoxious as they approached—fast and sudden, I saw blue lights flicker in our front yard. I rolled my eyes to myself when I realized that the next day the story would once again be: *What happened at the Grant's place?* I stepped over Jack, to exit the kitchen. I didn't have to, I could've used the hall door, but I didn't. I wanted him to know I was over him, and everything he brought into this house.

"Think about it, Grayson," he called out to me.

"Enough, Jack" I called back. "Play time's over."

The police arrested Jack Hanna, and as they pulled my best friend out of the house he'd played, slept, cried, ate, laughed, and practically lived in for the better part of our childhood, Alan and I sat on the front porch swing. After the police questioned me for the second time in the same twenty-four hour period, there was nothing left but for Alan and I to do but swing on the porch as the morning continued to grow.

"I'm sorry," I finally said, to break the silence.

"For what?" Alan asked, his voice dull and lifeless.

"It's not how I wanted you to find out about mom. I haven't known long. I didn't even want to tell you, to be honest. I wasn't going to—not until all that happened," I said, my head gestured to the kitchen.

"It isn't your fault, Grayson," he said. There was so much more to say, so much more to ask but it didn't seem right—not then, anyway. "You called me dad," he said, his tone higher, a little lighter, too. I chuckled, and so did he.

"Yeah, I did."

"It takes me almost dying for you to get sentimental," he said again, laughing awkwardly. The laugh was infectious. What started off as a hint of a chuckle grew between us. We found ourselves sitting on that swing, rocking back and forth and laughing.

"It actually takes a gun being pointed to your face," I teased.

"You threw coffee in his face," Alan said, suddenly finding the entire spectacle hilarious "it was like a Three Stooges sketch," he joked.

"No offense, dad, but that would have been the saddest Stooges sketch anyone would've ever seen." The laughing continued, and just as I felt some content—some closure on the events of a case so old it had morphed into the skeleton of our family, Alan opened his mouth and changed everything.

"It's true, Grayson," he said as his laugh wore down.

"What?" I asked, still a bit transfixed on the good moment.

"What Jack said, well, it was partially true." My heart sank and Alan waited, for either me to figure it out or to ask a question. I watched him, hoping that I wouldn't have to do either, but I knew I did.

"What are you talking about?" I questioned. Alan stopped swinging, now.

"Farmer, son. I killed him." The words were swift, unforgiving—bold. "He came here, not long after Elizabeth died. I suspected the two of them for a long time but he said she refused him. I asked him," Alan's lip trembled and his eyes started to water—patchy red around the lashes. "I asked if the rejection was enough to turn on her. He didn't like the implication that he killed her. I didn't believe anything he said. I didn't mean to, Grayson, I didn't," Tears were streaming down Alan's face, now.

"You really killed him?" I asked—I couldn't comprehend. The credits were rolling and the director had cut to black too soon.

"I did."

"You let all of that happen in there?" I yelled, pointing to the kitchen. "Not to mention jeopardizing this entire investigation. Why did you make it look like the Shoestring Killer did it? Shouldn't you know that it could have derailed the investigation? That in some ways you did derail the investigation? Above all, you took a life!" I yelled at him, uncaring of what eavesdroppers heard.

"It didn't derail it, though, did it? You still figured it out. I knew you would," Alan said, as if that was the only issue. "Listen, son. In the moment I really thought he was guilty. My eye had been on him for a while anyway. And when the next body popped up after his, you better believe I felt guilty. I felt very guilty. That's why I wanted to stop investigating."

"Stop investigating?" I questioned—growing more lost by the moment.

"Yeah, I wanted to stop. I wanted to punish myself for taking it into my own hands. But I couldn't, not until I could find someone else with a passion for it to pick it up. That's why I pawned it off to you, when I found out you'd become a private eye. That's why I could never make any headway on the case. I stopped trying. I just couldn't. I couldn't trust myself. It was different though for me, son. Judge me all you want but you weren't in my position. It wasn't the 'who', it was never the 'who', I just wanted to know why—now I know. Because she was a cheating whore, a sex offender, and so much more, apparently," Alan's words spat bitterness. "She's what—a rapist? I wonder if she even realized that is what she became," Alan said, in disgust.

"And you're a cold blooded killer," I snapped.

"Cold blooded? Cold blooded? My wife was taken from me. My boy's mother was gone. And I was looking into the eyes of someone I thought was guilty. There was nothing cold about it. I've been passion filled for twenty years, Grayson. You just recently took an interest, you just recently woke up. Not I, I've been up for a while," Alan claimed.

I sat in silence, dumbstruck and disappointed. My head spun, and I wanted to vomit on the porch, under the swing my parents use to swing on, hand in hand.

"I loved your mother," Alan started. "I still do. Even after—whatever sick thing she did." The domino effect of everything that happened from the early nineties, and how it trickled down to that day between Alan and myself on his front porch began to overwhelm me. I felt a hot, spiking sensation on the back of my neck, as sweat accumulated from the anxiety bubbling up from within me.

"Joseph Farmer knew what was going on at the asylum," I blurted out. "He knew Dr. Walker was breaking the law, because he was avidly trying to help those patients survive and escape. He knew what was going on with my mother, at least on some level, because he was around her every day all day, and he knew which patients were dangerous. He knew about the floor under the basement, because he was close to patients like Walt Rodgers. He had all of it, Alan. All of the information we needed. You killed him before he ever became valuable to the case," I stated.

"It was a mistake, son," Alan said—pools for eyes.

"He could've been stopped—Jody Farmer could've stopped this man way before I—or any of us. Think of all the lives Jody would've saved if you had decided to attempt justice and not vengeance. You know who, Alan? Jolene. Jolene would still be alive if it weren't for you," I said, coldly. I stood up from the swing and walked toward the steps. "Think about that next time you try to plead with me about doing it for the love of your life."

"Where are you going?" he called out to me, desperately. I looked back, to get one last glimpse of a man who forgot to raise me. He looked pitiful, alone, scared—that's because he was all of those things.

"For twenty years there was a big door between us, Alan. This door that is this case was always there, awkwardly ajar. Well, not anymore. Case closed—door shut." I concluded, and without another word from either of us, I walked down the walkway in front of the Grant house, and left behind an anchor that had never truly been released, until that very moment. I couldn't help but feel like something of a hypocrite as I walked away. I had come close, too close, to killing Franklin, myself, and if Alan had really believed Jody

411

to be the killer, then what was the difference? I thought of Lexi, for a moment, and how she was there to try and be a voice of reason, and though I wasn't sure she is why I stopped, I know that it wouldn't have hurt for there to be a voice of reason by my father.

That's the trouble with people, though, you can hardly leave them unchecked for very long, without fear that they'll reach into the dark corners of their self and pull out something just as grotesque as the thing they are facing. The difference though, between Alan and myself, is that when we faced that inner calling for true darkness, I flipped the switch on—Alan didn't.

Kiddy left that day for St. Louis. In his words, he'd seen enough of Virginia to last him a lifetime. Lexi, who carpooled with Kiddy, decided to stay with me, in Abingdon, long enough to attend a makeshift funeral for Walt Rodgers. It was sad, in more than just the traditional sense. There were few mourners. Old friends that remembered him from before his mental health worsened, a few people Rodgers knew at the bar. Mostly it was just people who knew him as the legendary *Irusan* and wanted to see what he looked like in person—the man who lived in the woods, the man who was almost the Shoestring Killer. The man who *fought* the Shoestring Killer. I was absolutely certain there would be a ghost story about him before I was able to get out of town. Lexi had taken Rodgers' death harder than anyone—his dying act was to save her, that's not something someone gets over, quickly.

I avoided as many people as I could—I was tired of questions and I was tired of being the poster child of current events in and around the small town. To make my avoidance meaningful, I walked the cemetery to Jolene's grave, and after paying a tear of respect, I walked down the hill to my mother's grave—a headstone I had never read, not even once. When my mother died, I taught myself not to obsess over visiting her grave. It was just stone with her name on it. Her body lay six feet below—cold and decayed. Yet, I found myself there, and I realized maybe I didn't let myself obsess because I knew if I started to, I would never stop.

As we parted from the gravesite, I told Lexi I was ready to leave. We got back in my car, me behind the driver's seat and Lexi riding shotgun, as she wiped her tears away from the most depressing funeral anyone had ever attended. Julius meowed in the backseat. Neither of us said anything for miles, and as we left Abingdon's welcome sign in the rearview mirror, Lexi looked back at it.

"Do you think you'll ever go back?" she asked.

"Door shut," I replied.

She grasped my hand for a moment, but only for a moment. It was a moment neither of us knew for sure if we wanted or if we should even have it. I couldn't help but feel like I was still not put together. I had left a piece of myself in my hometown. As I looked at Abingdon in my rearview mirror, I started to hope. I drove out into the vast horizon, hoping that there was a new piece of myself out there, and waiting for me. So, I pressed down on the accelerator a little harder—feeling my foot wiggle loose from my shoe, as its shoestrings slowly began to unravel.

END

Dear Readers,

I hope you enjoyed reading this book half as much as I enjoyed writing it. I have always enjoyed mysteries. I grew up watching and reading whodunits and always hoped to carve out a little corner of that world for myself.

I hope Grayson Grant's journey is one that sits on your shelf for years to come. If you are ever in the Virginia area, Abingdon is a lovely place to visit and the chances of a serial killer making you his next victim is highly unlikely.

If you enjoyed this novel, I encourage you to follow me on my social media accounts to keep up with my work and with Tamarind Hill Press for other talented authors and poets. And, as always, thank you for reading.

Robert T.R. Bradford

@robertbwrites
@robertbradfordwrites
www.roberttrbradford.com

TAMARiND HiLL
.PRESS